blood is thicker

blood is thicker

canadian authors association

iguana books

IGUANA

Published by Iguana Books
720 Bathurst Street, Suite 303
Toronto, Ontario, Canada
M5S 2R4

Publisher: Mary Ann J. Blair
Editors: Mary Ann J. Blair and Wendy Duff
Proofreader: Lee Parpart
Cover image: cartridge case by ankdesign
Cover design: Jessica Albert

Library and Archives Canada Cataloguing in Publication

Blood is thicker : an anthology of twisted family traditions.

Issued in print and electronic formats.
ISBN 978-1-77180-268-0 (softcover).--ISBN 978-1-77180-269-7 (EPUB).--
ISBN 978-1-77180-270-3 (Kindle)

1. Families--Literary collections. 2. Canadian literature (English)--21st century. I. Canadian Authors Association, issuing body

PS8237.F33B66 2018   C810.8'0355   C2018-902705-3
                                     C2018-902706-1

This is an original print edition of *Blood Is Thicker*.

Contents

introduction *vii*

the tiebreaker / Jennifer House *1*

the secret's in the sauce / Hilary Faktor *11*

deadly days in blossom city, again / Charlotte Morganti *30*

contract killer / Michelle Tang *42*

beating the odds / Arlene Somerton Smith *55*

pyrrhic victory / Robin A. Blair *70*

bloody reunions / V. E. Rogers *82*

time enough to heal old wounds / Michelle F. Goddard *102*

lorraine and the loup-garou / Joy Thierry Llewellyn *120*

a time to reflect / Colin Brezicki *129*

blood is thicker than scotland (until we leap) / Jess Skoog *144*

the race / Judith Pettersen *154*

costumes and wild mushrooms / Heather Bonin MacIntosh *164*

the metamorphosis of nova / J. F. Garrard *178*

rotting away / Karen Ralph *191*

introduction

On October 6, 2017, Kaarina Stiff of the Canadian Authors Association was visiting Toronto and I arranged to have lunch with her. We're both members of Editors Canada (which is how we know each other). And, among other things, I co-own Iguana Books.

I can't actually remember where we had lunch or what we ate. We got to talking about whether Iguana and CAA could somehow work together to publish previously unpublished writers. I do remember having ice cream for dessert. Over dessert, we came up with the idea of an anthology…

Far too often, not much of anything results from that sort of conversation. But in this case, people at CAA and Iguana ran with the idea and came up with a plan. In early December, we put out a call for short stories from new writers across Canada, giving them until February 28, 2018, to write an original story based on a single premise.

Instead of asking the writers to contribute to the cost of the anthology or raising the money first, we went the traditional route, covering the cost ourselves and paying contributors for their work.

When it came to the stories, there were only a few limitations. They had to be new, unpublished, and 3000 to 7500 words long. Most importantly, every story had to start with the same line, something I came up with: "It was February 29 again, and I was wondering which member of my family would try to kill me this time."

From there it would be a free-for-all. Writers could submit in any genre or style and could interpret the premise any way they wanted.

We had no idea if we'd attract a bunch of genre stories, or a mix of literary and genre pieces, and we didn't much care. We just wanted to challenge a bunch of new writers to test their skills and imagination on a single theme.

Based on what we knew about short fiction in Canada, we figured we would receive maybe thirty or forty submissions. Of that, we figured maybe ten would be worth publishing.

What happened next blew us away. By the deadline, we'd received eighty stories. As my editors and I read through the work, we couldn't believe our luck. There were new writers out there, folks no one had heard of, who could take a high-concept premise and turn it into gold. We were so impressed with what we found in our inbox that we wound up expanding the collection from ten to fifteen stories.

One thing we learned from this project is that Canadian short fiction is bigger and more varied than it sometimes seems. It may be known for its Morley Callaghans and its Alice Munros, but there's a whole other body of work out there, itching to claim its place within CanLit.

We also noticed that Canadian short fiction seems to be a little less identifiably Canadian than it has been at other points in the past. Although the stories were all written by writers in Canada, many of them seem driven more by imagination than by social setting.

As we put the final touches on this collection, I want to thank everyone involved, from the authors who shared their work with us to our partners at the CAA and the editors who helped me sort through the riches that became this book.

We had so much fun that we're thinking of doing it again next year.

Greg Ioannou

the tiebreaker

by Jennifer House

It was February 29 again, and I was wondering which member of my family would try to kill me this time. The first attempt was four years ago when my brother Joshua suggested I join the realm of the undead.

"Really, you won't mind being a vampire, Jess. Vampire mythology is grossly exaggerated. I mean, Stoker spent most of his childhood sick in bed letting his imagination run wild. And Stephanie Meyer's *Twilight* came to her in a dream. It's completely inaccurate. Look at me, Jess. Is my skin all sparkly? No. Am I burning to a crisp in the sunlight? Again, no. Even garlic is perfectly fine as long as you take an antihistamine. I mean, the wooden stake through the heart thing can pose a bit of a challenge, but that's a problem for anyone."

"Don't come any closer!" I said, pulling a vial of holy water out of my back pocket.

"Is that what I think it is? Seriously, Jess, didn't I just tell you that vampire mythology is a load of crap? But I'll back off. I have a date tonight and holy water gives me a rash. Besides, the Conversion Cup is only awarded to the family with the most conversions by consent. And since I don't have your consent, I'll be on my way. Dinner at my place Thursday?"

The Conversion Cup was the most highly coveted trophy among vampirekind. Much to the chagrin of my father, the Allaire family has held the Cup for the past sixteen years. Dad's greatest dream was to have the Habbershaw family name carved onto the trophy.

The Conversion Cup was instituted in 1884 by the Vampire Oversight Committee (VOC) to help stem the decline of the vampire population. They attributed low vampire birth rates to the fact that vampires preferred to mate with humans rather than other vampires. It apparently had something to do with the way humans smelled — like a fresh steak as opposed to three-week-old ground chuck. Since all children born to mixed-race parents were invariably human, the unfortunate consequence of humans smelling better than the undead was that the entire vampire species was threatened with extinction.

Thus, the Conversion Cup was born — a prestigious award that encouraged young humans to join the dark side. There were a few caveats. Children could only be *converted by consent* (italics mine), and consent could only be given at the age of twenty-one. One little problem that VOC didn't anticipate was that conversions were not entirely risk-free … in fact, they could be a little bit tricky to get just right. After all, it did take a certain amount of finesse to bite a human without sucking them dry. To mitigate the risk and put an end to the class-action lawsuits, VOC undertook an extensive study that correlated astrological charts with historical mortality rates. They concluded that when the sun was positioned ten degrees in the sign of Pisces, specifically on February 29, there were statistically fewer human deaths due to vampire bites. (Note: the significance threshold was set at .05.) Based on this irrefutable evidence, in 1994 the Committee passed a law that decreed conversions could only occur on leap days.

In our family, the twins Alex and Amy were the first to "take the leap" (so to speak). That was twelve years ago now, but I remember it like it was yesterday. "Two conversions on the same day!" my father beamed. "This is the proudest moment of my life. Your mother didn't want four kids, but she'll be eating those words when she sees the Cup on the mantel. The Habbershaws will finally go down in history! First up are Alex and Amy, and then by next leap year Joshua will be old enough to convert. That will bring us to a tie with the Allaires. Then it will be up to you, Jess. Jess the tiebreaker! Jess the victor!"

For the rest of the day, my father read up on proper conversion techniques. "Apparently, severing the carotid artery is considered passé," he said. "It's much safer to take blood from either the ulnar or radial artery at the wrist."

"Hmmm … interesting dear," Mom said. She was putting a pot roast in the oven. In case the twins didn't survive the conversion, Mom was putting her best effort into cooking what could potentially be our last meal together as a family.

"Alex and Amy, get over here!" Dad bellowed. "There are a few things we need to go over first. It says in the conversion manual that I need to disclose all potential side effects before you sign the consent form. Here, it's easier if I just read from the manual…

'The following is a list of potential side effects that may occur upon human death. These symptoms have been reported in at least ten percent of the sample population:

> Nausea and vomiting
> Headache
> Erectile dysfunction
> Extreme unyielding pain
> Loss of bowel control
> Hallucinations including seeing bright white lights

Note: In the unlikely event that a subject sees white lights during the conversion process please inform the subject not to follow the light. If said subject does indeed choose to go into the light, conversion will be unsuccessful.'

That looks to be about it. Sign here at the bottom."

The rest of the day was spent in nervous anticipation of what was to come. Alex aimlessly flipped through channels on TV, while Amy was absorbed reading *The Power of Positive Thinking*. Mom hummed away in the kitchen while Joshua sat on the couch sulking. God only knows what my father was up to.

"I don't get why the drinking age is nineteen, yet I have to be twenty-one to become a vampire," Joshua said. "Now I'll have to wait another four years before I can convert. I'll be twenty-three by then. That's so old!"

"Why do you even want to do this?" I asked Amy.

She put down her book and thought a moment before answering. "I don't know, Jess. You're still only sixteen, so I don't expect you to get it. Just look at the way Dad's face lights up when he thinks about winning the Cup. I guess it boils down to family responsibility."

"Yeah, plus vampires are cool," Alex said. He never was the brightest one of the bunch.

"What if it doesn't work? What if you actually die?" I asked.

"I trust Dad," Amy said.

As if on cue, my father walked into the room. He was wearing a black plastic cape from the dollar store and his hair was slicked back with either olive oil or mayonnaise. It definitely smelled more like mayonnaise. His left wrist was wrapped in layers of gauze, but the blood had already begun to seep through.

"Practising?" I asked. "On yourself? Seriously? And you people think this is a good idea?" Disgusted with them all, I went upstairs to my room and slammed the door.

I stayed in my room during dinner that night. I could hear them joking and laughing and clinking their wine glasses together. They were all completely insane. When the conversions started, I placed a pillow over my head to drown out the noises.

The screaming eventually subsided and I ventured back downstairs. I remember my heart was in my throat. What if they were both dead? I mean, Alex I could honestly live without, but Amy and I were tight.

Mom was sitting at the kitchen table sipping her wine. Her eyes were misty.

"Oh my God!" I said, running to her.

"No, no, it's fine. Everyone lived. Or died. Or rather, undied. Whatever. It worked."

"Then why are you crying?" I asked.

"Just grateful, I suppose. I mean your father ... well he ... well, it really could have gone either way."

I joined the rest of the family in the living room. Amy and Alex were sitting on the couch looking dazed. Joshua had a look of abject horror on his face. My father strutted around the room like a proud peacock … well, maybe not like a peacock. I've never seen a peacock strut while drooling blood.

"You've got a little something…" I said, motioning for him to wipe his mouth.

"Right, right. Of course." He dabbed his lips with his plastic cape.

"I knew that cape would come in handy for something," I said. "So? How'd it go?"

"How do I look?" asked Amy. She was always the vain one.

"Great. Fine. Not too bad," I said. Truthfully, she looked like she had come down with some frightful mixture of Ebola, influenza, and pernicious anemia all at once. "I mean, it's nothing a little bronzer couldn't fix."

"It was great!" Dad said. "Well, Alex may have a little scarring, but my technique definitely improved with Amy. What did you think, Joshua?"

Joshua opened his mouth and threw up on the carpet.

Given Joshua's reaction to the first family conversion, I was more than a little surprised when he decided to become a vampire the following leap year. He had just turned twenty-three. I was only twenty at the time and thankfully still underage.

Alex and Amy couldn't come home (something to do with jobs and mortgage payments and so forth), so it was just me and Joshua and our parents. When I returned home from college that afternoon, Mom was busy in the kitchen putting a pot roast in the oven. Another Last Supper.

"Your father would like you to watch this time," Mom said, handing me a glass of Merlot.

"Why?"

"Just so you know what you're getting into. It's too bad you're still too young. It could have been another double header. You'll be twenty-four when the next leap year rolls around."

I choked on my wine. "What on earth makes you think I'm willing to join the undead?"

"But with Joshua converted our family will be tied with the Allaires!

They don't have any more children. We do! You're the tiebreaker, Jess. With your conversion we could finally win that Cup!"

"I can't believe you support this!" I said. "You're not even a vampire!" In our family, that was actually an insult. I poured myself more wine and stomped out of the kitchen.

My father was already in the living room. This leap year, he had upgraded his plastic cape to a velvet one with purple satin lining.

"What do you think?" he asked, giving me a hug. "Is the cape too much?"

"It depends," I said. "Are you channelling Bela Lugosi as Dracula?"

"I was thinking more along the lines of Max Schreck as Count Orlok."

"He wore a button-down coat, not a cape," I said.

My father looked surprised. "Well, anyway," he said, "I ordered it online from some goth clothing store … *Deader than Death* or something like that. You've got to hand it to the goths — they've really got the whole death culture thing down pat. We vampires could really learn a thing a two…"

"Where's Joshua?" I asked.

"Upstairs getting ready."

I walked back into the kitchen and refilled my wine glass. Mom was now humming. I completely ignored her and headed upstairs to try and talk some sense into my last remaining human sibling.

Joshua's door was closed so I barged in. He was kneeling by his bed with his head in his hands.

"Are you praying?" I asked.

"Well, just in case … you know, with Dad and everything…"

"I know. It could go either way. Are you sure you want to do this?"

"We're so close to winning the Cup! When I convert we'll be tied with the Allaires. And you…"

"I'm the tiebreaker."

Joshua gave me a rueful smile. "I guess it sucks to be you," he said.

"You have no idea."

"Jess?" Joshua asked, as I turned to leave his room. "I could use some sisterly support tonight, you know … in case Dad messes up…"

"You want me to wipe up the blood and dispose of your body."

"Well, let's hope it doesn't come to that. I meant more like you could maybe hold my hand or something. Or sing that nursery rhyme that I used to sing to you when you were little…"

"Humpty Dumpty? I think that's a pessimistic choice given your situation. 'All the king's horses and all the king's men couldn't put Humpty together again…'"

"Right. I forgot about that part," Joshua said. There was a moment of silence.

"Fine. I'll be there," I said. "But first, I think I need to crack open another bottle of wine. Want some?"

"I'll pass. Dad says it thins the blood too much. He had a little problem with Alex the last time. He was a real bleeder."

"Come on, let's get this show on the road!" I clapped my father on the back and skipped into the living room. "Where's the best viewing area?" I asked.

"I guess you could stand next to Josh," Dad said.

Joshua was lying comfortably on the couch. After getting him to sign the consent form, my father picked up his wrist and began sucking. At the first drop of blood I broke into a roaring rendition of Foreigner's "Hot Blooded."

"How about no singing?" Dad suggested between sucks.

"But Joshua wanted me to sing!" I said. "And there are so many great songs for the occasion. I could do "Bad Blood" by Taylor Swift … or if you're feeling the punk vibe, I could go with "Bleed for Me" by the Dead Kennedys. "Raining Blood" by Slayer is another great choice, but I don't know if I can pull off the guttural heavy-metal thing."

"Just kill me, Dad," Joshua said. A few minutes later he was flopping around on the couch and screaming.

"I don't think he meant it literally," I said.

My father wiped his mouth with his cape and smiled. "Nothing to worry about, Jess. It's all just part of the process. Watch."

Soon Joshua stopped his fish out of water impersonation and lay perfectly still. Dead still.

"Um, Dad?" I was worried.

"Wait for it … wait for it … there!"

Joshua gave a little twitch and then sat up on the couch as though nothing had happened, but he looked like crap.

"How do you feel?" Dad asked.

Joshua opened his mouth and threw up on the carpet.

The past leap year was exactly four years ago today. It had been my turn to convert and I thought the pressure from my family to become a vampire would be unbearable. I was the last barrier to the Cup. The tiebreaker. The Habbershaw who would finally put the family name on the trophy. I was twenty-four and living on my own. The entire month of February I hid I from my family. On leap day, they sent Joshua to try to kill me, or rather, to have me consent to being killed. Semantics. But Joshua's discourse on the history of vampire mythology had been completely ineffectual. If you ask me, he really should have thought of a better argument. Now it was February 29 again and I was wondering which member of my family would try to kill me this time. My bet was on all of them.

At precisely one minute after midnight, my cellphone rang. It was Mom. I considered not answering, but Mom could be annoyingly persistent. How many times could I listen to my marimba ring tone without going completely insane? And if I turned the ringer off, she would just fill my mailbox with a series of inane messages. So against my better judgement I picked up the phone.

"Hi Mom," I said.

"Hi sweetie! How did you know it was me?"

"It's a cellphone, Mom. It has call display."

"Neato."

"So, what's up?" I asked.

"Well, your father and I thought it would be nice to get the whole family together for dinner," she said.

"Great. How about March?"

There was a long pause before she answered. "Um, well, March is actually booked up."

"The whole month?"

"We were thinking tonight would work," she said. "Alex and Amy will be home too. Isn't that exciting?"

It was definitely something. "I don't know, Mom, I'll have to think about it. Bye for now." I hung up the phone before she could get another word in.

Ten minutes later my phone rang again. It was Joshua.

"What do *you* want?"

"Is that how you answer the phone now?" he asked.

"It is when my whole family's trying to set me up."

"What are you talking about?" Joshua asked.

"Don't sound so innocent," I said. "It doesn't become you. I know what you're all up to!"

"We just want to talk to you, Jess," he said. "Besides, getting together with the whole family would be great."

"You don't even like Alex," I reminded him. "For that matter, I don't even like Alex."

"Yeah, but you and Amy are tight."

"I just saw her at Christmas!" I said. "Why can't this family reunion wait until after leap day?"

"C'mon, Jess. You're twenty-eight now. We all let it go last time, but you've got to start thinking of the family now. That Cup could be ours! You're the tie…"

"Don't you dare say it! If I hear that word one more time I'm going to throw up. On the carpet!" Ha! Low blow, but he had it coming. I hung up the phone.

The phone rang again an hour later. Mom's number again.

"Stop calling me!" I yelled into the phone.

"It's your father."

"Oh, hi Dad. I hope you didn't go to the trouble of ordering another cape?"

"I'm not even going to answer that," he said. "Why won't you come for dinner? Your mother is upset."

And there it was. He had found my Achilles heel. I was going to crack. I knew it. He knew it. He'd used the oldest trick in the book — a daughter's guilt. Judging from the sounds coming from his end of the phone, he was basking in his own cleverness.

"Is that a chuckle I hear?" I asked.

"No, no, just clearing my throat," he lied.

"Fine," I said. "You win."

"Really? It worked?"

"I'll come for dinner," I said, "but you have to promise not to kill me. And stop pressuring me about the Cup, OK? I'm not ready to become the newest member of the Habbershaw undead," I said.

"Great! That's great, Jess! No pressure here. We Habbershaws are pressure-free! You will be entering a pressure-free zone, a safe zone if you will…"

"Just let me talk to Mom."

There was a long pause and a lot of muffled talking before Mom finally came to the phone. "Hi sweetie. Your father said you've decided to join us?"

"Sure. Can I bring anything?" I asked.

"No, just yourself," she said. "Supper will be ready at five o'clock. Oh, and Jess? We're having pot roast."

Jennifer House loves reading and writing quirky fiction and has a penchant for all things supernatural. In addition to writing fiction, Jennifer writes practical things like bylaws, policy documents, and occasionally even a newspaper article or two. Jennifer holds a Bachelor of Arts degree in English and a Master of Arts degree in anthropology. She is currently working on her first novel.

the secret's in the sauce

by Hilary Faktor

"It was February 29 again, and I was wondering which member of my family would try to kill me this time," Neil says. His face is serious but for a twitch at the corner of his mouth.

Eva lets a snort escape and rolls her eyes good-naturedly at her son-in-law. Typical Neil. He has been married to her eldest daughter, Callie, for five years and Eva's grown quite fond of his exaggerated family tales.

"I'm being serious," Neil laughs. "You Sinclairs don't understand — my family is messed up." He sets aside his dessert fork to put an arm around Callie, gently rubbing her shoulder. She smiles down at her lap. "Every leap year my family has a huge party because me, my grandpa, also named Neil, and my Uncle Rick were all born on February 29. But with so many aunts and uncles, someone always seems to forget about my deathly peanut allergy." Neil shrugs. "I've escaped, what, seven attempts on my life?" He looks at Callie who turns to him with a tender smile.

"Come on," she says, "I doubt anyone's actually trying to kill you, hon. It's an honest mistake."

"That's what they always claim," Neil says, "but sometimes I wonder." He waggles his eyebrows at the table full of his wife's family.

Shayna, the youngest Sinclair sibling, sits at the opposite end with this season's boyfriend, Rhys. A dark-haired, dreamy sort of guy who, upon arrival, promptly announces he's vegan. Ed chokes on his beer, but Eva nudges her husband carefully under the table. *This one won't last*, she thinks. No sense getting all bent up over whether or not Shayna's boyfriend eats meat. Lucas, their only boy and a middle child, is dateless tonight. *It's probably for the best if there's a little space between girlfriends, after his last one*, Eva thinks.

The conversation moves onto the yoga class Shayna's been teaching down at the Y and an exciting new development she's been waiting to tell them about. Eva's eyes wander to her eldest daughter. While the others laugh along with Shayna's story about a bizarre request for nude yoga classes, Callie stares down at her hands, seeming lost in thought.

"Is everything okay?" Eva whispers. Callie looks up at her and Eva notices the dark smudges under her eyes. Callie was always a beautiful girl. While some women choose to colour their hair and wear makeup — Eva gladly doing both — Callie is a natural beauty who wears minimal makeup and keeps her sable hair simple and long. But tonight, Callie's shoulders are hunched and there's a tenseness about her that Eva can't understand.

"Everything's fine, Mom. We were late dropping Jeremey off and then I realized I'd forgotten to get gas, so we had to make an extra stop. Honestly, I'm just tired." She offers up a weak smile and leans back as a waiter sets a plate of calamari down in front of them. Eva notices Rhys push the plate away from Shayna and himself with one finger and stifles a smirk.

"You could have brought him," Eva says, her attention back on Callie. "I always have crayons and minicars in my purse and I would've loved having him here on my birthday. It is my day after all," she says, trying to lighten her daughter's mood. Callie works so hard. Between her shifts as a part-time ultrasound technician and taking care of her son, Jeremey, she doesn't have the luxury of quiet afternoons while the kids are at school, like Eva had. Eva treasured those days, but things are different now.

She leans over and pulls Callie's hand into hers, squeezing it gently before letting go. She gazes at her daughter's strong hand, lightly tanned like her father's, and wonders how the tiny fingers that clasped her hand every day on the walk to school are now the competent hands of an adult woman. Where did the time go?

"Well, order yourself a drink and relax now. I want to hear how Jeremey's practice went." Neil lifts his head. Apparently, there's a sweet story to go along with his son's first time at hockey. Everyone turns their attention away from their menus and back to Neil. Eva notices how his hand moves subconsciously to cover Callie's. He brushes his thumb over her knuckles and Callie seems to relax. The sight warms Eva's heart. Her dad was always an affectionate man with her mom — stolen kisses in the kitchen, a hug from behind. She remembers being small and hearing her parents laughing together. It pleases her that Callie has found the same kind of man her father had been.

She feels Ed shift beside her. Flipping his menu over, he listens attentively, nodding along with the story and laughing in all the right places. He's a very sweet man and an attentive father, but he's never been one for affection. It just wasn't his family's way.

Eva takes the napkin from her lap and dabs her mouth. The calamari is all gone and it's time to order the main course. She signals a waiter. "We just need to double-check that the chef knows my son-in-law has a serious peanut allergy. I called ahead, but we need to confirm." Neil gives her a grateful smile.

"I'd rather not die tonight, so if you could double-check, we'd appreciate it."

"Of course, sir," the waiter says.

After the food is eaten and Eva's blown out the five plus six candles on the chocolate cake — symbolic of her fifty-six years — and Ed's paid the bill, they make their way to the door.

Later that night in bed, Eva and Ed face each other. "I'm worried about Callie and Neil," she says. "I just have a bad feeling for some reason. I can't shake it."

Ed punches his pillow a few times. "Neil told me earlier in the evening that they lost the Larson contract."

"What? How?" The Larson project was a lucrative chunk of apartments that Neil's construction company was tasked with updating. It was going to be huge for his business.

Ed settles comfortably into the pillow. "Apparently there's more competition and fewer contracts to bid on. I think he's having a hard time with it. He seemed nervous."

"I feel so bad for them," Eva says. Poor Callie. No wonder she looked tired. "They're probably worried about finances. Callie can pick up extra shifts, but it might not be enough."

Eva is so anxious she can't get comfortable. She tosses around until Ed threatens to move to the guest room. "I'm fine," she whispers, willing herself to lie still. She's very fond of her son-in-law and hates the thought of her daughter being pressured to take on more shifts. She was only supposed to work two to three days a week.

She's beginning to relax when Ed's voice breaks the silence. "I forgot to mention that I saw Cal at the Co-op yesterday. He missed golf last week. Apparently, he and Lynn are done."

Eva sits up and leans over Ed, a hand on his shoulder. "What? Lynn and Calvin? Are you kidding me?" She's never going to sleep now. Lynn and Calvin, two of their closest friends, have been married for thirty years. "Why didn't she tell me?" Eva wonders aloud, pressing her head back into the pillow.

Ed yawns and turns over. "I'm tired, hon. Maybe she's embarrassed. No one likes to talk about divorce." The last word comes out as a whisper. Eva lies awake, staring at the ceiling, until the silent tears tickling down her cheeks finally dry.

"He was having an affair, Eva," Lynn confides the following day during their twice-a-week Zumba class. "I caught him texting the wife of a couple he sold a house to last year. The texts were so sexual there was no mistaking it. And he admitted it anyway," she says, tying the laces on her runners. Eva, Lynn, and their friend Sylvia have been going to Zumba and yoga together for years. Today, Sylvia is quiet. Her husband, Ian, died the previous year, and she's still very fragile. Eva worries that talking about marriage, even divorce, around Sylvia is cruel.

When Eva gets home, she finds Ed adjusting their TV, a football game starting up. "I saw Lynn. Cal was having an affair with one of his clients." She's waiting for him to show the same level of surprise and dismay that she's feeling. Ed barely looks up from the remote when he says, "That sucks, but Lynn would be a difficult woman to live with. I'm just surprised it took Cal this long to stray." He smiles as the surround sound kicks in and doesn't see the dark look of irritation flicker across Eva's face.

"I hardly think this is Lynn's fault," she says, hands on hips. "With Cal drinking and going out all the time, it's a surprise that Lynn didn't have her own affair." *Maybe she should have*, Eva thinks.

Ed, realizing he's on thin ice, sets down the remote and walks over to his wife. He pulls her into his arms in a rare but appreciated display of affection. "The guy's a prick, and I'm disappointed too, okay?"

The next day, Eva spends the morning volunteering at her church, making perogies, which they'll sell at their annual fall fundraiser. She wasn't able to reach Callie through text or calls the night before, so she decided to bring a container of soup over just before lunch. She pulls up next to Neil's white truck and hears voices from inside the house. *Strange, he's usually at work.* It's a sunny fall day, and the main door is open with the screen providing no sound barrier whatsoever. The voices get louder, with Neil's overtaking Callie's urgent whispers.

Eva waits, torn between leaving and not embarrassing anyone or staying and calling out *hello*. As Neil's voice gets louder, her heart begins to pound. She doesn't like the tone of this fight. For all of her and Ed's faults, they've never been the type of couple to use putdowns. Maybe raised their voices, but that's it.

But this is Callie's marriage. Eva is retreating down the steps when she hears Neil who's standing right by the front door. His back is to her, and he doesn't realize she's there. "Stupid bitch!" he shouts at Callie. Eva drops the soup. It makes a splat on the sidewalk, orange and red minestrone broth splashing everywhere. Neil jerks around. She expects him to look embarrassed or shocked, but his eyes are glassy and hard. He blows through the screen door, passes her, and gets into his truck. Eva looks down at the ground, stunned. She feels Callie before she sees her.

"Oh God, Mom. I didn't know you were here. You should have called or texted first. Shoot, here, let me help you." Callie bends over so her long hair covers her face. Eva tips the container upright. "It still has some soup in it," she says, shakily. She stares at Callie until her daughter is forced to look back at her. Callie's eyes are red rimmed, and one cheek is ruddy. Eva almost wonders … but no. Neil has shocked her today, but she doesn't think he would ever hit her daughter.

She puts her hand on Callie's arm, which is tight with nerves. "Honey, did Neil just call you a stupid bitch? Did that just happen?" She's asking aloud for herself as much as her daughter.

Callie stays quiet and then her shoulders slump. "I'm sorry you heard that. He's just under a lot of pressure. There's this job, and it's falling behind. His company could end up owing a lot of money." She puts an arm around her mom. "I'll hose this down, and then let's go inside."

Eva watches her daughter turn on the hose and aim it at the sidewalk, washing away all evidence of the spill. But she knows microscopic pieces of food will remain in the grass and in the cracks in the pavement, proof of what once took place. Just like the words Neil hurled at her daughter will leave their traces.

Callie holds the door open for her mom and Eva takes it upon herself to make them some tea. "Just sit down," she says to Callie, wondering if she'll ever get her to open up about all this. "That was very unlike the Neil I know," Eva says, while stirring a teaspoon of honey into Callie's Earl Grey tea. She carries it over to her daughter. "I didn't know he spoke to you like that."

Callie takes the tea and holds it with one sleeved hand covering the mug. She considers before speaking. "It wasn't always like this, Mom. He's under a lot of pressure. He never used to speak to me that way. But now, well, it's happened a couple of times. He feels really bad about it, though."

I'm sure he does, Eva thinks, aware by the set of Callie's shoulders that she's walking on dangerous territory. But she needs to know. "Does he talk to Jeremey that way?"

The question hangs in the air like a guillotine. Callie hesitates a moment too long and the blade comes down on the esteem Eva has always felt for her son-in-law. Severed forever. "No, Mom. Of course not." But she doesn't meet her mother's eyes.

"You guys should see someone, a marriage counsellor, or even a therapist, to help Neil through this hard time. We'd pay, of course," Eva adds, knowing money is tight.

Callie looks up at her mom. Eva studies the circles under her eyes, dark as bruises, and wonders how long her daughter has been keeping this secret.

"Thanks Mom. I'll mention it to Neil. And please don't judge him for today. He's going to feel really bad when he cools down. He loves you and Dad and he'd hate for you guys to lose respect for him."

Eva bites her tongue. She'd like to say that if Ed ever talked to her that way in front of *her* dad, he'd be in the hospital getting stitches. Peter Wright wouldn't hold for anyone mistreating his daughter, but maybe times are different. Maybe, like the way song lyrics have changed, the way people talk to each other has changed. Perhaps "stupid bitch" doesn't hold the same venom it did when Eva was a thirty-something. But she remembers the hate in Neil's eyes and it frightens her.

When she gets home, she wipes down the kitchen counters. Her spray bottle holds a concoction of water, vinegar and essential oils and she works feverishly to make the kitchen gleam as the fresh smell of lavender settles around her. This is a time-tested stress reliever for Eva.

Two hours later, Ed walks in from work, takes one look at the sparkling kitchen, and knows his wife is pissed. "What's going on?" he asks, slowly removing his jacket.

Eva pushes a lock of hair off her face. "I'm really worried about Neil and Callie." She tells him what happened at their house. Ed looks shocked and Eva is satisfied that she's not the only one horrified by what Neil said. "Okay, okay," Ed says, ever the mediator. "But what did Callie do to make Neil say that to her?" Eva chokes down her mouthful of tea so she doesn't spit it in Ed's face. "You didn't just say that. Is there anything she could have said to deserve being called a stupid bitch, Ed? I mean really." She's livid again and needs to walk around to blow off some steam.

"Hey," Ed says and gets up, placing his hands on Eva's tight shoulders. "Okay, let me talk to Neil. No one is going to speak to my daughter that way. Not even her husband. But they need us right now, Evie, so don't go losing it."

Eva would like to mention that she would have already lost it on Neil except she's a little scared of him in that state. The thought of his aggressive words being hurled at her daughter breaks her heart. If she was scared of him on the sidewalk, how does Callie feel when she's inches away from him and he's going off on her like that?

"We need to help them, Ed. Pay for a therapist or something."

"I agree. Therapy can work wonders," Ed says quietly. She feels her face warming and is sure they're both remembering what happened seven years ago: the business trip, the year of therapy, and her decision to forgive Ed's infidelity and stay together. Ruth. The co-worker Eva had never minded, but never really noticed either. Apparently, though, Ed noticed her. But that was years ago, now. They've moved on. Eva gets up and leaves the room. She hopes he doesn't follow her and is relieved to make it to their bedroom before finally allowing herself to cry.

One night, she's driving home from Zumba when her cellphone rings. It's Callie. Eva puts her on speaker. "Hey, honey. What's up?" Her pulse quickens. But it's silly to feel so worried. The young couple has been through a bad spell, but things are better now. In the last few weeks, Callie's eyes have recovered their sheen and she no longer looks as tired. "I just wanted to let you know we've been seeing that counsellor you recommended and she's just awesome. Neil and I both like her."

Eva doesn't mention that Sheryl was her and Ed's therapist, but she's glad it's working out for Neil and Callie. "How is Jeremey doing?"

"So good," Callie says. "He really seems to be enjoying kindergarten."

"That's wonderful, hon. But listen, I'm just driving home. Can I call you in a few minutes? I need to get that quinoa salad recipe from you."

"Oh, yeah, I'll text it to you, mom. It's really easy. But I'm actually calling to say Neil and I can't make spaghetti dinner on Sunday because his parents are in town. We'll come for a visit next week."

Eva's heart sinks. Ever since her children moved out on their own, she and Ed have hosted a monthly spaghetti dinner. Eva's grandmother started the tradition, followed by Eva's mother, and now Eva loyally keeps it going.

"Well, what if Kurt and Paula come over with you, too? That is, unless you want to have a quiet dinner with just the five of you."

Callie lets out a breath. "Really, Mom? That would be so nice. We'll come for six o'clock, okay?"

"Sounds like a plan. Night hon," Eva says. She's always liked Paula and Kurt and now they can have a big family dinner together. Eva loves entertaining; the more the merrier.

On Sunday, Ed sets the table while the sauce bubbles lightly on the stove. Grandma Sophie's original recipe had to be tweaked a bit, of course, due to Neil's peanut allergy. When Neil was invited to spaghetti night for the first time after he and Callie had begun dating seriously, Callie panicked because she almost hadn't mentioned his allergy. "What spaghetti sauce calls for peanut butter?" Callie griped, never having helped her mom out with this recipe.

"At least you told me before I made the sauce," Eva replied, a mix of irritation and relief running through her. She hadn't ever given much thought to food allergies. Her kids weren't allergic to anything and neither were she and Ed. Of course she couldn't add the peanut butter, but leaving it out meant it wouldn't taste the same. Eva didn't mind since Neil was becoming such an important part of their family, and she was genuinely fond of him. But sometimes she thought about the original recipe and the tangy softness the peanut butter added. She'd have to make a small batch sometime, just for her and Ed.

Eva opens a bottle of red wine. It's five thirty, and they are ahead of schedule. The water is set to boil for the pasta, and the bread is warming in the oven. She carefully stirs the Caesar dressing into the salad. Ed bumps comfortably against her, the ease of a team used to working alongside one another.

When the doorbell rings, she opens up to find just Paula, Kurt, and Jeremey. "Hey," Eva says, checking behind them as her grandson flies into her arms, wrapping his scrawny limbs around her. "Hello, there, buddy." She lifts him up for a bear hug before setting him down. "Grandpa's in the kitchen."

He stares up at her with his wide brown eyes. "I told Granny Paula and Papa they don't need to ring the bell because we're family."

All three of them laugh at his grown-up expression. Paula steps inside. "So good to see you, Eva," she says and embraces her, followed by Kurt.

"Where are Callie and Neil?" Eva asks. Her pulse speeds up just a little.

Kurt looks down, but Paula smiles tightly. "You know how it was when we were their age, with young kids. It's hard. They just needed a few minutes." She lifts a finger in the air. "I told them, nothing comes between you and your spouse. Nothing." Paula's eyes narrow and Eva is taken aback by her fierceness. What happened? She longs to see Callie and be reassured that her eldest daughter is safe.

It's after six when the young couple arrives as if nothing's wrong. Neil is full of charm, ruffling Jeremey's hair, slapping Ed on the back, and helping himself to a beer from the fridge. "Join us on the back patio," Ed says, and like that, the men retreat.

Eva studies her daughter as she gingerly removes her jacket, a pleasant smile pasted on her face, but her eyes are wild. *A mother knows*, Eva thinks. "Hey baby, what took you guys?" she asks quietly, while the others talk outside. "Neil and I had a fight," Callie whispers. She looks up and falls silent. Paula walks over to them, her small eyes focused on Callie. "Things resolved?" she asks, her voice tight.

"What needed to be resolved?" Eva says, suddenly defensive. She feels, rather than sees, Neil glance over at them from the deck. He's telling a story about a project he's working on, his dad and Ed listening closely.

"What needed to be resolved?" Eva asks again, her tone steely.

Paula steps closer. "Just husband and wife stuff, Eva. Leave it alone." She looks at Callie as she says this. This irritates Eva to no end.

"Well, I'm sure you'll understand this, Paula. The only thing as important as husband and wife stuff is parent and child stuff. And I'd like to talk to my daughter. Alone." She holds Paula's gaze, neither one breaking contact.

Callie whispers, "It's okay, Mom," but both mothers ignore her.

Reluctantly, Paula turns away, her cheeks red. Eva watches as she heads over to Neil and puts an arm around his waist. He looks down at his mother with a smile. This affection used to seem sweet to Eva. Lord knows she'd love for Lucas to put an arm around her once in a while, but now it just pisses her off. Her mind goes back to his "stupid bitch" comment and she turns her back to shield Callie. "What happened, honey? Please tell me." Then she notices how gingerly her daughter is holding her arm.

"Neil lost his temper. I forgot to pick him up from work, and he was embarrassed about having to ask an employee for a ride. It made him look bad, being the boss and all."

"Okay," Eva says slowly, not seeing the big deal at all. So Neil had to ask for a ride.

"I know it doesn't seem like a big deal, Mom, but it was. And he ... Well he..."

"He what?" The answer hangs in the air.

"He pushed me. Down the stairs. Right before his parents arrived."

"Oh, Callie. This has to stop," Eva hisses.

"Mom, please don't make a scene. Not with Neil and his parents here." Eva closes her eyes and presses her fingers against her temples. How has her daughter's life come to this? She gets pushed down the stairs by her husband. This doesn't happen in Eva's world.

"I can't sit at the table and look at Neil all night without saying anything," Eva says. "I just can't, Callie. How long is this going to go on?"

"We're getting help, Mom. I promise."

"Yeah, you're getting help. But he's the one who needs it." Eva is so mad she could spit. But Callie's pleading eyes force her to pretend, for now. Somehow, she manages to pull herself together and, with a strained smile, serve the spaghetti. Ed can clearly tell something is wrong, but he manages to keep the conversation flowing. Neil, the little pissant, has no problem laughing along with his parents about old family stories. Eva studies Neil's father, Kurt. She'd never given him much thought before, but now she can't help noticing the way he talks over Paula. The quick way she rushes to grab him another drink. Eva wonders how far the apple fell from the tree with Kurt and Neil.

During the dessert course, Eva makes eye contact with Shayna who lifts an eyebrow in response. She hopes Callie is confiding in her sister. She needs all the help she can get. It occurs to her there's probably a support group for loved ones of those experiencing domestic violence. She'll have to look into it.

Somehow Eva manages to make it through dinner, but she is in no mood for pretending. As soon as dessert is served, Eva jumps up. "Sorry to rush everyone out of here, but I have a killer migraine starting. I'm going to have to call it a night." She hopes the others will take the hint.

"Anything we can do, Eva?" Neil leans forward at the table, his brown eyes sincere. It gives Eva chills. It's like he has no idea of the pain he's causing their family.

Paula, seated beside him, gazes adoringly at her son. "We should go anyway," she says.

Kurt pipes up, "You can't be the big boss man and not get in a good night's sleep, I always say." Eva thinks she might be sick. Both parents looking so admiringly at their son, who just hours ago pushed her daughter down the stairs. Her baby. The same one she delivered after twelve excruciating hours of labour. The one she learned to breastfed through the pain of engorged breasts and then cuddled back to sleep when she woke in the night. Her baby girl is being harmed and what can she do about it? She grows dizzy in her distress and her vision grows spotty.

A plate shatters on the floor and everyone jumps. Eva rubs a tired hand over her forehead. "Sorry, everyone. We really need to wrap things up."

Ed comes over to her. "Get upstairs, honey. I'll clean up." Eva turns to look at Callie, but her daughter is busy wiping food from Jeremey's face, her slim shoulders tense. As Eva walks toward the stairs, she hears someone come up behind her. It's Neil.

"Eva."

"What is it?" She can barely control the venom in her voice. She hasn't realized how worried she's been about Callie and Jeremey until this evening. Now, they have to go home with this unpredictable man. It makes her physically sick. She looks straight in his eyes, expecting him to feel ashamed of himself. Or, at least contrite.

"I'm getting help. I'm going to beat this," he says before turning back to her family, the most precious people in her world. No one really explains that to new mothers, when they hold their small, fragile bundles of perfection. A day will come when you have to trust this part of your heart to someone else. You can only hope they pick the right person. But they might not.

Eva rolls over in bed. She's feeling shaky and there's a tiny, very tiny part of her that feels bad for Neil and his parents. Paula and Kurt are good people. At least, she used to believe that. They love their son. Naturally they want him to work things out with his wife and the grandchild they all love.

She wants to believe there's help for Neil, but she's not sure. Eva picks up her phone and searches "domestic violence." It comes up with basic things she expects, advocates detailing how to support a loved one and a list of women's shelters. Then she searches, "how often do domestic abusers stop?" And although there are a few articles, there's nothing concrete. The more promising ones seem to say that stopping relies heavily on the abuser being willing to get help. Well, Neil did claim he was trying, but…

Eva licks her lips and looks up as Ed walks in the room.

"What was going on tonight? You were acting so strange. I think you made Paula and Kurt feel uncomfortable." It rankles that Ed is upset with her. He has no idea; sweet, oblivious Ed.

She sets down her phone and straightens up. "Have you heard what your sweet son-in-law did to our daughter?"

A red flush works its way up Ed's cheeks, and she rolls her eyes. "No, he didn't cheat on her, Ed. It seems he's chosen a different path than you." She nearly spits the words out. Anger she'd forgotten pokes out from the depths of her sadness. "No, he pushed her down the stairs."

Ed's jaw hangs open. "In front of Jeremey?"

Oh God, Eva hadn't even wondered that. "I don't know. But as horrible as it would be if Jeremey saw that, it's bad enough on its own. Our precious little girl was pushed down the stairs by the one person who should always protect her." Eva is shaking. It's only when Ed grabs a box of tissues out of the bathroom that she realizes she's also crying. He passes her the box and she wipes her eyes. It feels good to cry. "I mean, how do we know he's not hurting her now?" she wails. Ed sits on the bed and pulls Eva into his arms. He smells like Old Spice. Even after thirty years, she still loves the feel of his arms around her, the scratch of his beard stubble against her cheek.

He kisses the top of Eva's head like she's a child. When she looks up at him, she sees that he's crying, too. "Oh Ed, I'm sorry. I didn't think about how you would feel." She passes him a tissue.

"What are we going to do?" she whispers. Eva doesn't really expect an answer. So much depends on Callie, and she seems content to make excuses for Neil. "Do you think it's even possible for Neil to stop?"

Ed sits up and adjusts his glasses. She's always thought this nerdy habit of his was sexy. Her engineer husband with his Clark Kent body. "Does Callie say this just started, or has it been happening for a while?"

Eva shakes her head. She and Callie haven't talked in depth about it. Her daughter always shuts down whenever Eva tries to bring it up. "I don't know. Maybe we should have her over, without Neil. A family meeting, Lucas and Shayna, too, not just to let her know we're here for her, but also to get to the bottom of things. What do you think?"

Ed rubs her back methodically. At first, she doesn't think he's going to answer, but then he says, "Good idea. Maybe we could invite Pastor Ron?"

Eva chews her bottom lip. Their pastor is a wonderful counsellor. He's been their family minister for the better part of twenty years, but Neil and Callie don't attend regular services, and his visit might seem too official for Callie. "Maybe not yet," Eva says and Ed's face falls. Although he's not big on religion, he's always been happy to bring in the experts. In this situation, he must feel like they need all the help they can get.

The day of the intervention, as Eva refers to it, she's chopping up some fresh fruit. *What does one serve at this kind of thing?* she wonders. She has water, tea, fruit, and cheese. And some strategically placed tissue boxes. Ed is trying to remain calm. He wants to act like it's just a regular get-together with their three adult children. It's not. Eva feels like everything hangs in the balance this evening. Yet, she's not even sure what they're hoping to do. Does she want Callie to leave Neil? Not if he can be helped. Being a single mother would be really hard on Callie, and what about Neil's parental rights? How could she sleep knowing Jeremey was spending time alone with someone so physically and verbally abusive?

On the other hand, she doesn't want Callie and Jeremey to continue living like this. As far as she knows, they've managed to keep the boy safe and ignorant of what's going on, but can you ever really keep this kind of dysfunction away from a child? They always know, don't they?

The best thing right now would be for them to convince Callie and Jeremey to stay with her and Ed for a month, giving Neil some time alone to figure things out. *And really, it might teach him a bit of a lesson*, she thinks bitterly.

With that in mind, Eva decides to call Callie. Make sure everything is set for tonight. They haven't described it as an intervention to her, but more of a family meeting. "Hey hon," she says when Callie picks up. "We're really looking forward to seeing you tonight."

Callie's voice is hoarse when she answers. "About that, Mom, I'm not going to make it. It doesn't work anymore."

"What? Why? You already agreed." Eva tries to keep the pleading out of her voice, but she feels a prickle of fear running along her neck. "Is this because of Neil? It is, isn't it." She hears a crackling sound on the other end and suddenly Neil's voice comes through.

"Hi Eva," he says.

"Neil? Were you listening to our call?" Eva holds her cell with both hands to stop her trembling fingers from dropping it.

"Whatever you have to say to my wife, you can say to me." His words are slightly slurred.

"Well, actually Neil. I don't feel comfortable talking to Callie with you there because of the awful way you've been acting." Eva's eyes sting. This is going all wrong.

Neil laughs, and she can picture the sneer on his face. "Before you called, I was telling my wife about the new job I took in Toronto. We're going to be moving next month."

Eva drops the phone then and scrambles to pick it back up. Her heart beats like a frightened rabbit's. The powerlessness she felt as a little girl, when her father died and her mom had a string of bad boyfriends, returns. Eva takes a deep breath. She has to keep it together. She hasn't lost control since that one night when she was a teenager. But that was self-defence. She pushes the night from her mind. *Focus, Eva. You can do this.*

"Put Callie on." Her voice is calm now, masking a fear she's just barely holding back.

"I'm here, Mom. You're on speaker phone."

"So, you're moving then? This is for sure?"

Neil chuckles. "Yes, Eva, unfortunately we won't be around for you and Ed to help, but we'll work things out."

Callie clears her throat and adds. "Neil's business has been struggling for a while, and this new job could make a real difference for our family."

"And your job? You'll quit, then?" Eva's barely keeping up; she feels slapped but doesn't let it show.

"Of course. I'll get a new one once we're settled." Callie sounds determined and for a moment Eva wonders if she actually wants to move. "It will be a fresh start for us, Mom."

"But you'll be across the country from your family, your support system." With each breath Eva's pulse slows, and she knows what she has to do. What any mother would do to save her daughter, because, if Callie and Neil move so far away with Jeremey, she'll have no way of keeping tabs on her family. No way of knowing if they're safe. She stares out the kitchen window at the bare tree branches dusted with snow and gives Neil one more chance.

"Is this really the best time to make a move? I mean, you're still in such a bad place as a couple." There's silence for a moment and Eva enjoys the feeling of her words being out there.

"It's not really any of your business, is it, Eva?" Neil says, and then the phone goes dead.

Eva leans back against the kitchen counter, gently setting down her wooden spoon, so as not to splash herself with spaghetti sauce. There are times throughout her day when she thinks about Neil's treatment of her daughter, and it riles her up so much she could scream. She drinks a full glass of water, hoping to drown her anger, but it's there, bubbling and trying to break free.

It's been two weeks since her phone call with Callie and Neil. One day since she stopped by Neil's work site and asked him to swing by today and fix the garage door for her. He looked utterly surprised by her friendly demeanour. "Don't mention to Callie that you're coming, okay? She would want to come and fix it herself and I don't want to bother her. Besides, you're the handyman in the family." She smiles, but her words are poison.

She's wearing a crisp white blouse with khaki-coloured slacks and her mother's pearls, the only thing of value left to her daughter. Eva takes strength from an orderly appearance. It's her armour, and today, she's a one-woman army. She checks the clock. It's almost Neil's lunchtime. He'll be here soon.

For the past few weeks, Eva has given an award-winning performance. She managed to convince her family that she's happy for Callie and Neil and this new chapter in their lives. It helped that Callie found a counsellor in Toronto that they can see once they get settled. At first Ed was skeptical of her cheeriness, but she has fooled even him.

Neil is still acting cold toward her, but she can tell he'd like to get back into her good books before he takes her daughter and grandson away. Without hesitation, Eva scoops a large spoonful of peanut butter and adds it to the sauce. She grabs the whisk and blends the mixture until no evidence remains. It would look like a very unfortunate mistake, if anyone found out. She doesn't think anyone will because Eva is careful.

Once the added peanut butter is completely mixed in with the sauce, she puts the jar away and washes off the wooden spoon. She carefully ladles sauce on top of the cooked spaghetti noodles sitting in the Styrofoam container. A takeout container she'd saved for today.

And then she waits. Eva is good at waiting.

"Eva?" Neil comes in through the garage. "I had a look at the garage door and I think it just needs a little lube. I'll grab some from my truck."

She turns and smooths her shirt down. Takes a deep breath and looks at Neil slouched against the granite countertop. He looks uncomfortable and shifts his posture, his eyes on the door.

"Thank you, Neil. I really appreciate it. With Ed out of town, I felt nervous leaving the garage door open overnight."

This has the effect on Neil that she hoped it would. "My pleasure, Eva." Is it just her, or does Neil actually look a little guilty? No matter, though.

"Before you leave, please take some lunch with you. I've made spaghetti — peanut-free, of course." Neil shrugs off his jacket and sets his cellphone down.

"Sure, thanks Eva."

He fixes the garage door and comes in to collect his personal items and lunch. Eva sets the container down in front of him and busies herself tidying some papers on the counter. She can hear the sounds of Neil lifting the lid and checking the spaghetti out. He closes it again and heads toward the door. "I almost regret taking your daughter to Toronto. But not really."

Eva's head snaps up. Neil's smiling but his eyes are cold. Eva cocks her head. "Goodbye Neil," she says and watches him leave.

Eva imagines he'll eat lunch when he's back on site. How tragic, they'll say. The spaghetti sauce from the unknown restaurant was contaminated with peanuts.

She hauls the recycling to the edge of the curb and then walks to check the mail, taking her time. She's in no hurry. Any who spot her will see a nicely dressed, middle-aged woman smiling warmly. After all, she has so much to be thankful for.

Hilary Faktor is a writer based in Calgary, Alberta. She doesn't enjoy trying new things and yet finds herself in random activities like adult gymnastics, downhill skiing, and canoe racing in Northern Manitoba. Hilary's work has been published in *The Globe and Mail*. She is currently querying her young adult novel about a girl who wakes up alone on the highway with severe memory loss. Follow her on Twitter at @hilaryfaktor or find her at **hilaryfaktor.com**.

deadly days in blossom city, again

by Charlotte Morganti

It was February 29 again, and I was wondering which member of my family would try to kill me this time. When the doorbell rang and filled the house with the opening notes of "Bad to the Bone," my self-preservation instinct took over. I grabbed my antique samurai sword and my Kevlar vest. Then I ducked and rolled.

I crouched under my armour-plated dining room table, listening to the repeated chorus of the doorbell and shivering from the cold rush of adrenalin roaring through my body as I fastened the buckles on my vest. The musical notes finally stopped, and all was quiet for a moment. Then I heard knuckles rap out "shave-and-a-haircut" on the bulletproof glass of the sidelight and a voice calling my name. "Chrys? Chrys, it's me."

I recognized the voice. "Persie?" I said.

"Of course. Who else would it be?"

I could think of at least one other person whose voice might sound exactly like that of my next-door neighbour Persimmon Worthing — my niece Dahlia, the celebrated impersonator. Dahlia was currently earning serious money, American dollars no less, as the opening act in Las Vegas for the Boys of Yesteryear. Still, it was a family tradition that we reunite every four years, so Dahlia was here in Blossom City, along with seventy-four other members of the Leap family.

I crawled from beneath my table and peered along the hallway toward the front door. The salesman from Dude's Home Security had given me a money-back guarantee that the door's reinforced-steel lining would stop a .600 Nitro Express bullet. I hoped, but didn't really believe, I could rely on that. He probably didn't care whether his words were as empty as our premier's assurance that the hike in the sales tax rate was only a temporary measure. If an elephant-stopping bullet came blasting through my door, I'd hardly be alive to collect on the guarantee, would I?

Instead of rushing down the hall and throwing the door open as I would do on any day other than Leap Day, I grabbed my iPad from the kitchen counter and tapped on the videophone app. The screen lit up and showed a grainy shot of a petite woman standing with her face smooshed against the sidelight. She was the correct build and her hair looked like Persimmon's — short black curls tipped with magenta. I exhaled in relief, tossed my iPad back on the counter, and hurried to the door. Just as I reached for the knob, a little worry squeezed its way into my brain. Were the tips of Persimmon's hair magenta this week? Or violet? I snatched my hand back. If it were my niece Dahlia who stood on my porch, she could have electrified the doorknob or affixed an explosive to it. Probably not even a Dude's Security door would withstand plastique.

I ran back to the kitchen, grabbed the iPad, and returned to the front door. I shouted, "Please look at the overhead camera."

The woman on my doorstep raised her head and stared at the camera lens. She looked a lot like Persie. Did I mention Dahlia was also a makeup artist?

The woman waved at the camera. "Chrys, hello? It's me, Persimmon."

"Please execute the dance steps we learned last week," I said.

The woman stood wide legged, arms akimbo, and glared at the camera. Her breath puffed out into the chilly Leap Day air. "I'm freezing out here; stop goofing around, and let me in."

"If you really are Persimmon Worthing, you know the dance steps, so humour me. Just think of it as extra practice. God knows you need it."

Her jaw dropped. For a moment I thought the woman was preparing to kick the door. Then her shoulders relaxed. She said, "What the hell, why not?"

She tapped her foot as she hummed the opening bars of "Boot Scootin' Boogie." Then she danced. She executed the opening heel-step section easily and even pulled off the leather-slapping step without losing her balance. I waited, watching for the slip that would tell me the woman on my porch was really Persimmon. It came during the second of the grapevine moves. She stepped to her left but then slid her right foot in front of her left.

"Oops, wrong," I said under my breath. Persimmon had made this misstep every time we'd run through the line dance at class last week.

Now she stamped her foot and turned to face the overhead camera. "Who cares about the boot shittin' boogie anyway?" she said, the same thing she'd said after every misstep in class last week.

I threw my door open. "Persie! It's you."

She stomped past me into the hallway, red faced. "Chrysanthemum Leap, you have lost your mind. I swear I was getting ready to call the authorities."

She marched down the hall toward the kitchen, peeling off her parka along the way. Before closing my door and double locking it, I did a quick scan of the street and thankfully saw none of my family lurking out there, behind trees or elsewhere.

I found Persie in my kitchen, staring at the granite-topped island and the black shield leaning against it. "Is that...?" she said.

"A riot shield, yes. It arrived two days ago, just in time. Honestly, Amazon Prime is a great deal when you consider how much you save in delivery costs."

A frown flickered across her forehead. "Just in time for what?"

I filled the kettle and set it on the burner. "Tea?" I said.

"Sure, but then let's take a walk. I need some exercise. So, the shield arrived just in time for what?"

I couldn't fault Persimmon for not connecting the dots. She wasn't a Leap. She was from the Branch and Worthing families, and both of those families took a sane approach to family reunions — they avoided them.

I rooted around in the cupboard, found the Earl Grey tea and plunked it on the countertop before answering her. "Our family reunion, cleverly named Leap Days. Three days of boring togetherness, culminating in the terror of the final day when one member of the family tries to murder me. Remember four years ago? If I'd had this riot shield then you wouldn't have had to spend six weeks fetching and carrying for me while my broken bones healed."

When the kettle whistled, Persimmon poured the boiling water over the tea bags in the pot and I grabbed a lemon from the fridge.

Persimmon set the teapot on the island. "I don't think that what happened to you four years ago was really an attempt to kill you, Chrys," she said.

When I raised my eyebrows at her, she said, "Well, yes, your cousin *did* try to kill you, but it wasn't you Jasper was fighting, was it? Didn't he say the pain medicine he was taking caused hallucinations and he thought you were a deranged harridan?"

"Oh sure. That's what Jasper said when *you* arrived on the scene," I said. "Before you showed up and called 911, however, he knew exactly who he was trying to kill. He even told me. 'Chrysanthemum,' he said, 'you've gone too far this time. I'm gonna bust every bone in your scrawny body and drown you in the Thompson River.' And then you come to the rescue and suddenly he's pretending to be delusional."

"But the police didn't charge him."

"Of course they didn't." I poured tea into our cups. "You know who his father was."

Persimmon nodded. "Jeremiah Leap."

"Exactly. Once the head of Blossom City's violent crimes department, not to mention a good friend of the mayor. You might think less of me for saying this, but when he died two years ago, I didn't send a card to my aunt. I couldn't find one that said "congratulations on your loss." And believe me, I looked."

Persimmon smiled and squeezed some lemon into her tea. "Okay, let's recap. Four years ago your cousin Jasper did, or did not, try to kill you."

"Did."

"Whatever," she said. "Isn't it a big leap, pardon the phrase, to go from one unfortunate incident that happened four years ago to the conclusion that someone in your family tries to kill you at each reunion?"

"My conclusion isn't based on just one incident."

"What?" she said. "You never told me there were others."

"It's not something you bring up when you first move into a new neighbourhood," I said.

"But we've been neighbours, and friends, for six years."

I nodded. "I probably should have said something after the thing with Jasper. But I didn't want you to think you lived next to a woman with would-be murderers in her family, or to believe I might be cut from the same cloth."

"Hah! I've seen you scoop bees out of your bird bath to save them from drowning. You're afraid of spiders but coax them to scramble onto a paper towel so you can put them outside rather than stomp on them. Your windows are plastered with reflectors to prevent bird strikes. You fainted last week when I sliced my finger on the mandoline." She peered at me. "See? You've gone all pale just thinking about blood, so no way could you try to kill someone."

I hung my head between my knees for a moment to encourage blood to move back into my brain. Then I sucked in a deep breath. "Yeah, I guess."

"How many other incidents have there been?" Persie said.

"Jasper's attack four years ago was the sixth time a relative tried to do me in. The first one happened when I was twenty-eight and Philippa Leap, another cousin, pushed me off Deception Ridge Viewpoint. Luckily, I landed on top of a snow-covered cedar that broke my fall. Philippa claimed I had tripped when I took my eyes off the trail. I tripped alright, but only after she placed both hands on my chest and shoved."

"Why did she do it?"

I shrugged. "I have no clue. Just before she catapulted me off the mountain she said something along the lines of, 'How could you do that to me?' Unfortunately, I was airborne before I had the chance to say, 'Do what?' I swear I never said or did a bad thing to her ever. Anyway, Philippa was the first of my family to try to kill me. Since then, I've narrowly escaped death from falling tree limbs, a venomous snake, a remote-controlled model airplane, and a toaster in my hot tub. And, of course, Jasper's baseball bat."

"Hmmm," Persimmon said. "And every one of those events happened at your family reunion?"

"Yes. But to be precise, they all happened on Leap Day itself. You have to admit there's a pattern there, eh?"

Persimmon nodded. "Certainly enough of one to conclude you have become your family's favourite woman-who-should-be-dead."

"Yes. And that is why I have a riot shield in my kitchen and am wearing a Kevlar vest."

She smiled. "I noticed the vest when I first came in the door. The fabric's pattern looks familiar."

I ran my hand over the vest, smoothing the green faux velvet embossed with crimson fleurs-de-lys. "I covered it myself with some leftover material from my living room drapes. I thought if I could blend in with my surroundings, it might save my life."

"Worth a shot."

I checked my watch. "If we're going for a walk, let's do it now," I said. "I have to be at our Leap Day Lunch by one. It's at Al's Deluxe Diner so perhaps you can walk there with me?"

We shrugged into our parkas and headed out. I thought about taking the sword and shield along but figured my relatives wouldn't try anything as long as I was with a potential witness.

Partway along the block, Persimmon said, "Listen, did you ever consider turning down the invitation? I mean, if you almost die at every reunion, why put yourself in harm's way?"

I stopped in my tracks to stare at her. "But it's a much-loved tradition. I can't not go. That would be a snub to the whole Leap family, especially my great-grandfather who dreamed up Leap Days."

I started off down the sidewalk again. "Nope, I have to attend. I'm fifty-two years old. I've managed to live through thirteen Leap Days so far, and I'd like to live through several more. I just need to figure out how to do it."

Persimmon jerked her head toward me. "Wait, I thought you said Philippa tried to kill you at the first Leap reunion."

"No, I said that was the first attempt to kill me, not the first reunion. Leap Days have been going on since before I was born. Relatives only started trying to off me twenty-four years ago."

"What changed? Why didn't people try to kill you at earlier reunions?"

I shook my head. "Beats me. All I know is that the 'let's try to kill Chrysanthemum' event is now firmly ensconced as part of Leap Days." I sighed. "And here we are, another leap year, another Leap family reunion, and today is Leap Day, so somewhere in Blossom City, one of my relatives is plotting their own deadly closing ceremony."

Persimmon said, "There must be a reason. Why weren't you a target before? If we can figure out what changed, perhaps you can avoid being a target today."

For the first time since I woke up this morning, I felt a glimmer of hope. Could Persimmon be right? How wonderful it would be to live worry-free and to spend my savings on trips instead of personal security devices. Still, I knew figuring out the reason behind all the attempts to kill me was a hopeless task, and I told her so. "For the last twenty-four years all I've done is try to solve the mystery. I can't think of a single reason why this would be happening."

"You know I love puzzles," she said. "So let's give it a try. What have you got to lose? Tell me about the reunions. What happens at them?"

We'd reached a small park not far from the diner. When I gestured at a bench we moved to it and sat down, turning our faces to the weak February sun. She was right. I had nothing to lose and everything to gain. I told her about Leap Days.

"What happens?" I said. "Everything that's boring. The first day there is always a potluck meal at a community hall. The little kids run shrieking around the room while their parents play horseshoes if the weather is half-decent and indoor beanbag toss if it isn't. The teens sneak off somewhere with a couple cases of beer that adults pretend not to see them lifting from behind the bar. One of the aunties from the

Danish side of the Leap family opens a huge jar of pickled herring and tells everyone that it perfectly complements the sausage and perogies the aunts from the other side of the family brought. The meal is topped off with peach pies made by various relatives and everyone votes on their favourite pie."

"And the second day?"

"More of the same. More food, usually casseroles. Definitely more pickled herring. More screaming kids. But colder than the first day because the second day's events usually take place in a town park or campsite by the lake. Apparently, great-grandfather Leap believed his family was a hardy lot and could withstand February in the British Columbia interior. The day ends with the announcement of the best peach pie. The winner gets a tacky ribbon."

"What about the last day? Is the final day of the reunion always February 29?"

I nodded. "Yes. On Leap Day the family meets in a local restaurant for lunch. Like I said, today Al's Deluxe Diner gets to play host. We have a feel-good chat time where everyone can tell the family what they admire most about their relatives. A few people, usually the same three, volunteer to organize the next Leap Days. That's probably why the reunion is so boring — those three Leaps are the dullest of the Leaps. Anyway, at the end of the lunch everyone exchanges promises to stay in touch and to get together soon, which of course they never do."

"That's it?"

I nodded. "Yeah, like I said, boring."

"Okay," Persimmon said. "Is that exactly the way the reunions have always been? Even before Philippa?"

I nodded again. "Yes."

"To recap, then. Day one, get together, share food, eat peach pie, vote on it. Day two, get together, share food, and congratulate the prize pie maker. Day three, get together, share food, have your mutual admiration chat, and say see you in four years?"

I'd been nodding along with Persimmon as she recapped the days.

Right up to day three. "Wait," I said. "Day three. Sharesies. I remember my grandfather started it. He thought Leap Days needed some oomph. He said we should think about why we appreciate each other and then share those thoughts as a way of supporting each other. He believed it would bring the family closer together."

"Sharesies? Is that the feel-good chat you mentioned?"

"Yes. It's the only change to our reunions that I can think of and I'm pretty sure the first one I ever took part in was the year Philippa chucked me off the viewpoint."

"Now we're getting somewhere," Persimmon said. "Do you think your Leap Day Sharesies could be the key to why you almost become a murder victim every February 29?"

I snorted in disbelief. "How could singing someone's praises be a problem?"

Persimmon was quiet for a moment as we trudged along. Then she said, "From what you've told me, some members of your family are excitable. You never know what they might perceive as a problem. Can you remember what thoughts you shared about the relatives who tried to kill you?"

"Not word for word, but yeah."

"Okay, what did you share about Philippa?"

"Philippa won the peach pie contest that year. She and her husband Jeff had been married just six months and this was the first pie she'd made during their marriage. When Jeff and I were dating, before he dumped me in favour of Philippa, I used to make him peach pie every Sunday. Jeff told everyone Philippa's peach pies were the best he'd ever tasted and that he'd married perfection itself. At Sharesies, I stood up and said I admired my cousin's ability to make an unbelievable peach pie that had the same flaky pastry as our Aunt Ethel's and a peach filling that tasted exactly like Aunt Ivy's. Philippa's pie duplicated the pastry and filling so well, I said, if I didn't know better I'd think she'd stolen our aunts' recipes."

"And later that day she pushed you off the mountain?"

"Yep. Go figure."

"Were you right? Did she steal those recipes?" Persimmon said.

"I never said she'd stolen the recipes. I said I knew better. But, you know, since then everyone who enters a pie in the reunion contest must give a copy of their recipe to Aunts Ethel and Ivy in advance. Philippa hasn't ever entered again."

"Let's think about the other attempts to kill you," Persimmon said. "You mentioned a venomous snake? What happened there?"

"Petey Leap, Philippa's younger brother, had a pet rattler. Somehow it got loose and found its way into my bedroom on February 29, four years to the day after the episode with Philippa."

"Did you share anything about Petey at that particular reunion?"

"Sure. I'd overheard him talking to Philippa at the sausage and perogy dinner. I was so impressed by what I heard that during Sharesies I told everyone I truly admired Petey's take-charge attitude and creativity when it came to trying to help his parents cut down on their excessive drinking. I said we all knew it was fairly easy to water down vodka, but not every teen would think to add food colouring when they watered down the scotch and red wine."

"How'd Petey react when you shared that information?"

"He didn't say much. Not that I could hear anyway. No one could hear anything other than Uncle Bert and Aunt Emily, Petey's parents, yelling obscenities." I mulled that over. "I always thought Petey had put the snake in my house. Do you think it could have been my aunt and uncle?"

Persimmon chuckled. "Could be any of them, maybe a joint decision. So what about the toaster in your hot tub, who did that?"

"Charise, my father's second and *much* younger wife. On that particular February 29, I told the whole family that I admired her selflessness in offering afternoon tea and solace not only to Reverend Greeley, whenever his wife went on one of her many European junkets, but also to Coach Draper, during the high school football team's several losing seasons. I said I was certain her efforts raised their spirits, among other things, immensely."

"I can see why she might want to jolt your system," Persimmon said. "You're fortunate you spotted the toaster before you electrocuted yourself."

"I never said Charise was smart. I spotted the fluorescent yellow extension cord stretching from beneath the water to the outdoor wall outlet. Actually, I tripped over it on my way across the patio." I puffed out a breath. "I guess over the years I could have offended the odd relative or two. Who'd'a thought?"

"So you shared something at Sharesies about each relative who has tried to kill you?"

"Without a doubt." I checked my watch again. "It's almost one. I should head to the diner."

We left the park, and once we were back on the sidewalk, I said, "At one reunion, I talked about my Uncle Jeremiah Leap — you know, the once-upon-a-time-big-time cop. Anyway, I mentioned how clever he was when he was the mayor's campaign manager and hired ballot stuffers. And at another I raved about my brother-in-law Larry's ingenuity in feeding steroids to his kids' 4H calves so they won all the ribbons."

Persimmon said, "How'd they try to do you in?"

"My uncle's remote-controlled model airplane, which had razor-sharp propellers, mysteriously went amok and dive-bombed me. And my brother-in-law made a few miscalculations when pruning the branches of a fifty-year-old oak just as I walked beneath it."

"You see a pattern in all this?" Persimmon said. "If you refuse to avoid your family reunions completely, then you need to stop taking part in Sharesies."

"Oh no, that would be seen as an insult. Everyone is expected to say something nice about someone."

"Okay, here's an idea. Simply stand, smile, and say 'I admire and thank everyone here for their generosity and love.' Then sit down and shut up."

I grinned at her. "Perfect! I can do that."

We arrived at Al's Deluxe Diner. All my relatives were inside, either at the bar or seated at tables. I said goodbye to Persimmon, entered the diner, grabbed a glass of white wine from a passing waiter, and took a seat at a table near the door — just in case I needed to boogie on out of there post-haste.

The meal was uneventful, as dull as every other Leap Day Lunch. Even though they had announced the prize pie winner the previous day, they congratulated her once more. It was not Philippa.

Then it was time for Sharesies.

When it was my turn, I walked slowly to the front of the room. I smiled at all my relatives. I remembered Philippa's words. I said, "I admire…," and then I caught sight of my sister Fern and her husband Gord, sitting beside their lovely granddaughter, and I remembered what lengths Gord had gone to in order to cultivate a close relationship with the new president of the very exclusive Primrose Primary School. No stone unturned, he'd said, when it came to ensuring little Melody would be admitted. No bedsheets unrumpled either, I thought. Did Fern know the president of the school was none other than our father's now-estranged but ever-present second wife, Charise?

I said, "I admire and thank everyone here for their generosity and love." I headed back to my seat and sat down. Everyone clapped. I stood again and bowed slightly. I noticed Gord sitting next to Fern but smiling across the table at Charise.

I raised my wine glass and said, "I also admire my brother-in-law, Gord. Let me tell you why."

Charlotte Morganti has been a burger flipper, a beer slinger, and a lawyer but always a stringer-together-of-words. She writes primarily crime fiction and when not writing (that is, procrastinating) you'll find her kayaking, gardening, lazing about, or making tourtières. Charlotte and her husband live on the Sunshine Coast of British Columbia where, as advertised, it's mostly sunny. Except when it's raining. Find out more at **www.charlottemorganti.com**.

contract killer

by Michelle Tang

It was February 29 again, and I was wondering which member of my family would try to kill me this time. I couldn't wait. My hands in constant movement, I adjusted my clothes like a nervous prom date, even though they fit like a second skin. I wore a leather motorcycle suit with sewn-in armour and steel toe boots. Ski goggles hung around my neck. I carried no weapons — I didn't want anyone to get hurt, least of all her.

My mother knocked on my bedroom door and, after a moment, poked her head in. Across the room, I tensed.

"Bruce, it's a quarter to midnight." As if I wasn't staring at the clock like my life (haha) depended on it. Still, moms will be moms.

"I know, thanks."

"We'll be in the basement."

"Right. Be down in a sec. Just … getting ready."

She tried to smile but her trembling hands were a dead giveaway. "I love you, honey."

"I love you too. It's going to be okay, Mom."

Alone again, I stared into the mirror one last time. Though I've been told I'm a good-looking guy, I only saw the deep bags under my eyes and my skin, paler than usual. I made a face at my reflection, put gel in my hair, and headed to the basement to await my anticipated murder.

Our basement is a large, rectangular, open-concept space. Opposite the stairs is an alcove with a bar we use for entertaining. I sat on a stool behind the bar, tapping my fingers on the lacquered wood like a nervous bartender, while the rest of my family members waited, one in each corner of the basement. I wasn't about to start distracting myself with my phone or a video game, so I stared into the centre of the room, monitoring any movement with my peripheral vision. I tried not to yawn, took a drink of strong coffee, and cursed my jet lag.

My sixteen-year-old sister, Erin, was lounging in a chair placed in the corner to my right. She was surfing on her tablet and taking selfies with her phone. Erin had claimed that corner because of its proximity to an outlet where she could keep her devices charged. My twenty-year-old brother, Trevor, was in the corner to my left, reading a textbook as thick as my bicep — for fun. My parents were in the corners closest to the stairs, staring at me with heart-breaking intensity. My father looked sick with guilt, as he always did on these days. After all, this whole thing was his fault.

Thirty years ago, Seiichiro Nakamura was an ambitious young human rights lawyer, so ambitious that he'd been made the youngest senior partner at his law firm. He was ready to sacrifice much to achieve his goals. Some things, like his first name, which everyone seemed to stumble over, were easily left by the wayside. "Call me Steve." He lost his accent and picked up local colloquialisms. Other things were harder to give up, like his sense of right and wrong.

When my dad reached the upper echelons of the firm, he became privy to information that made his skin crawl. Hush money flowed in, ensuring the named partners turned a blind eye to awful accounts of mistreatment. His firm had also been hired by corporations to "find" human rights violations as a means to pressure companies in the developing world into unfair deals. The worst part, the arsenic-laced icing on top, was that it hadn't been his skill or his work ethic that his bosses had noticed; he'd been set up to be the fall guy. Blame it on the overreaching minority. Why not, as long as the reputation of Dewey, Prophet & Howe was unsullied.

Well, good ol' Steve blew the whistle. It was a big deal in the media, tanked the reputation of the law firm, and it wasn't a surprise to the young Nakamura that he was soon jobless. He was waiting for the other shit-smeared shoe to drop: officers arresting him at the diner where he bussed tables or getting disbarred — when things got worse.

My mom, Wendy, became pregnant. She was fresh out of school with a degree in Nothing Employable; her parents had disowned her for marrying a man who could never pass as WASP; and their combined student debt was threatening to drown them both like the tsunamis Seiichiro thought he'd escaped when he left Japan.

The way my dad tells it, he was clearing a table at the diner when a woman walked up to him. When she said nothing, he paused in his work and looked up.

She was young, maybe twenty, with brown hair that fell in waves to her shoulders. Wearing no makeup, she was effortlessly beautiful. Her hands were in her coat pockets.

"Can I help you, Miss?" His own hands were still moving as he spoke, loading chipped, stained coffee mugs into his plastic bin. There was a lineup for tables and he couldn't afford to lose this job.

"Meet me out back by the dumpster in five minutes."

My dad always painted on the same expression when he told this part of the story. His thick black eyebrows drew together in puzzlement, his mouth opened to form a perfect *O*, and his small eyes moved left and right. He was the picture of shocked confusion. It was the only moment in his story that made us kids smile.

"I'm flattered, Miss, but I'm married."

"Meet me out back, Seiichiro. You're going to want to hear me out."

Not only did she know his Japanese name, long discarded in his efforts to succeed, she pronounced it as it was meant to be said, the way he had not heard it since he left Japan as a young man to study in Canada. That Japanese accent coming from the lips of a white woman intrigued him enough to leave the bustling restaurant in the middle of the breakfast rush and follow her outside.

"How do you know my name?" he demanded of the stranger as soon as they were alone.

"I have a proposition for you," she said, ignoring his question.

"What's that?"

"I would like to grant you one wish in exchange for a request of my own."

My father narrowed his eyes and looked around him, thinking this was a joke. They were alone, the stench of rotting food in the dumpster beside them ensuring their privacy.

"Who are you, that you can grant wishes?"

She gave a shrug rather than respond.

"What do you want in return?"

"The heart of your first-born son."

Seiichiro took a step back and really looked at the stranger. She was dressed in a long trench coat, the kind he'd always seen soul-trading demons wear on television. The effect was slightly marred by bright yellow rain boots, but it *had* been a wet spring. The woman looked young, and innocent, nothing like an entity that would barter for the heart of an unborn child.

"No deal."

Seiichiro began walking toward the kitchen door. "You need a shrink." Just like that, his feet stuck to the ground and he almost fell over. It was then he was certain that the woman was more than she appeared. She had supernatural powers.

"Seiichiro, this is your last chance. I have been impressed by your moral character. You are a brilliant lawyer. You can decide the terms."

My father thought of his pregnant wife and the child who grew within her. He thought of their debt and the roach-infested rented room they shared. He pictured himself bussing tables for minimum wage for the next few years, or worse, in prison for crimes his partners had committed while his wife and child starved.

Tears always came to my father's eyes at this point in his story. His sense of failure and guilt never abated, not once in twenty-five years. "I was so arrogant," he would whisper as he wiped his eyes with his ever-present handkerchief.

My mother placed a hand on his arm. "You were desperate," she said. There was never a hint of blame in her voice.

So, he struck a deal. Bargaining for a new life for his family, he considered every possible situation and made sure no word could be misconstrued. He made it as detailed as he could and as free of loopholes as possible. My father wanted success for himself and his descendants, and wanted us to achieve all our goals as long as they led to great happiness and they were morally sound. His children were to be born with intelligence, beauty, and kindness, with the extra attributes of charm and luck for me, his eldest son. He specified that only someone in my immediate family would be allowed to take my life and that I would be safe from all harm 365 days of the year. For everyone else in the family Seiichiro demanded safety and protection from major harm. "In exchange, you can try to take the life of my first son."

The strange woman stared at my father for a moment before shaking her head. "Seiichiro, I bargain only for possession of his heart."

"If you take a heart from a mortal's body, Supernatural Being, that is the same as taking their life."

"How peculiar," she murmured.

Terms decided, the two shook hands in the very Western way my father had become accustomed to. As the woman walked away, my father gasped in horror. Her long trench coat was unable to completely hide five white-tipped red tails. He had made an arrangement with a Kitsune, a mischievous Japanese fox spirit.

And so our lives became blessed. My father's former partners were found to be responsible for the crimes committed and his name was cleared. He started his own firm, which was successful beyond his wildest dreams, and many lives were improved through his work. My mother found that her degree was lucrative after all and became famous for her comic book art. It was the same for my siblings and me: whatever we wanted, as long as it wasn't harmful to others or ourselves, we were granted. Aside from the very natural drama teenagers inflict on their parents, our family was perfect — except for one day every four years.

My father hoped that by allowing only immediate family to take my life he could prevent strangers from being harmed, and it would narrow down the list of potential attackers. He thought when the woman agreed not to harm me for 365 days of each year that he had tricked her out taking my life. Who could blame him for forgetting about leap years?

To his credit, when my father realized his mistake, he spared no expense in my protection. I was trained in various martial arts, focusing on defensive skills and submitting opponents. He spent a fortune on equipment designed to protect me from my family members. The spirit that hunted me could only possess one family member at a time, but she was smart as hell. He bought a plexiglass containment chamber that could only be unlocked from the inside. I unlocked it pretty fast when my possessed mother turned purple from holding her breath. Next, he bought cages for each one of my family members. When my little brother Trevor started to strangle himself, it was tough to open his cell last so that other family members were free to protect me from his inevitable attack. In the end, we decided that the safest thing we could do was stay together. When no one was imprisoned, the spirit only had eyes for me. She didn't hurt anyone needlessly, and, with the three other family members to subdue the would-be murderer while I stayed a safe distance away, we could afford to be gentle. That was our modus operandi, and it had worked the last couple of leap years. I hoped that tonight would be different, that my plan would work. My hand touched the small object inside my jacket pocket, a gesture meant to reassure me, but it caused another surge of nervousness.

My sister stood up and stretched. Like a team of synchronized swimmers, we turned toward her. Erin took a step toward me, and, in that small movement, it was apparent that the Kitsune had possessed her. Erin normally stomped about like she was wearing combat boots, even when barefoot. Now she was too graceful, moving like a flower on the surface of a pond. My family stood up at once and pulled her back toward the stairs, far from me. It was only when the host body was restrained that I could see the Kitsune's face. It separated from Erin's in its attempts to regain control. She looked like a Japanese woman in her twenties, with dark flowing hair and pale skin. Her eyes were almond shaped and glittered with intelligence. The spirit was beautiful, as all shape-shifters must be. If you could choose the form you had, would you not choose a pleasing one?

The first time I'd seen her, I was nine. My parents told me she hadn't come in the previous years. My young mind confused fear with awe and her face burned itself into my memory. I couldn't think of her without my palms sweating, my heart pounding. How could any mortal girl compare with a creature that inspired such a visceral reaction at the mere thought of her? Yes, she was trying to tear my heart out, but the attention seemed almost flattering.

Over the next four visits, I only grew more and more enamoured. My father worried that she had somehow glamoured me with her power, yet another reason for guilt. My mother wasn't so concerned. I was healthy, had friends and other interests, nothing like a character in those folk tales, wasting away, pining for love. She suspected that the Kitsune was not a Nogitsune, a malicious spirit, but was in fact an Inari. Inari were benevolent celestial beings that often rewarded great acts. My mother told me that if it weren't for all the assassination attempts, she would quite like my visitor. The assassin certainly had more class than a lot of the other girls I had dated, Mom said, wrinkling her nose.

Last leap year, the spirit did not try so hard to take my heart. Instead, we talked, and as long as my family remained silent, she seemed to forget her purpose. The spirit had a gentle voice, a slight Japanese accent, and a bit of a lisp that I found absolutely adorable. Although she would not answer questions about the Kitsune who had sent her or how to escape the agreement, she told us many tales of her kind and of her life. She was a young spirit, with only one tail, which might have explained why she was easy to distract. When the alarms on our phones went off at midnight on March 1, I swore she looked reluctant to leave. I hoped this would be the last time the Nakamura family sat in vigil. My heart was racing, and I didn't know if it was from fear or nerves.

"Please, Honoured Guest, will you not sit down?" I gestured to a stool in the centre of the room. After a moment of hesitation, she parted from Erin's body and crossed the room to sit down. Like the stranger my father had bargained with, she appeared solid, even casting a shadow on the wooden floor. In this form, she was no danger to me, since my father had stipulated only a member of my family could harm me. Still, my hands shook and sweat sent an itchy trickle down my back.

"I've done some research since I saw you last," I said. I fought the urge to pat my jacket pocket again for my secret weapon. "I learned your name, I think. Kiyomi?"

Her almond-shaped eyes widened in surprise. She shifted her weight on the stool like a deer ready to flee. I did not try to calm her, nor did I press my advantage. I waited, mouth dry, for her response. It was an eternity, or perhaps only a few seconds, before she settled again on the stool. She gave a shallow bow of acknowledgement.

"That is my name, yes." Her simple admission was a sign of her courage. There is power in knowing a person's name, more so if they are not anchored to this world with mortal bodies. You could use a name to curse someone, or pray for them, or draw them out of a crowded diner to change their life forever. "How did you learn of it?"

If you've ever tried to find a person who doesn't have any social media accounts, you'll understand the trouble I had. The entire Nakamura family devoted its considerable intellect, determination, and finances to finding out about Kiyomi. Our advantage was that we had four years to come up with a plan. Since we were destined to succeed in any worthy cause, we soon had leads. Last year, my father and I went to Japan so I could learn about the folklore surrounding the Kitsune, and that extra luck I was granted as part of the bargain was hard at work during that trip. I hoped it, and the extra charm I was granted, would serve me well now.

"We went to your home last year. You are quite a legend, you know." Indeed, the locals my father spoke to considered it very lucky to see

Kiyomi in either of her forms. In the many bars and restaurants we visited, I recalled leaning ear-first into conversations as if that would help me understand the rapid-fire Japanese that was spoken.

Her pale skin whitened further at my words. Her single tail flicked around her, the only movement she made. I came around the edge of the bar to approach her, legs shaking so hard it was difficult to walk. I kneeled before her, vulnerable. "Twenty-five years ago, your mother made a bargain with my father." She drew a sharp breath at my words, but really, once we had figured out her name, it wasn't difficult to connect the dots. "In exchange for one wish, your mother asked my father for the heart of his first-born son. My father interpreted that to mean you were to take my life."

Kiyomi stared at me with dark eyes that sparkled like she held the light of stars within them. There was the tiniest hint of a smile on her soft lips.

"My mom and I believe that your mother was being mischievous. Are we right?" Heaven help me if we weren't, because if I'd formed the wrong conclusion, I didn't have a plan B. Technically, a Kitsune who had only earned one tail couldn't hurt me without possessing a body, but I'd really rather not gamble.

"We Kitsune can be very playful," she said.

"I think your mother wasn't looking for my death. I think she was playing matchmaker for her daughter."

The colour of ripe peaches suffused the spirit's cheeks before she nodded. "Seiichiro Nakamura has done many great deeds for mortals. His son would have the same sense of honour."

"Kiyomi, you don't have to take my heart. You had it when I first saw you, so many years ago. And I will give you my life, willingly, if you spend the rest of it with me." My mom had helped me with my speech. I felt it was a bit cheesy, but it seemed Wendy Simpson hadn't lost her sense of romance. The stars in Kiyomi's eyes gathered until they spilled over her long lashes, caressed the sharp curve of her cheekbones. Her smile widened.

Erin, who had been immersed in her world of pixels and bytes while the family had been planning the last four years, objected. "Not to burst your bubble, Bruce, but um … what? Have you forgotten the number of times she's tried to kill you? Remember when she almost made Mom pass out? Or when she made Trevor choke himself?"

There was no remorse in Kiyomi's face at my sister's words. She met my eyes, her features beautiful but blank, and I was reminded that the being before me was not of this world.

"I would ask you to marry me, Kiyomi, and extract an oath from you never to harm me or my loved ones."

"Kitsune don't have to tell the truth. It's not like we can call the police on her ass if she kills you in your sleep. Um, yeah officers, the murderer turned into a fox and ran away."

My mom shushed Erin, but Kiyomi never flinched. "On what should I swear? A bible?" Her beautiful eyes sparkled with mirth.

I reached for the small object burning a hole in my inside jacket pocket. From the way the spirit woman froze, I knew she realized what was inside it.

"My Hoshi No Tama," she said. Kiyomi nodded her head at me in a gesture of respect. Her graceful hand stretched out as though to take it from me before she stopped herself. "Well played. How did you get it?"

I opened the ring box to reveal a large pearl that glowed with its own internal light. "I went to your home two days ago. I just got back yesterday." The timing was tight; if I'd taken the Hoshi No Tama too early, Kiyomi would notice. The trick was taking the magical jewel just after Kiyomi departed for our home, but without being caught by her mother, who also lived there. Luck had been on my side. Or, perhaps her mother approved.

The legends our family had researched spoke of the Kitsune's prized objects in which they stored their souls or their magical powers, depending on which book you read. To be separated from these precious stones for too long would kill the Kitsune. It was said that the person who returned a Hoshi No Tama could extract a promise from the fox spirit that it would be bound to keep.

"I return to you your Hoshi No Tama, Kiyomi. In exchange, I wish that no harm will come to myself or my loved ones. No more attempts on my life."

"If I agree, as I must, what of your offer of marriage?" She stared at me over the iridescent sheen of her pearl.

I dipped trembling fingers toward the perfect white stone and picked it up. I had had a jeweller set the Hoshi No Tama into a ring. "It must be of your own free will," I said.

Her smile was so radiant her magical pearl seemed dull in comparison. "Then I accept your proposal, Bruce Nakamura."

She took a tentative step forward and slid into my arms, and she was as solid and warm as any human. I saw the exact moment when her fox tail faded from sight.

My mother was the first to embrace us, murmuring welcome to Kiyomi. Trevor joined in, laughing with delight. My father stood apart, tears streaming down his face.

"Do you mean to say that all these years, you would never have really hurt Bruce?"

My fiancée turned to face my father, her small frame still sheltered under my arm.

"Oh no, Seiichiro. I would have killed him if I could. But, that was not my mother's initial intention — that was the condition you had set for my mother, and she had to adhere to it. In a way, it was a test. If you allowed your son to be killed, then neither you nor he would be worthy to have an Inari Kitsune marry into your family."

Regret warred with shame on my poor father's face. I was reminded that benevolent though these spirits must be, their sense of mischief was not to be taken lightly.

"Dad, it's over now. None of us would have the awesome lives we do now if it weren't for you and your bargain."

"It was your honour that first attracted my mother, Seiichiro. Few mortals are so blessed."

"Come and welcome your new daughter," my mother said, holding her hand out to her husband.

"I have never had a father, Seiichiro. I could not have picked another whom I would respect more."

My father walked like a man to a guillotine, as though he was evaluating his life with each step. When he reached our little group, he looked into my eyes.

"Bruce, are you sure you want to marry this fox spirit?"

I tightened my hold on the small woman and nodded. "I've loved her since I first saw her, almost two decades ago."

He levelled a look at Kiyomi that he reserved for the most morally-bankrupt criminals he brought to justice. "And you, Kiyomi, you swear you will keep my son safe and happy?"

She smiled at him, at everyone. "I vow to take the heart and the life of your first-born son, and fill both with joy and love."

Only then did my father accept that I was finally safe and that his mistakes had not cost me my life. He wept as he embraced us both, shaking with emotions too strong for his body to contain.

"Are you kidding me?" Erin stood apart, eyes blazing with indignation. She stood barefoot, arms crossed, her voice three octaves past screeching. "We're all just going to forget that she made our lives hell every four years? She didn't even apologize for possessing us!"

Kiyomi's cheeks coloured again, and she lowered her head in a bow. "I am sorry for the harm I have caused you and your family, Erin. I was fulfilling the agreement that was laid out by our parents."

"Well, I don't care! I'm not going to have some fox as my sister-in-law. That's just gross! Bestiality much?" Erin glared at me with such intensity I was glad my mother stood in the way, and then my teenage sister ran up the stairs sobbing. Moments later, we heard her room door slam.

"Man, she looked like she wanted to kill you," Trevor said, whistling.

I looked down at Kiyomi, who smiled up at me with the same expression of love mirrored in her beautiful eyes. I replied, "Meh. Wouldn't be the first time."

Michelle Tang is an oncology nurse by day and a procrastinator by night. She writes speculative fiction and lives in Toronto, Ontario, with her husband and son. She is a recovering World of Warcraft addict. In her spare time, Michelle enjoys reading movie spoilers and wrestling her ideas onto paper.

beating the odds

by Arlene Somerton Smith

It was February 29 again, and I was wondering which member of my family would try to kill me this time. Turned out, it was you.

ODDS OF DYING FROM A FALL: 1 in 2739

NOTE TO SELF: Repair step.

Charlie came up with the brilliant idea on my birthday, February 29, 2016. The day I turned twenty-four — or six, depending on how you look at it.

You remember that day.

"We need to digitize our old home movies," my brother said. "Before the VHS rots to nothing. We can surprise Mom on Mother's Day."

It was a little past noon when he announced the plan. He waited until after lunch but before Mom got home from work. It was the first one of my "actual" birthdays when Mom had gone to work with Dad. Before that she had always taken the day off to hover and fuss around me. "This day only comes around every four years," she'd say. "We have to make the most of it."

She'd gone to work, but I suspected she had assigned Charlie the hover-and-fuss duty, because he hung around me in a weirdly un-Charlie-like caring way that day.

"Come on," Charlie said. "Let's go find them."

He ran down the basement stairs and I trudged behind, the heels of my plaid bedroom slippers slapping on the wooden steps. By the time I reached the bottom, he had already crawled into the storage area under them and tossed aside his old hockey bag and a tub of Matchbox cars to retrieve the dusty cardboard box labelled *Movies* in black marker. He blew off the worst of the dust and set the box on the coffee table our father had made out of used forklift pallets from one of his building sites. We sat side by side on the sectional basement couch and opened the cardboard flaps. The box felt damp and smelled of mould.

Most of the tapes were identified: Baby Charlie smiles, April 1987; Baby Charlie's first haircut, September 1987; Charlie's first steps at nine months! November 1987; Charlie's first birthday, March 1, 1988; Charlie skates! Only three years old! February 1990; Charlie's first day of school, September 1991; Charlie goes skiing, February 1992.

"Did you fart without them recording it?" I asked.

Charlie laughed. "Jealous much?" He tossed his blond curly hair. Even you have to admit his hair deserves the word *lustrous*. It defies biology and all sense of justice that his blond hair gets thicker every year while my hairline is receding.

It's one more way in which we couldn't be more different, even though we share a birthday, sort of. As you know, he was born on March 1, 1987, and I was the leap-year baby born on February 29, 1992. That would have been March 1 in an ordinary year. Three years out of four Charlie had to share his birthday with me, and he didn't like that.

It feels to me like Charlie was born fully formed, as if he walked out of the womb tall, blond, and confident. His jeans somehow magically highlight his toned leg muscles as if assigned the job. T-shirts hug his pecs. Even clothing can't slouch around Charlie.

I didn't walk out fully formed. (I don't think I'm fully formed yet.) I'm shorter than Charlie by four inches, and I'm pudgy, dark-haired, and always struggling to keep up.

ODDS OF BEING BORN ON FEBRUARY 29: 1 in 1461

NOTE TO SELF: Those are pretty good odds. Why do I feel like I'm the only one?

Charlie crawled back into the storage area to dig out the old VHS player from under the boxes of his Brio train set. We disconnected the DVD player from the big screen and hooked up the old VHS.

We picked tapes out of the box, reading the labels as we went. There were no videotapes for the remainder of 1992, 1993, or 1994, as if the video recorder had been lost, stolen, or hidden out of reach for a time after I was born. There were no tapes with my name. No record of Kevin's firsts.

I picked up a tape and read the label out loud. "Niagara Falls, March 1, 1995."

Charlie searched for the memory of that date. When he found it, he yanked the tape out of my hand. "You don't want to watch that one," he said.

"Why not?"

"You just don't."

I grabbed it back. "I do now."

"No!" He tried to snatch it back, but I hid it behind my back.

"I'm watching it," I said. He tried to tackle me, but for once I was too fast and I was closer to the machine. I fought off his attack with one arm and popped the Niagara Falls tape into the slot with the other.

Charlie fell back onto the sectional couch as sixty-five inches of snowy static crackled across the big-screen TV. After a few seconds of rolling images, the tape heads aligned and the static crackle softened into the roar of the waterfalls. The screen showed us a hazy mist pluming over the curlicue metal railings beside Niagara Falls. An eight-year-old Charlie, wearing the new blue and silver ski jacket that later became my frayed and dirty hand-me-down, leaned against the railing. He turned his face toward the camera as it zoomed in. His blue eyes and long lashes filled the screen. Then the camera zoomed back out to capture the arc of a rainbow over the falls. My left arm and then half of my three-year-old body appeared on the edge of the screen as I tried to lift myself up by a knee onto the cement footing.

"Careful, Kevin," my mother yelled, but her voice sounded a long way off.

"Wave to the camera, birthday boys," Dad said. The image jiggled as he waved with the hand that wasn't holding the camera.

"It's not *his* birthday," Charlie said. He reached out one hand and gave me a push at the same second I found footing on the cement ledge and straightened to turn and wave. The half of my body that could be seen disappeared off-screen as I lost my balance and toppled over the railing. The last shot before my father dropped the camera to the ground was Charlie's mouth forming an O.

"Jealous much?" I said.

"Ha."

ODDS OF FALLING OVER THE RAILING AT NIAGARA FALLS: 1 in 34,000,000

NOTE TO SELF: Buy a lottery ticket.

The tape kept rolling after my father tossed the video camera to the ground. Yelling erupted all around and feet stampeded past the viewfinder in the direction of the railing. "Jesus!" my father shouted.

"Kevin!" my mother shrieked, still far away. (What the hell had she been doing?)

"He's OK. He's OK," said a male voice I didn't recognize. "I got him. Up and over little guy."

"Oh, thank God," my mother's voice, closer finally. "Kevin, are you okay? Do you hurt anywhere?"

Charlie said, "Kevin fell."

My childish voice said with surprising vehemence, "MY bir'day."

Static filled the big screen as the recording cut off. I pressed *Stop* on the player. "I don't remember that," I said.

"You were only three."

"And what's this about Kevin 'fell.' You pushed me. You could have killed me."

Charlie tilted his head and gave me his impish grin. The one he practises. "I think the important part of that sentence is *could have*."

"Not funny. How come no one ever told me about that?"

"Yeah, well." Charlie twisted his mouth to one side and rubbed an eyebrow with his finger. "I wasn't exactly going to brag about it."

"Right. The Golden Boy." I rolled my eyes. "Forget it. What's next?"

I scrounged around in the box. Scout Camps. Ugh. No. My Grade 8 graduation. The acne peak of my life. I don't think so. Christmas several years. Nah. Most of the tapes were lined up neatly, labels up. On the bottom of the box, one tape without a label lay separate and sideways.

"I wonder what this is?" I slotted the tape into the machine.

I couldn't figure out what I was seeing at first. The soundtrack bursting out of the surround-sound speakers consisted of a protracted grunt of exertion like a mountain climber making a final push up a precipitous slope. And the cleft on screen did resemble a rugged peak and sloping valley.

"Is it time to push yet?" My father's voice. Excited. Impatient. "He needs to be born before midnight."

He was drowned out by another animal grunting growl, like a wolf chewing its own leg out of a snare trap.

"SHUT UP. SHUT UP. And DON'T tell me when to push," my mother said through gritted teeth. "I … am in … FUCKING … AGONY here."

"Jesus. Fucking. Christ," my brother said.

Nausea stirred in my stomach as my brain pieced together the peaks and valleys of the image and I realized what I was seeing. A big screen full of…

Mother of God. No, no, no.

My face contorted in disgust. No child wants to see that. My brain told me to stop the machine immediately, but my body didn't compute. I couldn't move. I was suffering from PRE-Traumatic Stress Disorder. I couldn't move to stop the pain because I was immobilized by horror.

"Now, honey. We agreed," my father soothed "Natural birth at home. You told me to not let you change your mind. Breathe through it."

"YOU FUCKING BREATHE," my mother said in a voice that could have won her casting as a demon. (How did she make it reverberate like that?) "I want DRUGS! My back is FUCKING KILLING ME."

I had never heard my mother swear, keen like a she-beast emerging from the bowels of Hell, or impersonate a wounded animal quite so accurately.

A hand and shoulder moved into the right half of the screen. "The baby's facing the wrong way. I need to turn the head." A midwife, or nurse, or one of those doulas.

The camera zoomed out and there was my mother, splayed out on the old double bed my parents had when we were kids. The bed had been stripped of its sheets and blankets and covered with a piece of blue plastic decorated with yellow fish. My mother was propped up, bloated and ungainly. Her dark hair was sweat-soaked and matted on one side of her head. Substances that I didn't even want to speculate about smeared her legs. She was wearing an oversized navy blue sweatshirt that read, "My favourite breed is RESCUE."

The red digital numbers on the clock radio on the nightstand showed 11:52 with a red dot by PM.

The midwife, or whatever she was, leaned into her work and my mother howled in the same way she did one time when she stepped on the pointy Transformer I had left on her bedroom floor.

The midwife stood up suddenly. "Get the car. We're going to the hospital."

"What?" my father said. "That will take time."

"Now," the midwife said, quiet but firm. "The baby's heart rate has dropped. The cord's around the neck. We're going to…"

The tape stopped and static and crackling noised filled the basement.

Charlie and I sat together, stunned.

"Je-sus," he said.

I scrunched my eyes closed and ground them with the heels of my hands. "I can never un-see that, can I?"

"You and me both, brother."

I sank back into the sagging cushions of the couch. I had always known I was born at 12:02 a.m. on February 29. I had always known that I was born in the hospital. But my parents had never told me about the planned home birth. Our house was five minutes away from the hospital. Apparently the doctor didn't waste any time yanking me out once I got there.

"Huh," Charlie grunted.

"What?"

"I always wondered what happened to that shower curtain."

I turned my head slowly toward him. "*That's* what you have to say about this?"

"I loved that shower curtain. You ruined it."

"You think I ruined it? I didn't ask to be born at home on a bunch of fish. It's not my fault."

I glared at him and tried to piece together the shine of his life and the shit luck of mine. "Why did Mom want a home birth? I could have died."

My brother shook his head and shrugged. "Who knows? But I think the important part of that sentence is *could have.*"

Thank Christ there was no HDMI in 1992. That's all I can say.

ODDS OF MEDICAL DIFFICULTIES WITH A HOME BIRTH: 1 in 2300

NOTE TO SELF: Birth videos: How to traumatize your child for life in one easy step.

"Well, I think we'll take that one out of Mom's happy birthday mix," Charlie said. He leaned forward and pressed the eject button.

"Can we burn it?"

He tossed the tape at me and it bounced off my belly. "I leave it in your hands. And don't worry. If you don't do anything eventually it'll rot away, or the machines will all disappear and there will be no way to play it anyway."

"I can only hope." I leaned my head on the back of the couch and stared up at the water stain on the ceiling tiles from when I clogged the toilet with a mini Frisbee. The stain was the exact shape of Florida, complete with a panhandle along the wall.

It reminded me of our family trips to visit our grandfather in Florida every few years. I had an actual birthday there in 2004. My twelfth, or third, depending on how you look at it. Grandpa treated us to a day at Busch Gardens. My father and Charlie loved rides, so they disappeared almost immediately to find the roller coasters and pirate ship. I always threw up on rides, so I was stuck with Grandpa and Mom on the Serengeti Express and Skyride. Big whoop. When we met up at the end of the day Charlie had barbecue sauce on his T-shirt from the ribs they ate for lunch. Mom had made us eat with Elmo and friends because she loves a buffet. "So much variety!"

The last stop of the day was the Congo River Rapids ride. Water rides were okay for me, because our bodies are mostly water, after all. What the water in the ride could do, my body could do too. Grandpa bought the tickets and we shuffled to the loading area in the afternoon heat behind a group of spring break college students from Pennsylvania. They had the builds and high energy of basketball players and the vocabulary of pissed-off kitchen workers. My grandfather made a sound exactly like *harrumph*. Before that I'd never thought that harrumph was something people could really do but he changed my mind.

"Impertinent college brats," he muttered. You never knew my grandfather, but yeah, he was the kind of guy who used the word *impertinent*.

When it came time to load, of course, we ended up sharing a raft with the rowdy college kids. They pushed each other and jockeyed for position. I stepped around them and sat in the first seat to the right. My grandfather followed me on but didn't get as far as a seat.

"Let's fucking DO this!" The loudest and tallest student raised his arms above his head. You'd have thought he was heading an expedition to conquer the real Congo instead of stepping onto an amusement-park ride.

"Do you mind?" My grandfather was standing right beside him at the entrance to the boat. "Watch your language. There's a child present." He reached a hand down and placed it on my shoulder.

I turned brighter red than even my sunburn would account for. Sure, I was small for my age, but *child*? I shrugged off his hand and shrank into the seat.

The college guy leaned sideways to peer around my grandfather at me. "You don't mind, do ya, kid?"

I shook my head ever so slightly.

He smiled and straightened up. "See, gramps? He's cool. He's heard it all before."

Murmurs of discontent had begun to grow on the landing as people grew impatient with the lack of line progress. "Get a move on, people," a man yelled.

My grandfather puffed out his chest. From behind I watched his shoulder blades contract and the leather belt holding his khaki pleated trousers strain. "Don't call me gramps. Show some respect."

I stood up. "It's okay, Grandpa," I said. I pulled on his elbow.

The college guy's eyes narrowed. "What is your problem, old man?"

The puce colour started at the collar of my grandfather's golf shirt and travelled up his neck over his cheeks and past his hairline.

My mother said, "Dad, let it go." But my grandfather's arm shot out and delivered a sharp shot to the loud college boy's throat. Like a ninja. It was impressive. I'd always known my grandfather was a military man, but to see it in action was something else. My jaw dropped open.

The college boy choked and brought his hands to his throat.

"Wow, Gramps!" Charlie said from the loading dock. That's what was weird about this. Charlie called my grandfather "Gramps" all the time.

The ride supervisor shouted, "Hey!"

The college students shouted "Hey!" Apparently that's the word for the situation. The students surged toward my grandfather, and the lead one gave him a push with both hands.

My grandfather kept his balance by spreading his feet. He rotated his body and brought back his arm to ready his right hook. When he did so his elbow caught me in the face and I staggered sideways into the loading opening as another one of the college boys tackled my grandfather. The raft rotated and my body fell in exactly the right way to lodge it between the edge of the raft and the solid railing of the loading dock. One of the metal bars gouged my side and drew blood. That's where the C-shaped scar on my side came from.

In all the mayhem, no one paid any attention to me, jammed and fighting for breath. I had started to turn grey by the time the Sasquatch-sized security guards dragged my grandfather away by his underarms. My father finally noticed me and said, "Kevin, what are you doing in there?" As if I'd slipped in there for a spot of relaxation. I gaped at him like a stranded fish until he jostled the raft away from the edge. It took considerable force, and he said, "Well, you were certainly wedged in there good, weren't you?"

All I could do was nod. And as I looked at the stain, it occurred to me that I could have died that day because my grandfather didn't want to hear that he was old.

But I guess the important part of that sentence is *could have*.

ODDS OF INJURY ON AN AMUSEMENT PARK RIDE: 1 in 16 million

NOTE TO SELF: Even water rides aren't safe for me.

My grandfather had celebrated more birthdays than anyone in our family at that point. That did make him old, I guess. That also made him lucky, in my book. People like me who don't get to celebrate their birthdays on the proper day like "normal" people notice the discrepancy. If getting old means lots of birthday parties, sign me up!

On my sixteenth birthday, my brother got me drunk for the first time. He was in university then, and he took me along with his friends to a keg party at one of the University of Toronto residences. That year we started what has become an every-four-years tradition on my actual birthday. In the seconds leading up to midnight Charlie says, "Happy birthday, little bro." At the stroke of midnight we clink glasses, and then I say, "Happy birthday, big bro," after the calendar has changed to the new day.

We toasted each other that night at midnight, and I remembered it clearly. A few glasses of beer had done me no harm. But then his friend, Bull, brought out a bottle of tequila.

Just remembering the experience brought on a new wave of nausea. I raised my head. "Hey, Charlie, remember the time you got me wasted at the keg party?"

Charlie held up a hand. "Whoa, little bro," he said. "I didn't get you wasted. You wasted yourself. I didn't pour tequila down your throat."

"Yeah, but I was sixteen. I didn't know what tequila would do. You should have warned me."

Charlie shook his head emphatically. "No way. Some things you have to learn on your own."

I sat up and leaned forward on my knees. "So the first time you drank tequila you got sick too?"

He gave me a "you've got to be kidding" look of disgust. "Of course not. I never get sick. My body is good at metabolizing."

I fell back into the couch cushions and sprawled in defeat. "Of course it is. If there's a genetic gift in this family, you inherited it. If there's a genetic curse in this family it homed in on me like a freakin' heat-seeking missile."

He laughed. "Don't be ridiculous," he said. "Anyway, I do remember that night. Dad was *pissed*."

I grimaced. "I remember. Between the tequila hangover and Dad's death stare I thought I was a goner."

"The tequila didn't kill you, but Dad could have."

I laughed. "But the important part of that sentence is *could have*."

ODDS OF A TEENAGER VOMITING AFTER DRINKING TOO MUCH TEQUILA: 1 in 1

NOTE TO SELF: Nothing good comes from drinking tequila after midnight.

So there I was, sitting in the basement on my twenty-fourth birthday with my mind reeling from traumatic birth videos, sibling confusion, and hangover memories. It was February 29 again, and I was wondering which member of my family would try to kill me next time.

Turned out, it was you.

We met later that night. We had my favourite birthday dinner of real macaroni and cheese, baked in the oven with lots of sauce. I blew out twenty-four candles on my birthday cake. (Never skimp on my birthday candles. I insist on every last one.) I opened the new pair of work boots from Dad, a dress shirt from Mom, and a new iPad from Charlie. After that he dragged me out for drinks at the Queen and Beaver.

He deposited me at the bar with a slap on the back and instructions to the bartender to "Take care of my little bro. It's his birthday." I could have had free drinks all night — leap year babies get that a lot — but I sat at the bar and nursed a lager while Charlie made the rounds with a regularly refreshed glass of bourbon.

The first thing I noticed about you was your coat. A real one. Warm. It was February, after all, and I had no use for girls who thought that freezing to death somehow made them more attractive. The hood of your coat tucked up around your chin and framed your pixie face. The rest of it hugged your silhouette. Stunning.

You held the door for a man who was going out as you and your friends were coming in. When you all arrived at the crowded bar, you offered up the last two seats to your friends and stood to the side.

I slid off my stool. "Here, take mine," I said.

You waved a hand. "No, no. It's okay."

"I insist."

You smiled and my heart vacated the building. I was a goner.

"Thank you," you said. You climbed up onto the high stool and ordered a glass of white wine. I leaned on the bar beside you and tried to think of something to say that didn't sound lame. I was still sifting through options when Charlie spied us from across the room and made a beeline for us. I could almost hear a buzz. I sighed, resigned. When women saw Charlie I automatically became less appealing.

He sidled up between us. "Hi, I'm Charles," he said to you. He always pulled out "Charles" when he wanted to impress girls.

"This is my brother, Charlie," I said. I turned and leaned on the bar. I assumed there would be no further need for me. Out of the corner of my eye, I watched for the usual reaction. The turning of the body toward Charlie. The tilting of the head and tossing of hair. The chest pushed out.

But none of that happened. You said, "Hi," but you pivoted away from him and toward the bar. You left him hanging. I couldn't hold in a big grin.

Undeterred, Charlie persisted. "The boys and I are going to the site to check on the progress of my building. Would you like to come?"

My smile faded. If his good looks didn't do the trick, the "architect designing a trendy building" card always reeled them in. I prepared myself for a lonely night.

"Your building?" you said.

"Yes, I'm designing the new commerce centre down the street. The lobby is taking shape, and it's spectacular."

Yep, I was done for. I was sure of it.

"Huh, interesting," you said, but you didn't sound interested. "But I'll pass. I'm happy here."

I turned sideways and re-evaluated. I examined you closely. A rare Charlie-resistant lifeform. You looked back at me with those big, dark brown, honest eyes and confident poise. The most beautiful thing I'd ever seen.

Charlie glanced back and forth between us and raised his eyebrows. "Okay then," he said. "I'll just be waiting over here." He gestured vaguely out toward the rest of the pub. We nodded, but we didn't take our eyes off each other.

"I'm surprised you're still here," I said.

You cocked your head. "Why?"

"My brother is a magnet most women can't resist."

You pulled your eyes away and looked across the room at Charlie, laughing with one of his architect friends. "Him?" You grimaced. "Not my type. He's so ... big and ... blond." You shuddered.

I'd heard those words so many times from other women expressed in such a different tone of voice that I didn't know how to respond. I didn't know what to do with disdain. I kept staring at you as if you were an exotic species of unicorn.

"So, what do you do?" you asked.

"I'm a carpenter," I said. "My dad has a construction company. I work with him."

"I like that," you said. "I like a man who's good with his hands."

We stayed at the bar long enough to be polite, and then we hopped the subway. I could barely breathe as we climbed the steps to the second-floor entrance of your apartment. I followed you up, which gave me a perfect opportunity to admire your shapely legs and to imagine how they would hopefully soon wrap around me. At the top step, you stopped abruptly and turned. I was so caught up in my imaginings that I didn't react in time. I ran smack into you and lost my balance. I swung my arms like an idiot and clambered for the railing but couldn't get a grip on the icy metal. I fell backwards down the stairs, clunk, clunk, clunk. My foot broke through the rotten wood of the second last step, and I flopped headfirst on the cement sidewalk. Out cold.

ODDS OF HAVING SEX AFTER SUFFERING A CONCUSSION: 0

NOTE TO SELF: I am one unlucky bastard.

I'm a little nervous tonight, so bear with me. You can keep these notes if you want. They're good reference material.

Did I ever tell you that my mother named me Kevin after the character in *Home Alone*? The day we met, when I re-lived all my past narrow escapes, it made me wonder if the name had set me up for a life of narrowly averting disaster.

But no. The *Home Alone* Kevin defeated his foes with ingenuity. I'm anything but ingenious. I'm just good at beating the odds. I was born to be "The 1 in..." that no one ever thinks they're going to be.

And now it's time. I'm hoping it's time for me to be The 1, period. The One.

Two years have passed and my not-quite birthday is coming up. Charlie and I will celebrate together tomorrow. It would be the best almost-birthday present ever if you would agree to spend the rest of your life with me.

I'll repeat the first words I said to you. "Here, take mine." Take all of me.

If not, it might kill me.

ODDS OF MEETING "THE ONE": 1 in Who-the-Fuck-Knows-How-Many?

NOTE TO SELF: I am one lucky guy.

Arlene Somerton Smith is a television and video producer turned freelance writer who specializes in video scripts, speeches, and web content. She also writes short stories, and her work has been published in *Descant* and a *Writer's Digest* compilation. When she isn't writing, she can be found in her other happy place — her part-time job at the Ottawa Public Library. To her knowledge, no one in her family has ever tried to kill her. **somertonsmith.com**

pyrrhic victory

by Robin A. Blair

It was February 29 again, and I was wondering which member of my family would try to kill me this time. Four years ago today, I fought tooth and nail to survive. My eldest son came for me with the fading light, death his grim purpose. Our battle was bloody and brutal. When darkness fell, my son Gabral lay dead. Though I mourned his loss, I gloried in my victory. Four years ago, I yearned for life. Not this year. This year, I craved death.

Reluctantly, I crawled from my bed and went forth to face the day. My summer home, high on the stony slopes of mighty Tanakara, provided a view to the east. Dawn light was shining bright upon the mountain top, the surrounding rocks and stones gathering the early morning heat, while the lowlands were still shrouded in mist and shadow. Many seasons past, I had cleared away dense stands of grey-barked photara and tall umir that grew near the front entrance. Wildflowers and soft grass now filled the open space. Here and there, a few of the larger trees remained, providing cool shade at midday. I came here now to sit and to consider my death.

The rising sun warmed my face as I watched the slow tide of golden light illuminate the landscape, perhaps for the last time. Scanning the horizon, I scratched my brow with a long bony finger. Pain laced through my shoulder as I moved. I was accustomed to such pain by now and would hardly have given it any thought, but, today, it was a reminder of why this year was different. Today, this small pain aroused thoughts of the larger pain, the pain that had become too great to bear.

Whence the pain came, I knew not. It began as a mild annoyance but grew steadily from season to season. I felt it now as an ever-present ache. Each small movement brought sharp stabs of discomfort. Larger exertions resulted in blazing agony. My nights were wracked with fevered dreams and offered little restorative sleep. By day, my thoughts were slow and dull.

In the beginning, I was ever hopeful of recovery. By the end of the third winter, hope had melted away like snow in spring. I began to consider the release of death. At first I thought to bring about my own end. Then it struck me. Soon enough, the most ambitious of my family would be plotting to kill me anyway. I had but to let nature take its course.

Leadership of the family bloodline was my primary focus. Whoever became Virka needed to be someone strong, someone who could fight off challenges for the next few cycles at least, someone who could win rich territory at the Wyrding Council. My sister Avral was my first choice. Unfortunately, she was perhaps the most peaceful member of my closest kin. I could give her cause to hate me, of course, something vile enough to rouse her to deadly anger. But then, she might turn on my progeny after I was gone. I also feared that, despite her great wisdom, she lacked the viciousness needed to be the Virka our clan needed.

Rasa was the most clever and cunning of my siblings, but she was busy hatching plans of her own and vying for power within her mother's clan. My younger brothers, Olvar and Adran, were large and strong. Countless times they had fought, one against the other, though seldom in true anger. I had often wondered if they were preparing for an eventual challenge to my rule, but nothing ever came of it. Though both had matured in recent years, they still lacked the focus and ability to think about the future. At least not in the way being Virka required.

From its hidden nest deep among the boughs of an umir, a piwakeke sang out a sweet song, greeting the sunrise. The sky had brightened as my mind wandered in search of answers. The dawn light revealed a thousand jewels scattered among the wildflowers. Soon enough the little folk would gather them up and hoard them deep within their secret halls. Warm rays were burning off the morning fog, revealing shades of emerald and gold in the landscape. Fields and scattered woods stretched out from the foothills below to the distant coast. A light haze from the morning fires hung above Seltspraw and lay curled atop the hills that sheltered the harbour.

I gnashed my teeth as I tried to shift my body into a more comfortable position. The constant pain made it hard to keep my thoughts focused. I must think. My mother, comfortable in her northern retreat, was an unlikely threat. While she had been formidable in her younger years, she was no longer in fighting shape. I had already killed my father, of course. Once he became too weak to hold his position on the Council, I had no choice but to challenge him.

The battle had been brutal. I attacked from the east, the blinding light of the morning sun behind me, hiding me from view as he made his way toward the sea. Perhaps he merely wished to swim or to fish. Or perhaps he planned to spend the day away from land, thus making it hard for others to track him down. If so, it was a sure sign he lacked confidence in his ability to fight off challengers.

It was my initial blow that led to my final victory. A staggering strike to the head, blinding my father in one eye. We struggled up and down the wide stretch of golden sand. Waves crashed upon the shore as we collided and broke apart. The cries of the gulls mingled with our roars of pain and fury. Great blows were struck, no quarter given. Once the challenge was made, neither could suffer the other to live. Slowly but surely my father's strength eroded; the tide of battle turned in my favour. Then, at last, the body of my sire lay broken upon the shore. I gazed upon it for the final time. The light of the rising sun was reflected briefly within his remaining eye, then faded away to darkness.

Eventually my sisters found us, taking us both for dead at first. Discovering I still drew breath, they dragged me home to recover. My injuries were extensive, blood seeping from a dozen wounds. Several ribs were broken. It took many months to fully heal, part of the reason a new Virka cannot be challenged until the next day of ascension.

I shook my head to clear memories of past suffering. Stretching my neck, I attempted to clear my current stiffness and discomfort. Focus. Who else might offer challenge? I had many grandchildren, all far too young to pose any threat. By Wyrding law cousins were not given the right to challenge. Most of my grandparents, uncles, and aunts were already dead. Two were in exile. Only one uncle remained. Suffering from his own grievous injuries, the legacy of past battles, he would offer no challenge this year.

Five of my six children yet lived. Along with my brothers and sisters, they were the most likely threat and my best chance for release. My silver sons, Aagar and Doran, taking after me in appearance, were full-grown and strong. My golden daughters, Roshin, Vaki, and Rakell, took after their mother, full of energy and endless endurance. I could seek any of them out and attack. Simple self-preservation would force them to fight back. But, if they lacked the confidence to initiate a challenge, I doubted they would have what it took to claw their way to a place within the Council. Confidence and strength of will were vital to hold a place among that den of vipers. Ruthless cunning and bargaining skills were required in the never-ending quest for rich territories. Lush and verdant islands, such as those my clan now ruled, were won through intimidation and guile.

My nieces and nephews totalled seven in number. Often we had wrestled playfully when they were small. They had wriggled and squirmed all over me with much delight. I recalled how they would squeal in gleeful terror as I growled and roared in mock anger. Olvar's oldest daughter, Pendra, was the most precocious of them all, constantly stirring up trouble. She had a nasty habit of biting me with her sharp little teeth when I least expected it. Now, of course, they had grown much larger and more dangerous. Though not yet full adults, any one of my seven nieces and nephews might decide the day had come to attack. The fresh vitality of youth, combined with a growing sense of potency, often made the young feel invulnerable, able to conquer anything. Lacking the prudence that came with age, they tended to bite off more than they could chew. Still, I felt it unlikely any of them would seek to challenge me this year. While it was true they might have a chance of defeating me in my current state, I had taken pains — Ha! — to hide my condition from the world at large. For all my family knew, I was as potent and lethal as ever.

I rested my chin on my forearms and huffed in frustration. So far, I had uncovered no gems of wisdom. Just then I glimpsed a flicker of movement on the trail below. A flash of ruby light where a switchback emerged from shadow. Alert for any threat, I focused my attention on the motion instantly. As two small forms became clear, I relaxed. It was only Yeoman Gardener and his young wife, slowly making their way up the path. Allying ourselves with the people in the towns and villages of the archipelago had been one of Pendra's schemes. The Yeoman, as usual, was dressed in drab greens and browns. His copper hair was cropped short above the sharp features of his hatchet face. His body was grizzled and lean, leathery skin tanned nut brown from long days in the fields. The woman had platinum hair, worn in a long braid down her back. Her round face matched the plump juicy curves of her tender young flesh. Both were bearing large bottles showing enticing ruby sparkles as they passed through slanting shafts of sunlight. The weekly delivery of wine. The local vineyards produced a delightful red, fruity with a hint of golden honey, burnt spices, and an earthy tang of iron. I recalled cracking open the last bottles to share with Olvar. It was likely the last time I would enjoy his company or the taste of that fine vintage.

"My Lord," called Gardener, the bittersweet smell of terror he gave off tickling my nose. "We come with gifts and to wish you well on this glorious day."

"I accept your offerings," I growled. "You may leave them and depart." I waved them away impatiently. While I seldom spent much time in conversation with the townsfolk, today I was especially keen to avoid distractions. The two villagers placed their cargo on the ground. They moved with haste, but also with great caution, taking care not to break any of the bottles. Once done, they bowed briefly, turned, and fled back down the trail. By the time their footfalls had faded from hearing, the breeze had cleared away the reek of fear.

I ignored the wine. If any of my family did perchance slay me this day, they would inherit it, along with whatever other treasures I had hoarded over the years. I needed to keep a clear head. The wine might provide a welcome dulling of pain but would also further dull my thoughts. Although, the more I looked for a solution, the less clear my options became, sober or not.

I remained sitting as the sun crawled across the crystal blue sky. An errant gust of wind harried small clouds about the peak of Tanakara. A falcon spiralled and dove as it hunted nimble hare and bright-eyed prossa in the fields far below. I wondered, if any among my kin came, would it be in open challenge, or would they strike like the falcon: silent, swift, and sudden?

All through the long day I waited, the tension building. It gripped my mind like a shadow, setting in my limbs as molten iron cools into rods. The great fire of the heavens was bleeding crimson into the clouds when my ears perceived faint footfalls. I recognized her lithe movements and soon picked up the familiar scent of sulphur that seemed to follow her like a malodorous shadow. Quiet as a cat, she stalked up the trail, moving quickly from tree to tree, not hidden, but stepping softly, as though stealth was her natural mode. The dark bulk of the mountain cast her face in shadow, large eyes and teeth gleaming within the darkness.

"Greetings, Virka Moldaga," Pendra whispered softly, white teeth showing further as she grinned wickedly. "How are you this fine evening?" she asked, a mocking tone to her voice. I eyed her sharply, puzzled by her behaviour.

"I am as good as gold, young Pendegara," I replied, using her full name in echo of her formality. "And yourself?"

"Oh, I'm feeling excellent, Uncle. It has been a beautiful day, and I feel perhaps tomorrow will be even better. Wait, what's that?" Pendra suddenly dashed behind a large boulder and out of sight. I glanced warily about the clearing. What was that scoundrel up to?

Normally a youngling such as Pendra would offer little chance of defeating me in battle. It was true that, given how rapidly I fatigued and how much each movement pained me, she could indeed win. But unless she knew of my condition, it would be folly for her to attack. Her presence and behaviour were making me suspicious, but I could not fathom her intent. From the corner of my eye I caught a flash of movement. Pendra had clawed her way several feet up the slope of the mountain and was now surveilling me from above. "Let's wrestle, Uncle," she cried, launching herself down toward me.

She landed heavily on my back with a laugh, driving the wind half out of my lungs. My back muscles spasmed as they absorbed the impact. Sharp spikes of pain, like the strikes of a dozen swords, ripped through my body. I clenched my teeth and hissed. I rolled, trying to trap her under me, but she was too quick. Slithering to the side, she turned with a smirk. Quick as a snake, she leapt for my neck. Her momentum spun me around. It took some effort to throw her off and prevent myself from crashing into the wide trunk of a nearby umir. In a flash, she charged back, forcing me to keep moving. The effort of trying to conceal the agony I was in continued to grow. I was tiring fast, but, so far, Pendra had not drawn blood nor attempted any lethal strikes. It seemed a poor time to play-fight, but I was still reluctant to attribute malicious intent.

Finally, Pendra dealt me a wicked blow. Using her full body weight, she drove me onto a rocky outcrop. Small creatures fled deeper into the woods as I let loose a bellow of agony and frustration. Pendra moved back, an evil gleam in her eye. "Why Uncle, surely I have not managed to hurt the mighty leader of our great clan?" she purred, her breathing still smooth and unlaboured. I tried to conceal my desire to gasp for breath and wondered if she could hear the pounding of my heart.

"I have been feeling a little under the weather," I growled. "It will pass soon."

"That is a shame; after all, today is the day of challenge. Ascension day! But perhaps it's something you fed upon?" Pendra looked slyly toward the large pile of bones that lay nearby, all that was left of the kine I had recently consumed.

"What do you mean, child?" I asked, a sense of unease beginning to coil within my gut.

"Perhaps there was something wrong with the herd. Perhaps they ate something unwholesome?"

"What would cause you to suspect such a thing?" I stared at her intently, but otherwise stayed quite still. I wanted nothing more than to lie down and try to let the pain fade, but I had to remain motionless. If I moved, I would be unable to conceal the stiffness and cramping that had begun to set in. My gaze was locked on her, unblinking.

"Well, Uncle, on the island where I live there are certain pools: pools fed by hot underground springs. The water in these pools is a beautiful aquamarine. The rocks nearby are coloured like jewels: topaz and turquoise, amethyst and emerald. But alas, no fish live in these pools, no flashing of silver scales, no tasty morsels to eat. For the water, you see, is noisome. There are certain minerals dissolved in the water that ... But perhaps this is boring for you. I see your eyes beginning to glaze over. Perhaps you would like to wrestle some more instead, yes?"

"On the contrary, child, this is most interesting," I said, both curious to hear where this was leading and reluctant to engage in further combat. I knew that drinking fouled water could make one ill. I had also seen pools like those of which she spoke. Among the emerald isles of the Sapphire Sea there were several regions that vented steam and noxious fumes from time to time. Like most of my kind, I had given them little thought.

"Well," Pendra continued, sitting at ease and looking pleased with herself, "these minerals can also be found in the soil near the pools. I found through experimentation that if I fed too much of these minerals to a small animal, it would sicken and eventually die. But if I fed it just a little at a time, the creature survived. But even more interesting, if you feed a little of the mineral to lots of animals, squirrels perhaps, and then a wolf eats the squirrels, the wolf begins to sicken and eventually dies. Most interesting, don't you think, Uncle?"

I looked over at the pile of bones again, the shape of her scheme beginning to form. The kine came from the villagers, part of their monthly tithe, along with payments of wine, gold, and silver. A payment in return for which we agreed not to raid the herds at will, taking what we wanted. Nor would we attack the villages and towns as we once did, simply for the joy and chaos of it. And it was Pendra's idea to form this agreement. Pendra with her experiments. Pendra with her new ways of thinking. At some point she must have convinced the nearby villagers to poison the cattle they brought me. Over time the toxins had accumulated within my flesh. Over time my agony had grown and my strength faded.

I glared at her through slitted eyes. I knew then she planned to challenge me. The wrestling had been another ruse, designed to tire and enfeeble me further. She had counted on my restraint, on not seeing her as a true threat. Only two questions remained. Could she defeat me, and did I want her to?

"Your tricks may have weakened me, you deceitful snake," I growled at her. "But how will you gain a place within the Council? Or perhaps your mind is so twisted you wish to see your clan doomed to ruin and starvation?"

"Don't worry about your dear Wyrdmates," Pendra snarled. "I have plans for them, those old fossils, so stuck in their ways. They deserve to be extinct!" I felt a heat building within me, a fire fuelled by anger and horror. A growl arose from deep within my chest.

"You meddle with our ancient ways and traditions. You will bring our clan, and all our kind, to ruin!" I roared at her.

"Bah! You simply fear change," she scoffed. "I see a glorious future ahead, one in which we rule the world!"

"You mean where you rule the world?"

"Yes, and why not? Why should it be the strongest in muscle and limb and not the strongest of mind and thought who rules?"

"And what of the villagers and townsfolk? What will stop them from using what you have taught them against others of our kind? They fear us now, but their numbers are great, and they too can be cunning." I saw the tiniest spark of doubt ignite in her eyes. For a brief moment hope kindled within me. But then her greed and self-confidence rose up, fanning the spark into the flames of ambition. My hope vanished like smoke. I knew I must try to destroy her, even if it meant another four years of suffering and misery.

I took a deep breath. My lips curled back, baring my teeth. My eyes narrowed, and my nostrils flared. Muscle and sinew erupted in searing fire and stabbing pain as I tensed myself to leap. This would be a desperate attack. There would be no subtlety to it. Pendra could see it coming, knew I was hurting and exhausted, but knew also I had nothing to lose. She was braced, ready for me, trying her best to appear calm and confident, but I saw she feared me yet. I was larger, older, and more experienced. Muscles along her jaw twitched involuntarily, but her gaze remained steady.

I raised my head and roared long and loud, the echoes reverberating from the mountainside, small stones shaking loose and clattering down. Further down the valley, I heard deer startle and flee. Flocks of piwakeke rose from the canopy and whirred off in all directions. My tail lashed back and forth, once, twice, and then I leapt, wings snapping wide, tooth-filled maw open, diving for Pendra's scaled neck.

Pendra hissed and dodged, quick as a viper. My jaws snapped shut on empty air, but the weight of my body caught her. There was a wet cracking sound, like that of a bough breaking, as bones snapped in her shoulder. She let out her own roar of pain and defiance. Her wedge-shaped head swung around and she bit, long teeth sinking deep into my forewing. Compared to the agony I was already in, I barely felt it. I twisted as her claws raked at my underbelly and her razor sharp talons skittered off the thicker scales on my chest. Wrenching to the right, I felt her front claws shred the delicate membranes of my wing. I was heedless of the damage, uncaring if I never flew again.

Sinews screaming in protest, I struggled to bring my greater weight to bear. Finally, I managed to wedge her against the trunk of a large umir, trying to stay clear of her hind legs as she attempted to rake at my underbelly once more. I bit down hard on her shoulder, hearing broken bones grate together, tasting the hot iron of her blood.

Pendra let out a shrieking howl as she thrashed desperately, trying to break free. With a horrific tearing sound, the great trunk splintered. Several scales tore loose as Pendra ripped herself from my grip and coiled around to strike again. I struggled to stay close, drive her forward, and pin her against the rocks on the opposite side of the clearing. I tore off more scales and left four great gouges down her side, but she slipped away again.

My heart was thudding in my chest, lungs on fire, muscles burning, breathing ragged and hot. Every movement was torture, but I drove myself to keep going, for the future of my bloodline and of all the clans.

I scrabbled about, but I was too slow. Pendra hunched and sprang, jabbed her talons into the softer hide below my forearm. With a jerk, she ripped open a deep wound, sending great gouts of blood onto the stony ground. It spread like wine from a shattered cask, the sticky blackness steaming slightly in the cool evening air.

I collapsed, exhausted, the last of my strength draining rapidly. Pendra backed away, watching me warily as she slipped from my sight in the twilight gloom. I felt I had failed my kin. I hoped that I was wrong. I hoped our great clans would continue to rule the lands, seas, and skies for many generations to come. But all I could see was the long night approaching. The shadows seemed to stretch out along the ground, the blackness clawing its way toward me. I felt cold, colder than I had ever felt before. The sky was swiftly darkening to shades of deep blue and bruised purple.

A furtive motion drew my eye, almost directly beyond Pendra's large horned head. Beside a tall buttress of rock further up the mountain I glimpsed a flash of copper and platinum. The Yeoman and his wife. Returning to witness how effective Pendra's poisons had been. My niece would become Virka, but how long would her reign last?

As the last light faded, I felt immersed in a great enveloping warmth. All the pain slowly lifted away like the breaking of a fever. A sweet euphoria washed over me in a long silver wave. The heavy beat of my heart became a soft, slow pulse.

Slower and slower.

Slower.

Then, stillness.

Robin A. Blair was born in the South Seas, and then lived for many years in a magical land down under. He moved to Canada in his youth and studied biology in the cold wastelands of Northern Ontario. His career has spanned anthropology, web design, and e-learning development. Robin now lives with his exceptional wife and lovely son in Toronto. He enjoys camping, hiking, drawing, painting, and writing, as well as playing role-playing games and strategy board games with his family and friends. His son is now old enough that "Family Game Night" has become a regular thing.

bloody reunions

by V. E. Rogers

It was February 29 again, and I was wondering which member of my family would try to kill me this time. Every four years, on or around February 29, we have a family reunion. I don't know when this dangerous tradition started, but I think it was Uncle Ted who thought it would be a good way to make sure we all got to see each other "before too long." Nothing else is going on in February anyway.

So every four years, my family and I fly from Toronto to an unnamed Vancouver Island location. I'm not going to tell you exactly where it is because I don't want to give you a bad impression of the place. Most people who live there are very nice, and the scenery is beautiful. My family? It wouldn't matter where you put them, they'd stand out for all the wrong reasons.

I had asked to be excused from the family warfare this time, claiming a lack of funds. I *was* between contracts. But when my parents offered to pay my way, my excuse no longer held water, and I found myself committed.

Trapped on a plane bearing our country's emblem, I watched the safety video as we taxied toward the runway. Aghast, I rolled my eyes and looked at my family across the aisle for affirmation. To my annoyance, all three looked placid and content, waiting for this onscreen national embarrassment to end so they could select their choice of inflight entertainment. I looked at Mom in the aisle seat opposite me.

"What?" she asked, removing her earbuds.

"Can you believe this?"

Her eyes widened a fraction but she made no sign of understanding.

"Do you remember our flight to New Zealand two years ago?"

"Yes…"

"Do you remember *their* safety video?"

"Yes…"

"Don't you remember how much better it was? It was actually funny. It didn't even take place on an airplane. It had celebrities in it and a good soundtrack. *Really* good."

"You know, you're sounding a bit spoiled, Patrick. Not everyone gets to go on nice trips with their family."

What? Had she heard what I said? "I don't mean *that*," I said. It has nothing to do with…" I tried to squelch the anger threatening to derail the conversation, and my point.

Trying again, I said, "It's just an observation. I mean, if there's a better example out there, why are we still doing *this*?"

"I don't know, Patrick. It's just not who we are."

"Are we mind-numbingly boring?"

"I don't know. Maybe."

Suddenly, I felt very claustrophobic. How could I make it through the next five days when this tête-à-tête represented the mere tip of the iceberg in terms of the intellectual discouragement I could expect? I gaped at her, but my silence must have signalled the end of the conversation. She replaced her earbuds as serenely as she had removed them.

Not who we are? Who are we then? We're a lot more interesting than that safety video, I hoped.

My girlfriend had wanted to come with me on this trip and now I wished I had let her. She would have needed to pay her own airfare though, and that's a lot of money to blow just to spend time with my relatives, in combat. Jules, my middle sister, was in France on an exchange, so she got out of it. I looked over at my youngest sister, Prudence, having a great time watching the latest Disney movie with Dad. Sixteen and she was still into that, and so was Dad. Whatever.

I fished in my backpack for one of the books I had brought, and comforted myself knowing that at least I would have a little time for reading on this trip. Settling into my seat, I opened my book near the beginning. I hadn't noticed Mom take out her earbuds again, but suddenly, her mouth was somehow across the aisle and almost in my ear.

"I hope you're not going to read during the whole holiday again," she said. "You remember what happened last time?" She was smiling. I wasn't.

"Yes, of course I do!" I said.

Struggling to refocus on my book, I found myself in a worse mood. Reading was much better than what we'd be doing once we got there. It was hardly a holiday. I don't know why I had to participate in *that* part of the reunion, but Mom had said not participating would be too insulting to Uncle Ted. He "puts so much work into it."

The rest of the flight passed without any other conversation directed at me, which was the best I could hope for. Walking through the Vancouver airport at least lifted my spirits. This was an example of something we did well, and I tried to enjoy it, despite an uncomfortable feeling telling me that we tend to celebrate seemingly authentic Aboriginal art more than living Aboriginal culture.

We had elected to take the ferry to the island and fly back. "The ferry is *so* great," Mom had said before the trip. "We wouldn't want to miss it completely. Plus, I always seem to run into somebody I know."

What difference that made when she probably wouldn't see that person ever again, I couldn't understand.

Once on the ferry, though, I started to see its appeal. At first the grey day meant there was nothing much to see. But, when the ferry's horn sounded, and my mom squealed "Active Pass!" I looked up from my book to see islands closing in on us from all sides.

"I'm going out on deck," I said.

As soon as I was outside, I stopped regretting the trip. The almost spring air, though still cool, was amazingly fragrant. Breathing in deeply, I started to feel more relaxed again. I reminded myself to appreciate the nature aspect of the trip, if nothing else.

Passing by the window where my family sat, I saw that Mom had indeed met someone she knew. At least I assumed that she knew this woman who looked to be about Mom's age. They both had a look of amazement on their beaming faces, as if neither could believe their uncanny good luck running into each other after such a long time. Mom gestured out the window toward me. I was forced to wave and smile, but I was definitely not going in there. The woman could meet my sister instead.

After another turn around the deck, I ascertained that the woman had cleared out, and I returned to my seat.

"Why didn't you come in?" Mom asked. "That was Janice from when I used to work for the government here. She's *so* nice."

"Lots of people, in fact most people, are nice," I said. "It doesn't mean it's serendipity."

"Oh, Patrick."

The drive from the ferry terminal to the cabin was pleasant enough. My sister and I sat in the back seat and did impersonations of various family members. Hers were decidedly less mean-spirited than mine, but it didn't matter. We were both in hysterics.

"Quack, quack!" was the one that kept us in fits — Uncle Ted's signature greeting. Each impersonation of it became louder and louder, and deeper and deeper. We even got shushed by Mom.

As we entered the outskirts of town, though, I started to sober up with the prospect of our arrival — the often jarring first encounter. The last time we were here, I realized just how much Mom changes around them. The moment she crosses the threshold of the family cabin, she ceases to be my mother, Elizabeth Lin, and she becomes Liz Bunton, the unmarried woman who left these parts thirty years ago. She might even have some device implanted under her skin that releases a five-day brain virus, changing her interests and her vocabulary.

The cabin is thirty minutes outside of town. My eyes glazed over as Mom recited her customary lakefront childhood stories: the time Uncle Gary got stuck in the middle of the lake on a sailboat and had to get towed in, the time Grandma fell through the ice in winter, the time Uncle Ted led them into a hornet's nest and they all got impetigo later from scratching the bites. In the evening, after a few drinks, we might be treated to stories like the time a campfire got a little out of hand or the really hot night when Aunt Rebecca and some of her friends went skinny-dipping. These family stories have almost taken on the qualities of myth. Often repeated, word-for-word, by other family members, they hint at greater meaning, but I'm not sure anyone actually knows what that greater meaning should be.

The gate to the property was open, so we pulled in and drove all the way down the long driveway. I looked at Prudence for solidarity, but she looked happy. For her, this trip was still a bonus holiday away from school, and I think she was actually looking forward to it. I exited the car, alone in spirit.

A concrete path beside the house leads to the front door, passing by a large floor-to-ceiling picture window. This uncovered window belongs to the cabin's only bathroom. And, you can often spot someone sitting on the toilet as you walk by.

Who would put a bathroom with such a large window right by the front door? And, why would you not put up a curtain? But my family's attitude is: if people have an issue with it, that's their problem. Whenever I'm at the cabin I try to keep in mind who's coming over that day, and at what time, because I don't want to be indisposed on the toilet when someone's expected at the front door.

However, that vigilance doesn't stop other people from coming in to use the toilet while I'm brushing my teeth, for example. Uncle Ted did that last time.

"You don't mind, do you, Patrick?" he had said. "I've been holding it awhile." Seeing the shocked look on my face, he had continued, cranking his head around to look at me while he peed, "It's hard to think of this as a private place at the cabin, Patrick. There're just too many of us here to ever have it all to ourselves." He had struggled with his zipper; then, seeing that the sink was in use, he had left without washing his hands.

Mom knocked on the front door. Stuck at the back of our group, I couldn't seem to get past that awful window, no matter how much I smooshed up against my sister.

The door opened and Uncle Ted's round frame and rosy, moustached face appeared in the opening. I cringed, hoping and wishing please, please let him not do it this time. We don't *have* to do it, not *every* time.

"Quack! Quack!" Uncle Ted bellowed.

Jesus.

"Quack, quack!" Mom returned.

She was a cyborg.

Uncle Ted lunged through the doorway, giving Mom a big hug. "Quack, quack, David!" he said, turning to Dad.

"Gobble, gobble," said Dad.

That sure got Uncle Ted's belly jiggling. He came out to greet and hug everyone, reaching me last.

"Quack, quack, Patrick!"

"Hi, Uncle Ted," I said.

Uncle Ted looked at me for a moment, a pudgy, warm hand lingering on my shoulder.

"Well," he said at last, "is everyone ready for battle?"

"Always!" said Dad.

"Looks like we've got a stretch of good weather, too," said Uncle Ted.

Lightheaded, I looked down at the cement path and felt like I might fall over sideways. I thought if I divide the trip into chunks of time, discrete segments, maybe I could get through it: breakfast to lunch, lunch to dinner, dinner to bed. I didn't have to participate, I just had to be present.

Upon entering, I was greeted by the cabin's distinct elementary school smell, a combination of peanut butter, bananas and linoleum. The odour's saving olfactory grace was the aroma of burning cedar running through it like a vein of sanitizer. I eyeballed some of the plush, reclining chairs by the fire and fantasized about sitting in one and reading, undisturbed, for an entire evening — a fantasy that would never come true.

Uncle Ted's family was already there — Aunt Lori, their daughter, Tanya, and their sons, Joshua and Marc. My three cousins have spouses and children of their own, and they were all there too. Already we felt like quite a big group, with still more to come.

"Little Liv probably isn't old enough to join in yet," Aunt Lori said later, sitting down next to me on the couch. "But in four years time? Maybe."

"I thought you had to be at least eight," I said, looking at the tiny person who was using Aunt Lori's thumbs to practise walking.

"Well, that's true. But she might be able to take on other roles. *You* know," she said, and winked. I had no idea what other roles she could possibly be referring to. I also didn't care. After a pause, Aunt Lori asked, "So, what about you, Patrick — how's your business going? What is it exactly, some sort of tech company?"

"I'm just a freelance website designer," I said. "It's going well for the most part, but I'm finding that these days it's so easy for people to just do their own websites. I might have to go back to school for some extra training. Get more into the development side of things."

"Is that right?" she asked. "But that's not what you went to school for, is it?"

"No. Funnily enough, I took anthropology—"

Aunt Lori didn't hear me. Just at that moment Mom's younger sister, Rebecca, appeared with her husband and teenage girls, Madison and Brooke. Aunt Lori scooped up the little person and jumped up to greet them, uttering a quick "Sorry Patrick" over her shoulder as she left.

With Aunt Rebecca and her family settled in, we were left waiting for Uncle Gary to arrive from the Yukon. To pass the time, some of us drank tea or played cribbage — pretending to be English, in a Bunton sort of way.

"How about you, Patrick?" said Uncle Ted. "Will you play the winner?"

"Sure," I said. I don't mind cribbage. I think it reminds us all of Grandpa, who passed away five years ago. Cribbage was more "his style of sport," he used to say. Personally, I always found these quiet evenings all the more bizarre, considering the mayhem that was to come tomorrow.

After my game, I went back to sit on the couch. I wondered where Prudence had gone. I looked over at my older cousins, Marc and Josh. Laughing about something, they gave each other hard high fives. I realized they must have been talking about tomorrow. Blood sport always brings out the high fives. Marc must have momentarily tuned his radar into the worldwide web of consciousness, though, because just as I was having that thought, he twitched his head, like a rabbit listening for footsteps, and looked directly at me. *Shoot*, I thought, *here he comes.*

"Hey, *Cuz*," he said, plopping down beside me on the couch. "Bring any good books this time?"

My face froze.

"Just kidding," Marc said, bodychecking me into the couch.

"Oops, sorry. I didn't think you'd fall over."

"That's OK," I said, sitting back up again.

"We're going to have fun this time, right?"

"Yeah. Sure we are."

"You sleeping here tonight?" he asked, nodding down at the couch.

"I don't know, am I? That would be fine."

"The kids are gunna be up *so* early tomorrow," he said. "But I'll tell them not to bug you."

"Thanks," I said.

"They're so excited though," Marc continued. "It's Hudson's first time. He's only just eight, right, so we didn't think he should do it last time. But we've been taking him out to practise a bit lately and he's like, 'Die, everybody! Die!'"

At that thought, Marc burst into a belly laugh to rival Uncle Ted's.

"Whew," he said a moment later, wiping tears from his eyes. "Kids are seriously fun."

I tried to smile. "That's great," I said. "He seems like a really nice—"

But Marc must have felt inspired after our little chat because he stood up, raised his mug, and looked as if he might give a speech. Instead, he just took a good look around the room and yelled, "To the Buntons!"

"To the Buntons!" everyone yelled in return.

"Quack, quack," said Uncle Ted.

Marc slapped me on the shoulder before going off to greet Uncle Gary, who had just arrived.

"Good timing!" Aunt Lori said, to anyone who was listening.

Taking advantage of the commotion created by Uncle Gary's arrival, I snuck outside and walked down to the dock. I took my phone out of my pocket and prayed to god that cellphone service had made its way to the Bunton family cabin. I had one bar — one wonderful bar. I called my girlfriend, completely forgetting about the time difference. As soon as I heard her sleepy voice on the other end of the line, I felt terrible.

"I'm *so* sorry," I said. "I wasn't thinking at all. I just really needed to talk to someone normal."

"I'm glad you think I'm normal," she said.

At least she wasn't angry. "I don't know how I'm going to do this," I went on. "I don't even know who these people *are*."

"It's just five days," she said, "two of which are travel days and don't even count, right?"

"That's true," I said.

"Just hang out and have fun in the woods. It's kind of what we do, isn't it?"

"I guess..." I said. A small voice in the back of my mind started wondering if maybe she was more like these people than I had previously thought. Still, I felt better as I took my time walking back up to the cabin. Just have fun in the woods, though? Maybe I hadn't described the situation well enough.

"How's your *girl*friend?" Marc said as I got inside. I assumed he must have seen me down on the dock through the patio doors. Luckily, Uncle Ted was just starting a bedtime announcement, so I didn't have to answer. "We've all got a big day ahead of us tomorrow," he said. "We're gunna need our rest. We've got lots of air mattresses all blown up and ready to go. Sleeping bags are there too so—"

The rest of his talk was drowned out by loud chatter. At first I wasn't sure that anyone had taken his bedtime advice seriously. Sure enough though, everyone started to disperse to bedrooms down the hall, air mattresses and sleeping bags in tow. My family and I were left alone in the living room, with Uncle Gary.

"Well, I guess I'll just sleep here then," said Uncle Gary, gesturing to the space behind the couch that bordered the dining area. "Give you guys some *privacy*."

No one acknowledged the joke, if it had actually been a joke. Everyone in my family, except Prudence, was feeling the effects of being in a different time zone.

While our family made arrangements to bed down for the evening, Prudence somehow managed to corner me by the front door, in the predatory way that only a teenage girl wanting to share gossip can.

"Brooke's boyfriend is coming tomorrow," she whispered.

"OK," I said.

"He's bringing a friend, maybe two."

"OK," I said again, annoyed to find out that there would be even more testosterone in the woods tomorrow. I was also annoyed that the family reunion always had to include a few randoms. Uncle Ted could be a bit too welcoming sometimes. "What's this got to do with me?" I asked.

Prudence seemed to realize that she had hit *enter* on her post a little too soon. She blushed and looked unsure of what to say. "I don't know. I just thought you'd like to know there'll be more people."

"There *always* seems to be more people," I said. But, seeing the hurt look on her face I tried to smooth it over. "Thanks for letting me know. I'm just really tired. Which couch do you want to take, anyway?"

As I slunk into my chosen sleeping bag, I was glad I was wearing long johns and socks. I sensed that the nylon lining wasn't as sleek and slippery as it should be. Why hadn't I thought to bring my own bag?

As I waited and hoped for sleep, I realized that the dinner-to-bedtime segment of day one was complete. How many more segments did that leave? On the last day, we'd be leaving before lunch, meaning only a breakfast-to-lunch segment that day. With three full days, at three segments per day, that made ten more segments of time left to endure. Some would be easier to get through than others.

In the morning, I woke up to the sound of loud screams. It sounded like a child had fallen and hurt themselves.

"That's some alarm clock," I heard Uncle Ted say from the other end of the house. "Oh well, time to get up!"

Soon bacon and pancakes were on and so was the radio, although I didn't know why, because beyond being able to tell that it was a newscast, no one could make out what the announcer was saying. Maybe someone was half-listening, though, because all of a sudden everyone started talking politics over coffee. These people might not be totally in my political camp but they were close enough — I could handle this. They started to sound a bit disgruntled about what was going on in Ottawa, and I was about to get onto a bit of a soapbox when Uncle Ted got onto his instead.

"OK, everyone," he said. "I can see we're all having a nice little discussion. But it's not getting any earlier out there. Let's start to get organized. A few family friends will be joining us in an hour, so we can get suited up and go over everything then."

I made a mental note of the time so that I could plan my bathroom visit well before the visitors were due to parade past the window.

When everyone arrived, the living room got super loud and there was a huge bottleneck as we all tried to get out the patio doors and down to the storage room under the deck. Uncle Ted told everyone to form a line outside so that he could hand over all of the equipment. I was near the back, of course. Prudence was near the front with Madison and Brooke, and Brooke's male friends. Prudence kept bouncing up and down, looking up at Brooke every two seconds for reassurance. I had never seen her smile and laugh so much.

Once I got closer to the front, I saw that everyone's suit and equipment was on its own coat hanger, with the person's name displayed on a piece of paper punched over the top. It must have taken Uncle Ted ages to organize all this. I imagined him coming out here on weekends to spend time in the cold storage room, his nose running while he matched up suits, goggles, and masks, wrote names, and stocked ammunition. I was conflicted; I felt a surge of love for my uncle, and an even greater hatred of what we were about to do.

It took a while for everyone to get into their gear and select their weapon. I looked over at Dad. He sure wouldn't have been doing this back in Beijing. He was already wearing his goggles and mask, but I could tell he was smiling. Dad just smiles a lot around my mom's family and sometimes I wonder if he's just being polite. He already thinks Canadians are kooky, and I honestly don't know whether he realizes there's a difference between the members of our family and everyone else. Surely there *is* a difference.

Dad nodded at me. I gave him a thumbs up and I started to feel just a little bit bad about what a good sport he always is — and what an awful sport I am.

Once we all had our gear on, we went around behind the cabin onto the field, or "terrain," as my family likes to call it. I noticed that Uncle Ted had added some extra props this year — giant blue barrels. The tires had been there last time. I wondered how many hundreds, if not thousands, of dollars all this stuff represented.

"Now," began Uncle Ted, "Is there anyone who *hasn't* played before?"

In a stupid fit of spontaneity, I raised my hand. "Very funny, Patrick," laughed Uncle Ted.

"What are you doing, *Cuz*?" said Marc, nudging me several times, laughing in my face, and waggling his head around like a crazy person. I hadn't noticed he was standing beside me.

I chastised myself for trying to participate. I was just trying to make it through the day two breakfast-to-lunch segment, nothing more.

A few other hands had gone up. Uncle Ted responded by giving a rundown of the rules.

"And, of course, no face shots," I heard him say. "Unless it's an accident."

At this statement, most of my family, including Uncle Ted, looked at me. Marc put a hand on my shoulder, his face wearing an expression of attempted sympathy. "Sorry Paddy. It was a total accident. I couldn't see that you didn't have your goggles on. I had no idea you were reading."

"That's OK," I said nodding. "I'm sure it won't happen again."

"No, it won't happen again," said Aunt Lori.

Marc must have thought I meant the reading part wouldn't happen again because he started patting down my body in a pretend impromptu frisk. "I don't know," he said. "Are you *sure*? Any books hiding in there?"

I did have a book in there and I did intend to read it. I just had to find a better hiding place this time — like inside the cabin.

"Stop it!" I said. "I meant the face shot part. Not the reading."

"I feel awful," Marc said, recovering himself. He seemed a bit awkward, like he had never been in this situation before.

"Well, I shouldn't have taken my goggles off," I said. "That was stupid."

I allowed Marc to fist bump me in a spirit of truce so that we could just get on with the freak show.

Uncle Ted got everyone's attention again. I held my gun beside me, in the same noncommittal fashion that I might hold a dead fish. While he talked, I started thinking about my book again, and my gaze drifted back toward the cabin. When I swung my head back to the front, I caught Dad looking at me. We locked eyes for an instant, through those stupid goggles that he didn't need to be wearing yet. It had only lasted a split second, but I wondered if Dad knew what I had been thinking. It didn't matter anyway. It was just my backup plan.

"This is a serious sport, a matter of kill or be killed. People can get hurt. So let's all remember to play fair," said Uncle Ted, wrapping up. "But, in its defence, paintball does have one of the lowest injury rates of any sport."

I thought I might fact check that little tidbit later.

"OK, everybody!" Uncle Ted said. "Let the games begin!"

I had sort of listened to most of Uncle Ted's spiel, so I knew whose team I was on. We were just going to play some simple games of capture the flag as a warm-up for a more complicated scenario the next day.

Once the game got underway, my team devised a strategy. Most of us would pair up and attack along the borders, while the rest, including me, would hang back as defence.

As the game progressed, I was relieved to find that my team was doing great. The other team was on the back foot, and that made my job of defence much easier. Surely I could just go sit near the back border for awhile, undisturbed. I wouldn't read necessarily. I'd just have a chance to enjoy nature in my own way, in peace.

I was inching backward on a diagonal toward our corner border when I spotted someone from the other team coming forward. The person ducked behind a tree about fifty metres away. No one else was on that side of the field and I weighed the option of pretending not to notice them. We were nowhere near our team's flag, so, did it really matter if I turned a blind eye? I found my own tree to hide behind, while I decided what to do. With a sigh, I realized that this person had probably already seen me, and I resolved to attack, but when I looked out again, the person from the other team was only five metres away — nearly at my tree. Panicked, I started to take aim, but he raised both hands. "It's just me, Patrick," he said.

How had Dad gained ground so quickly? He's almost sixty. I knew that he wouldn't shoot me. In fact, I knew what he was doing there.

"Hi, Dad," I said.

"Hi, Patrick. I came to see how you're doing. Are you all right? I hope you're not trying to disappear."

"I'm fine," I said, squirming a little.

We both sat down on the ground.

"Look Patrick, I wanted to talk to you about this trip. I know it's not your favourite holiday and you'd probably rather be doing anything else right now. Am I right?"

I nodded.

"Well, I was thinking, why don't you try to, I don't know, take it all a little less seriously? Think of it as trying to be a bit more like *water*, and a bit less like *rock*."

For a moment I braced myself, waiting for an expanded version of this lesson. When he didn't continue, I felt relieved. I already knew what he meant anyway. But why do *I* have to be the one to change?

"I know what you're thinking," he said. "Why are you the one who has to change? What you don't see is that other people are changing for you too. All the time. You might not notice it, but they *are* trying. You saw Marc earlier?"

I nodded again.

Dad got more comfortable and leaned back on the ground beside me. "You know what I admired most about your mother when I first met her?" he asked. He didn't wait for my response. "Her flexibility," he said.

He paused and I pushed ungracious thoughts about my parents having sex out of my head.

"She was adaptable. That's a better word," he said, as though reading my mind. "Adaptable. She could make friends with anyone. That's how we started to be friends. Canadians are nice people, but back then I didn't have many Canadian friends. She made me feel like it was totally normal that we should be hanging out."

As if on cue, we heard a "Whooooop!" — Mom's victory yelp. We looked out from behind our tree to see Mom tearing back in the direction of my team's territory, brandishing the opposing team's flag.

"Look at her," Dad said, happiness vibrating in his voice like a freaking harp.

The opposing team was close behind her, though, and before she could get safely back into our territory, she was shot in the back. She stumbled and landed hard on her elbows.

"Ouch," said Dad. "She's tough too. Watch, she'll get right back up."

We watched her get up; then Dad got up too. "I better get back in the game," he said. "And so should you, Patrick. Remember, more water, less rock!"

As he ran away, hopping over branches, I remembered back in kindergarten when some of my friends had asked me if my dad knew kung fu. I had told them that he did and that he was training me. To prove it I started making up kung fu moves on the spot — karate-chopping trees, jumping and kicking, rolling around on the ground. I had no idea what I was doing, but they had been impressed.

The flag had to go back to the other side, and my team reconvened in our territory to strategize. Feeling a bit inspired by my recollection of knowing kung fu and, again, forgetting the pact I had made with myself to not participate, I volunteered to do something.

Uncle Ted paused, clearly taken aback, but then, with more enthusiasm than I was expecting, he said, "That's wonderful, Patrick. No one will suspect *you*. You can be our secret weapon."

We already knew where the flag was. Uncle Ted laid out a plan to draw as many of their team away from it as possible with a fake attack from the rear, followed immediately by a second fake attack from the left, leaving the flag virtually unguarded. "Meanwhile, Patrick, you'll sneak up the right side, and if you see an opportunity, just go for it!"

I immediately wished that I hadn't volunteered. Why had I? I didn't think the entire plan would hinge on me.

This isn't going to work, I thought, as I crept along the right border, deep into enemy territory. To my surprise, though, the first attack drew half of their guards to the back border. I was behind a tree and in line with the flag. With the second fake attack, I managed a long dash toward the flag, bringing me just steps away from it.

My heart thumped hard against the tree that I was leaning on. I couldn't do this. I didn't want to. I caught a whiff of the tree and the mossy things growing on it, and I wished that I could let the smell of it lull me into a state of relaxation, like it normally would.

Looking up again, a small part of me couldn't help but feel impressed by how well Uncle Ted's plan had worked so far. There were two people left guarding the flag, but as a call for help came from the other side of the terrain, one more went to investigate. I thought it was Tanya's husband left guarding the flag, but I couldn't be totally sure in the suit, mask and toque. I couldn't even remember his name. I was certain, though, that whoever Buddy was, he remained completely unaware that I was so close. Another distressed yell from the left piqued his curiosity, and he took a few steps in that direction, away from the flag.

Two thoughts, "Maybe I *do* know kung fu" and "You're a freaking idiot for thinking that," occurred simultaneously in my brain. Nevertheless, I realized it could be my only chance, and I left the cover of my tree to take the five quick leaps necessary to reach the flag. I grabbed it. Buddy was already turning and taking aim, but his first shot zipped past my shoulder. I turned too, and I ran like hell through the woods.

"Help!" I yelled as I went. I looked behind me and saw Buddy get shot by one of my teammates. I was virtually alone as I ran back to our territory. As my teammates cheered, the book I had tucked into the belt of my pants came loose and started to travel down the inside leg of my paintball suit. Good god. I felt it coming out the bottom, and I tried to kick it out and away from me.

Kicking and running at the same time, in the woods, with a falling book in play, proved more complicated than I could handle. My other foot caught on something and I fell forward. I managed to get one hand out to stop my fall, and an elbow, but that doesn't matter much if there's a big rock in between them, which there was.

My head walloped the rock with a crack and everything turned black. I might have been out a second or two, but I soon recovered enough to lift my head and feel the place where it had hit, just above my mask. I was relieved to find that I didn't have a cut. I had a dent. Oh my god, I had a dent in my head. Then the blood started flowing. The next time I removed my hand from my head it was sticky and red.

I heard Uncle Ted's voice way behind me, "My god, Patrick! Are you OK? Can you get up?"

As he was speaking, I was getting up, unaware that the flag was still in my other hand, the one not covered in blood. "I think I need stitches," I said, but no one could hear me.

Uncle Ted, way behind, couldn't see the blood. All he saw was me getting up and walking toward our team's territory.

I was thinking about getting to the cabin. I needed a towel and the blood was getting into my goggles. "Mom?" I said, but she was too far back too. Uncle Ted saw me walking and must have noticed, though I certainly hadn't, that my earlier sprint had brought me within ten metres of our territory line.

With a thunderous voice that resonated through my bones, through my throbbing wound, and right to the centre of my skull, Uncle Ted yelled, "C-O-V-E-R HIM!" Every single person on the lake that day must have heard his command.

Without smiling, I actually started laughing in disbelief as I stumbled toward the cabin. This family was insane. Completely freaking off the rails. And I hated them.

With me only a few metres from our line, my team came out from all sides to cover me, attacking any would-be opponents. I needed a towel, badly, and I removed my goggles. "Mom?" I said again.

"Keep those on, for god's sa—" I heard someone on our side start to say. "Oh my god!" they continued. "Patrick's hurt!" they yelled. "He's bleeding!"

"Ew, blood!" I heard some of the kids screaming.

"Patrick?" I heard Mom's voice say. She sounded closer than I expected.

I turned around and saw Mom, a few metres away.

"That's definitely gunna to need some stitches," she confirmed. "But — could you just take a couple more steps first?"

WTF?

"I'm not still playing!" I screamed, but, as I did, I caught sight of the cord — the yellow nylon cord that Uncle Ted had pegged down the entire width of his two-and-a-half-acre woods.

"Argh!" I said, but I took the steps anyway and crossed the boundary. We had just won the game. And, I was so angry.

Mom came rushing up and gave me a big hug, ignoring my injury. "Patrick, you did it!" she said. Then pulling back, she added, "But, what on earth have you done to your face?" She was smiling. I saw that she had a patch of blood on the shoulder of her suit now and for some reason, at that moment, I found it funny too. I started to laugh.

She was laughing, and I was laughing. Uncle Ted, Dad, Prudence, Aunt Lori, Marc, Brooke and Uncle Gary joined in too. Soon, the whole gosh darn family, spouses, kids, and assorted strangers gathered around. Someone, thankfully, got a clean cloth, which got put on my head. But, we were all still laughing, and I wondered how long it could go on for.

Finally, Uncle Ted said, "Well, Patrick, looks like you're going to get some time for reading on this trip after all!"

At that, everyone laughed even harder. And our laughter filled the woods, and spilled up into the hills and back, and I felt a warmth I hadn't felt since childhood.

Later that night, after dinner, and after I had come back from the clinic, Uncle Ted got us all together in the living room. He proceeded to ad lib a hokey ceremony in which I was knighted "Sir Patrick." He said that, in recognition of my acts of bravery, I was hereby granted a lifetime exemption from participating in another Bunton family paintball game.

The ceremony was embarrassing, and I would never tell my friends about it. What happens in the woods, stays in the woods, I guess.

I don't know if it's our country's best characteristic, but it's true —

we do tend to like hanging out in the woods having fun. Maybe we should do it a little more safely. Maybe we should have more fun in other places, too, like airline safety videos. But still, it's something.

Everyone congratulated me after the ceremony, and I felt happier than I had felt in a long time. It didn't even occur to me that the dinner-to-bedtime segment of day two was almost complete. Instead, I was reflecting on how this story might get retold by my family in the years to come: The time Patrick cracked his head open on a rock but won the game anyway.

Everyone seemed to be waiting for me to say something, but I didn't know what to say.

"Thank you," I said, simply.

"You still have to come to the reunions, though," Aunt Lori said.

"Fine," I said. But no one could hear me. They were all laughing too freaking, bloody loudly.

V. E. Rogers lives in Victoria, British Columbia, with her partner and their two kids, all of whom inspire her creatively. Currently a stay-at-home parent, she loves hanging out in the woods having fun and wishes she could do it more often. She enjoys writing stories of all kinds and hopes that some of them will make people laugh. **www.verogers.com**

time enough to heal old wounds

by Michelle F. Goddard

It was February 29 again, and I was wondering which member of my family would try to kill me this time. I scanned the clearing. The first hint of dawn cast the participants in a half-light, their shadows like onyx daggers lengthening behind to stab bare trees and shrubs. Breath misted the air as whispers floated through the woods, terse greetings flavoured with bravado. A few heads leaned together for more weighty conversations, eyed by onlookers with shades of avarice and worry.

I held myself apart and tried to read each face, searching for any familiar landscape. Was that my chin, my nose, my eyes? Occasionally I landed on common ground; a stance, a tilt of a head. Someone even had my messy tangle of dark curls, though I wore mine close cropped, a dark stubbly cap against my brown skin. The two dozen or so Leapers that had made it this year came in every human shade and shape possible, but I could still parse where maybe some long ago pairing had spawned this family of strangers. But wasn't every family made up of strangers?

The hairs on the back of my neck rose in warning. I turned to find Piers staring at me. A Viking of a man, he had on jeans and a T-shirt, much like everyone else here, but he filled both out as if his body were keen to conquer more territory. I might be considered leonine, the necessities of my life spawning a catlike slyness in me. Piers had only a few inches on me, but he was bearlike. He nodded with a slight jerk of his chin as he approached. He hadn't aged in four years, the boon granted by the maze, but his body was more taut and muscles strained at the fibres of his clothes. He had prepared for today. But so had I.

I shifted my weight, feeling even the balls of my feet awakening to the threat. I didn't know what the rules were exactly, but it would be naïve of me to think he'd wait until we were inside the maze to strike.

"Surprised you showed," Piers said, leaning down to whisper. "Thought you'd have second thoughts, after what happened last time."

"It's my right, isn't it? Felt the call."

"But you didn't have to answer. Why not have a nice normal life, instead of this death match every four years."

"It didn't kill me the last time."

Light in the clearing grew, but it did not come from the east. Everyone turned to face a glow that bloomed on the nearby rock face. Black stone caught the sun and shot it back with a sparkling radiance. I yanked my hand up to shade my eyes.

I tensed as Piers moved as well, but he, too, must have been blinded by the glare. He had turned away from the rock to peer down at me. "Maybe this time you won't be so lucky."

I stared up at him, his bulk a barrier blocking the brilliance. I shrugged, trying to broadcast my swagger to anyone who might consider testing me. If we were lucky, they might just leave us two top predators to test each other before braving a fight with the survivor. "Guess we'll have to see."

Piers spun back around as the sun rose and the light faded to tolerable levels.

"Now, I might like to try my luck with her," Piers said, nodding at a lean figure picking her way to the front of the crowd.

I stared at him, surprised by his sudden chumminess, but held my tongue, not keen to provoke him.

"Good morning," the woman said, addressing the crowd. She carefully smoothed her long black ponytail over her left shoulder. She wore jeans tucked into boots and a wide-necked sweater. She glanced around the clearing as if counting heads, her dark almond-shaped eyes darting from one face to another. Her gaze met mine, pausing for a moment — or was it my imagination? — before taking in Piers, who folded his arms and smiled at her with a toothy grin.

"I'm Francine. At least, that's the name I'm owning now." A few chuckles greeted her comment, but her full lips betrayed no hint of amusement. "Most of you know why you're here, but these words must be spoken." Taking a breath, she spread her arms wide as if to embrace the crowd. "We are a family, connected by this ritual, linked by this opportunity, bonded by this pull. We leap into the maze with only ourselves for protection. If we are strong, if we are clever, if the maze finds us worthy, we will be given the boon." Francine lowered her arms. "Once the maze is open, you will have until the last rays of sunset to find your way out of the maze. There are traps. There are obstacles. Both are deadly. But the biggest threat is each of you. The boon will only be granted to a few, and the maze decides how many. The boon is time: for the next four years, those who receive it will only age one. Do not waste opportunity. Do not waste energy. Do not waste time."

With a nod, Francine returned to the crowd. I stared after her. She looked to be in her early thirties, but what did that matter here? There was a suspicious lack of laugh lines and grey hairs among those gathered here, and their eyes harboured a conspicuous glint of wisdom. Somehow, she had earned the position of greeter, as if this were some fluorescent-lit supermarket and she a blue-bibbed sales clerk. She took a position under a leafless maple, arms folded, one hand holding the end of her ponytail as if it might gallop away. Her gaze met mine but then flickered away.

Piers chuckled beside me. "She's checking me out."

I had been distracted by Francine and had almost forgotten he was there. I felt a flush of anger. Hadn't I learned from the last time? Four years later, the wound still itched and burned, a ghost of the near miss that had almost ended me.

"Too bad I'm already committed," Piers said. "But maybe you should do her a favour and make an alliance. Not that it's going to help either of you."

He walked away toward a group gathered at the far side of the copse, shouldering a wiry man aside to greet one who stood in the centre.

"He's a senior," Francine said. "The one holding court."

I jerked back, startled by her proximity.

"Sorry," she said, hands held up in surrender.

"What do you mean by a 'senior'?" I asked.

"Someone who's been at this a long time," Francine said. "He's working on an alliance."

"And that's good?"

"If you can trust it. And know when to betray it." Francine turned and stared at me. "You don't have to do this, you know."

"Everyone seems so concerned," I said, giving my sneer full rein.

Silence fell on the glade. As one, we turned toward the pull. An opening appeared in the rock, a darker stain against the ink of the stone.

"Last chance," Francine said.

"What do I got to lose?" I said.

She flinched as if slapped, but then nodded before turning to the hole in the rock.

The group filed in. Francine and I followed, not together but not apart. I held my breath as we moved through darkness and into dim light, steeling myself against the otherworldly chill that had so shocked me four years ago. The grey walls arched upward to an equally grey ceiling stretching several body lengths overhead. Light from an unknown source washed the space in a cold glow, doing nothing to make the cavern less intimidating. Tunnels curved off to the right and left, disappearing into the maze.

Francine was a presence beside me. It seemed we were the only ones admitted into this section of the labyrinth. For a moment, we stared each other down, hands balled into fists before letting them relax at our sides. It was the wave of air rushing toward us that alerted me.

Piers appeared, a bristling storm that blasted toward us, arms flailing as if to prevent any escape. I moved to one side, taking Francine with me. Spinning her free, I turned to face Piers. He smiled as if glad he had lost the element of surprise. Piers kicked off the wall, fists falling like an avalanche toward me. I let him come, waiting for the last moment to move. I sprang to my right, jumping off the wall and sending my body up above the towering man. I grabbed his head and added my weight to the momentum already bringing him down. The effort sent me staggering along the corridor, but I heard a satisfying crack when Piers met rock.

"Come on," I said, grabbing Francine by the elbow and propelling us to the opposite side of the cave. I steered us toward the path on the right.

"That move was impressive," Francine said, straightening her clothes and smoothing her hair as we dashed through the maze.

"This ain't my first rodeo."

"No?" She glanced at my face. "But you don't mean here, do you." I shook my head. Her head bowed as if she were searching the floor. "You've had to do something like that before." I nod. "But Piers isn't dead."

"I don't think so. Killing a man with your bare hands isn't necessarily quick. I thought we weren't supposed to waste time."

"No. You're right. Of course."

I let go of her elbow as we slowed, though neither of us made any move to separate from the other.

"I suppose, if we aren't going to try and kill each other," Francine said, "we can try to make our way together."

"Until it's time to betray each other."

"Until then," Francine said with a smile far more affable than circumstances would merit. She stuck out her hand. "Francine."

"Gerald," I said.

I took her hand and she covered mine with her other one, pulling me a little closer. "I am so pleased to meet you, Gerald," she said. She searched my face, perhaps seeking the same signs of familiarity that I had looked for earlier. Whether or not she found any, I couldn't tell.

I let Francine lead for the first few forks, having no better inkling myself. As we moved in silence, my hard-won stealth was easily matched by hers. I wondered if it was more than just time that gave her such grace. Around us, the maze clung to silence like a lover, jealously and tightly.

We took a turn and found ourselves in a short corridor that ended in a wall. I moved to retrace our steps, but Francine pressed her hand to my chest to stop me. She marched toward the end of the tunnel. Skeptical, I lagged a few paces behind. Francine took a step to her left and then moved right and disappeared. I stumbled to a stop, my heart beating so loudly that I couldn't even hear my voice call her name. Francine's head poked out of nowhere. Her hand reached toward me and pulled me behind a thin overlapping rock partition into a new corridor.

I looked back at a blank wall. "How?"

"If you listen, the maze will speak to you." I narrowed my eyes. Francine grinned as she yanked on my T-shirt to get me moving. "Start by making no assumptions."

We trekked through the endless corridors. When we arrived at forks, or came upon openings that led off the path, we chose our way without the need for words.

"I have some questions," I said. "Several, actually."

"About time. I was finding you even less talkative than I expected. Especially, all things considered," Francine said, her hands gesturing toward the walls of the maze.

I noted the word *expected* but it felt too trifling a thing to deter me and left it lying by the wayside.

"But if it's about the maze itself," Francine continued, "I don't have any answers for you. At least nothing definitive."

"Fine. Not about the maze. What about the people."

"You mean the family."

"The family," I said, trying not to choke on the word. "Fine. Let's start easy. Why would anyone create an alliance, knowing that betrayal is inevitable?"

"They're hedging their bets that they'll be the one to make it to the end," Francine said. She reached a fork and took the path on the left. "And you can be well looked after by a senior during the four years between leaps."

"Looked after?" I asked, considering the two roads myself. Finding no reason to counter Francine's choice, I followed.

"Time affords you many things," Francine said. "The opportunity to make lots of money is foremost. You get a senior out of the maze and you might be well compensated. If you survive."

"And you? What can you do for me, if I get you out? And survive."

"Very little, unfortunately. But I can share what I know. My experience. Advice."

"Like?"

"How old do you think I am? Actual age. Not how old I look."

"I couldn't hazard a guess."

"I'm in my sixties. I answered the call in my early twenties. You look to be mid to late thirties?"

"Actually, I just turned thirty. I've lived a hard life. Lots of wear and tear."

Francine pulled up and turned to look at me. She raised one hand toward me but then grabbed the end of her ponytail instead. She gripped it tightly as she looked into my eyes. "You didn't answer earlier?"

"Only once. I felt the pull before that but I couldn't leave where I was."

"Sometimes a person can feel so trapped they…"

"I couldn't leave because of the bars on my cell."

"Oh." Francine spun on her heal and walked away. "I didn't realize."

I followed, keeping a healthy distance. "I suppose you're rethinking this alliance about now."

"No. I'm not." Francine stopped and looked to her left. A passageway led away from our route. She glanced over her shoulder. "What do you think?"

I joined her at the tunnel entrance. I felt the slightest tug from the opening and moved onto the new path. Francine moved in step with me.

"As I said, I'm in my sixties but look like this. How long do you think I can stay in one place, one job, before people start asking questions, before I have to move on? So how do we live in the world like this?"

"False IDs," I said with a shrug. "That's easy."

"But there's more. Those seniors with their entourages. They are rich and powerful and that takes some finessing too. None of them would be too happy to have to walk away from their lives and start fresh, with nothing."

"Some people would. Some might like it."

"I suppose, but it's not an easy decision. And do you ever really start with nothing? Don't we all carry..."

Her voice trailed off and our steps faltered. Ahead the smooth surface of the ground turned craggy. Spikes from the floor and ceiling stretched toward each other, teeth in mid-chomp. I heard Francine gasp as we got closer. A figure stood just at the edge of the first row of spikes. I smelled the blood before we got close enough to see who it was. But even close up I didn't recognize the face. Or what was left of it.

"Trap. Obviously," I said, examining the site.

"So, what do we do?" Francine asked.

I knew what she was getting at. The longer I was in the maze, the more I felt the pull, like an irresistible tide, drawing me on. I jerked my head toward the tunnel beyond the field of spikes. "Go on."

"And if that's the way," Francine said, "there must be a way to get across."

I tried to ignore the pulpy wetness of the body and bitter iron pong of the blood that even now dripped onto the ground, adding to the puddle growing at the Leaper's feet. He was held upright, mid-stride, by one thin stalactite that had entered through the top of his head and a rough stalagmite that had pierced right up through his body.

"Stay back," I said, reaching out with my arm to make sure Francine hadn't gotten too close.

"What are you doing?" Francine asked.

I stretched my hand out into the field. Nothing happened.

Francine grabbed my arm and yanked it back. "What are you thinking?"

"I'm helping my senior get out."

"Don't be stupid. And I didn't ask you to do that," she said, her face pulled into a worried scowl.

"I've got an idea," I said, turning away from her concern. I sat down half a body length away from a tall spike. I looked up at Francine. "Stand here and brace me."

"What are you going to do?" Francine asked, moving behind me and pushing against my back. I reached up, and she gripped my arms firmly.

"Kick out a spike," I said, doing just that. The spike broke off a hand span from the floor, leaving a flat, round base. The broken spike sailed across the floor, bouncing once. Where the spike hit the ground, two new spikes shot out, one from the floor and one from the ceiling. "I guess we know what happened to him," I said, climbing to my feet. "I'll go first."

"Why you?"

"What do I got to lose?" I said.

Francine opened her mouth, but I didn't give her time to argue. I stepped onto what remained of the spike and grabbed for two hanging from the ceiling, prepared for a hasty retreat. I wobbled, hands suddenly slick with sweat. I heard a gasp behind me but didn't look back. Gripping the rough stone tighter, I regained my balance. I took a breath to steady myself, then, aiming as low as I could, kicked out another spike. I stepped forward onto the newly broken base, holding the two closest ceiling spikes for balance.

I glanced over my shoulder. "Seems to be working."

"Nicely done," Francine said. She waited for me to get a few paces ahead before stepping onto the first base and reaching up for ceiling spikes. "But don't go rushing into things like that." She steadied herself for a moment before following. "You've got plenty to lose."

"That's a strange sentiment," I said before knocking out another spike. "Wouldn't it just be easier for you if I stumbled and got myself impaled? One less Leaper to worry about."

I glanced back, a wry grin on my face, but Francine only scowled, not even indulging me a little. I resumed my efforts. I seemed to be getting the hang of it, but the sound of the spikes skittering off through the corridor made me wince. So far, however, it was just me and Francine. And the dead Leaper.

"What's that?" Francine asked. "Looks bad."

I glanced back to find her staring at my torso. I finished my stretch for a spike, feeling the pull of the scar that ran along my side, a memento from four years ago.

"We may age slowly," Francine said, "but scars don't go away. That will be with you for life."

I shrugged. "Got plenty of others to keep it company."

"Oh? From prison?"

I focused on kicking and stepping and grabbing, not eager to get too intimate with this stranger, no matter she called Leapers family.

"You know, the more I know about you," Francine said, "the better I can help you."

"I thought you couldn't do much for me."

"Yes. I suppose you already know people who could doctor up some IDs," Francine said, pausing for a moment.

"I'm not in any need of that yet."

I reached again and felt my scar pull, a warning not to get too cocky. I didn't really know much about this family, and I didn't have much acquaintance with the concept to begin with. I reached the last row and jumped clear. I turned around to find Francine only a few paces from the end. She took another step, looking far steadier than I had felt crossing, and then jumped neatly from her last position. "You may have to consider a new identity sooner than you think. The people in your life will start to wonder."

I stepped back, sending a spike skittering away with my heel. I hurried after it and picked it up, testing the weight of it in my hand. "Is that what you do? Just walk away from the people in your life?"

"When they start wondering why we don't age, we *have to*."

"Maybe it's better people like us don't have families at all." I gathered some of the spikes. Laying one of them on the ground, I propped up one end of it using another spike, then stomped on it until it broke in two. I picked up the piece with the sharp tip. It now measured about a foot long and fit nicely in my hand. I stomped on a few more.

"That bit of wisdom comes too late for some of us," Francine said, standing and watching me work. "And there are plenty of reasons for leaving that have nothing to do with the leap. Good reasons."

"I suppose it's easy to say, when you're the one doing the leaving." I now had about a half dozen of the shortened spikes. I handed a couple to Francine. "Anyway, I don't got anyone in my life to leave. They already did that for me."

"So, there's no one?" Francine asked, as she stuffed them into the back of her jeans.

"No," I said, handing her one more.

Francine held up the spike and examined the point. "Well, I must say, you've got a knack for turning obstacles into opportunities."

I turned away from her compliment, sliding a few spikes into my jeans. Four years ago, Piers had managed to get his hand on something sharp enough to do serious damage to me. It was nice to feel the security of these found weapons. I wasn't sure how I felt about killing anyone, but slowing them down, or giving them a reason to go bother someone else, appealed.

"We've got some interesting family traditions, don't we," I said. "Assault. Abandonment. Those extra years worth it?"

"You tell me," Francine said. "You're here, aren't you."

"I got a chance to make up for lost time. Why not."

"Couldn't agree more."

We crept down the corridor. Again, I noticed how silently Francine moved. "Is everyone as stealthy as you?" I asked. "Is that why it's so quiet in here?"

Francine grinned. "I think it might be a combination of things. It might be something intrinsic in our DNA. We are family, after all. Or it might be something the maze does to us. Or a side effect of our extended years — a skill we all manage to gain through experience. I, too, have so many questions about this, I wonder if I can earn enough time to answer even one."

"And that's why you're here? Curiosity?"

"Why not? Knowledge was a luxury not available to me when I was younger. Then the call came. I've made up for that over the years."

"So, I'm to believe you have lofty goals."

"Believe what you like," Francine said with a shrug that was annoyingly similar to mine, and just as dismissive.

We made our way along the corridors of the maze and I felt my pace increasing. Some sense of urgency had been added to the pull. "Are we running out of time?"

Francine cocked an eyebrow. "Is this really only your second time? Impressive. Yes, we are."

"And I don't understand how the only people we've run into were Piers and the dead guy hanging on the spikes."

"Maybe the maze *wants* us to get out."

It was as if she had spoken a curse. As soon as we turned the next corner, we found a hole that stretched from one wall to the other and over two body lengths to the other side of the passageway. I crept to the edge and looked down.

Francine stood beside me and whistled. "Now, that's a hole."

"If there's a bottom, I can't see it," I said. "I'm not too keen on testing this to see if it's a trick like the dead end."

"I don't think it's a trick," Francine said. "I'm not going to be able to jump it."

"I don't think anyone could. That's the point though, isn't it?" I knelt down. Pressing my hands against the floor, I inched toward the edge. When I got there, it felt like the ground had been sheared clean off, the sides of the hole smooth as far as I could reach. "The edge is sharp here but look where it meets the wall. The edge is not so perfect. It's almost like there's a ledge."

"A thin one," Francine said.

Facing the wall, I pulled out a spike and thrust it into the wall with all the force I could manage. The spike went in half of its length. When I rested my full weight on it, it seemed secure. With a hefty twist, I managed to free it from the wall. I stepped back and regarded

Francine. "Ever do any rock climbing in all your extra years?"

"Yeah, with a harness. And safety gear. And a team whose job it was to get me through it alive," she said, inserting one of her spikes into the newly-made hole. She let herself go limp and hung for a moment. "Feels secure when I'm nice and safe here." Francine stood up and wrenched her spike from the hole. "Like you said, though, there is a ledge." She stared out across the expanse. "I think it goes all the way to the end." She shifted her weight and toed her left foot out her boot. "Bare feet will be better, I think."

I was already unlacing my boots. "I wish we had grabbed more spikes. Do we go back?"

Francine shifted her weight from one bare foot to the other as she looked back. She shook her head. "We can only carry a few with us as we cross." She picked up her boots and tossed them across the crevasse. "And time's running out."

I nodded, feeling prickly between my shoulder blades and eager to get going. I threw my boots to join hers and then faced the wall to my left. I stabbed the wall with two of my stony spikes and set my toes on the ledge. I reached out and stabbed farther along with the third. Before leaving my spot, I twisted the first spike free.

I looked back at Francine waiting near the edge, arms folded so tight I wondered how she could breathe. "You push yours into the hole I've made," I said. "Don't move unless it feels secure."

She nodded, her eyes wide. I slid my foot along the ledge and stabbed again. Behind me, the abyss sat, a great hungry toad waiting to swallow me whole. I pressed my face against the wall, my torso and pelvis too as if it were a lover. Only my arm hovered over the crevasse. I couldn't even spare a glance for Francine, but there was no need. She was so close I could feel the warmth of her breath on my neck.

I crawled along the wall, silently begging the edge to hold us, praying that the spikes would carry our weight. We were halfway when footfalls slapped through the corridor behind us. For this, I had to turn my head. Piers ran around the corner. He saw us and skidded to a stop. His eyes narrowed, and he grinned.

"Damn it," I said, as Francine stared at me. "Piers."

I could see him assessing the scene and then he took a step back. He nodded and then spun on his heel running back the way he had come.

"I guess he knows how to get across now," I said.

"Go," Francine said, pleading with her eyes. "Go."

I resumed my crawl, stabbing a spike and sliding my feet, twisting a spike free before stabbing it into the wall a little farther along. I resented the fact that I was making this very easy for Piers. Not that he'd be the type to appreciate it at all. I could feel myself straining to hear, imagining the sound of broken, skittering spikes echoing down the corridor of the maze toward us. Sooner than I would have liked, Piers returned with what must have been an armload, the sound of spikes tumbling onto the ground, a rolling thunder clap.

"Don't stop," I said, hearing Francine moan. Then she cried out. I turned my head in time to see a spike flying toward us. I knocked it away, barely managing to hold on, and bruising my forearm in the process. I kept silent, holding my pain in, but I saw it reflected in Francine's eyes. The first one must have hit her.

"Even if you make it this time," Piers said, striding to the opposite wall, "you're going to have to watch your back for the rest of your life." He aimed the spike like a javelin. It spiralled erratically, the weight of its base making it wobble. It hit the wall below us and shattered into fragments that tumbled into the hole.

"Seems a fair trade off," I said, batting at another spike from Piers, this one headed for Francine. "This little adventure, for extra time." Piers tossed the next spike. I pressed myself to the wall and felt a glancing blow on my shoulder.

"I'm not talking about the maze," Piers said. "You know what I'm talking about, Francine. A few of us missing?" Piers tossed another weapon, higher this time, probably hoping to have it land on our heads. I grabbed it out of the air and immediately slammed it into the wall. I heard Piers swear. He glanced at the ground. He must have brought eight or so spikes back. Now he had two. He'd have to decide whether knocking us off the wall was as important as getting across himself. Of course, he could always go back for more spikes.

"We can't just stay here," I said to Francine in a low voice. "Can you crawl past me?"

"I don't think so," Francine said, glancing down and shuddering. "You should keep going. I'll watch for Piers. I don't think I'll be able to catch anything he throws at us, but I can at least warn you."

She turned her head toward Piers. I turned mine in the other direction, toed my way across the ledge and reached for the newly placed spike. I tested it and it held.

"Incoming," Francine said. "Got it." I heard her quick inhale and then the sound of a palm slapping stone. The spike clattered against the other wall and then down into the rift. "Watch out," Francine said. I felt her lean against me. I heard a grunt and a quick, gasping inhale. We stood frozen for a moment and then she said my name in a high, strained voice. She pressed something against my chest. "Take it. Use it."

It was another spike. I fumbled with it, trying to get a grip, its surface coated with something wet and warm. I looked down to find my hands slick with blood. Her blood. I gripped the spike tighter and drove it more than three quarters of its length into the wall. I took Francine's hand, brought it up to the spike and tried to ignore the blood that dyed her fingers red. "Hold tight. We're almost there."

"Piers?" she asked.

Looking past her, I saw that the corridor behind us was empty. "Gone. Probably to get more."

"Hurry," Francine said, pressing her forehead against the wall. "Hurry."

I reached back and twisted Francine's spike free. I passed it to my other hand and stabbed it into the wall. I guided Francine onward, encouraging her to move her leg in front of mine so that I could pin her. I could feel her shivering, but focused instead on freeing the spikes and then stabbing them into the wall. At one point, I had to bring her hand across again, fear or weakness making her hesitate.

We only had a few feet left, but when we got to the end, I was shaking and sweating. Francine stepped onto the path and stumbled to her knees. The left side of her sweater was dark with blood.

"Come on. Piers will be back soon," I said, draping her arm over my shoulders and helping her to her feet. "I've got you, but you'll have to use your hand to keep pressure on that wound." She nodded, or at least I thought she did. As we ran down the corridor, her head bobbed on her neck as if it was barely attached. "That was meant for me, wasn't it? You moved to block that spear. Why did you do that? Why are you even helping me?"

"It's not that bad," Francine said, though her face was a sickly shade of green.

"We've got to stop the bleeding." I lowered her to the ground, propping her up against the wall. I knelt at her side and peeled off my T-shirt, the cold, or nerves, or just plain old fear making the hairs on my arms stand at attention.

"Gerald," Francine, her hand reaching out to touch the long, winding scar that ran from my hip and along my ribs. Her hand jumped to my bicep where another scar pulled at the skin, purple and puckered. "This one is older. Much older." She pressed her hand against it as if it was still bleeding, as if it were possible to go back to my childhood and staunch the flow of blood. She searched my face, her eyes welling up with tears.

I tore my gaze from her tear-streaked face. I began to rip my shirt into strips. "Francine," I said, holding out a wad of cotton. "Press this on your wound."

She eased forward and away from the wall. I lifted her sweater and I recoiled. The injury was bad enough, but above it was a trail of scars that led upward. The scars, long healed, were the remnants of serious stab wounds even worse than mine. "How far up?" I asked as she stared at me, her hand sweeping her ponytail over her left shoulder. It didn't completely hide another scar on her neck ending at her collarbone. "Did you get those here?"

"No," Francine said. "When I felt the call, I thought staying young and beautiful would make my husband happy, but even that, he resented. I was supposed to be satisfied with life as he defined it. I couldn't stay, Gerald. I'm sorry."

I started wrapping the strips from my T-shirt around her midsection "What? What are you saying? Your husband did this to you?"

"I couldn't stay." She sagged, and her eyes fluttered. "I couldn't…"

"Francine. Come on. We're close, aren't we?" I felt the pull as if someone had tied a string to my navel and was yanking for all it was worth. "Can't you feel it?"

"You have to go," Francine said.

"What about *we*?" I asked, tying off the ends of the bandages.

"I'll slow you down. Piers. He's right behind us. You've got to go."

I said nothing as I got her to her feet. I swung Francine into my arms. She lay there like a child, head resting against my shoulder. She was close, closer than she had been the whole time in the maze. I felt her hair, her hand resting on my neck. I smelled her. There was something so familiar, so intimate about this closeness. Somehow, I recognized it, like it was a memory. Though I had been the one being carried.

"We're almost there," she said.

I felt something wet against my neck but was too focused on the sight ahead to pause. A light brighter and warmer than anything found in the chill of the maze revealed an opening, and beyond that a dusky sky. The setting sun winked through tree branches. We passed from the greyness of the maze into the twilight of the woods.

"Is that it?" I said, turning to look behind. The entrance was gone. There was only a rock face. I picked my way carefully, bare feet not at all happy about the rough path and the cold. "Did we make it?"

Francine nodded and wiped at her face. "My car is just over there. I've got a first aid kit. Water. Blankets. What did you say? This ain't my first rodeo?"

Once we got to the car, I wrapped myself in a blanket. I watched her re-dress her own wound, stapling the skin together, her hands shaking with fatigue, but sure of what had to be done. Finally, she leaned back in the seat and stared up at me.

"Thank you, Gerald. Thank you."

I stared down at her, scanning her face and wanting to understand so much more. "Why did you help me? What do you want from me, Francine?"

Francine sighed and shifted in her seat, wincing in obvious pain. "There must be something more to this. A greater purpose to the maze, to the leap, to us. I'm studying our DNA. Everyone who's willing to give me a sample, that is. I'd like yours."

"That's all?"

"Do I have a right to want anything more?" She peered into my eyes, staring so hard I felt the effect like a stone lying on my chest. "To know the son I left behind? To have your forgiveness? No. I don't have the right to ask that. The only thing I can hope is that now that you're here, you might understand why I left. And maybe in time—"

"Time," I said to this stranger who was my family. My mother. "The one thing the maze gives us is time." I smiled. "And what do I got to lose."

Michelle F. Goddard is an AWADJ (artist with a day job). She is a receptionist, but she is also a musician who has played around the world and a composer with credits to her name for songs performed in musicals and films. She is presently working on a science fiction novel and one of her short stories has been recently published in an anthology. Find her at **michellefgoddard.wordpress.com**.

lorraine and the loup-garou

by Joy Thierry Llewellyn

It was February 29 again, and I was wondering which member of my family would try to kill me this time. It wasn't that we weren't happy, and we don't *actually* want to kill each other, at least not in the traditional sense of murder, massacre, and carnage. And there's really only one member I have to be careful around; as they say, "one person's meat is another person's poison." In fact, I don't think I've ever been happier. I have a cozy home, work I enjoy, a fearless running partner, and I've never eaten a more delicious or varied carnivorous menu in my life. I both blame and credit the flitterbit.

Looking out at my forest view, it's hard to believe it's been one year and 101 days since I used to begin each morning writing in my gratitude journal. My life at the time was based on the perky belief that problems always worked themselves out. I liked my barista job — most days — and lived with the love of my life, Pierre, though he said things like, "It's the similarities that attract people but the differences that keep them together." That meant he played Dungeons & Dragons on Wednesday nights with his friends while I stayed home and watched French films on Netflix.

The problem one year and 101 days ago? I was running out of French movies.

Maybe I should both blame and credit Pierre as the one who shook everything up in our lives by deciding it was time to finish his opus, *How to Find Your Purpose in the Labyrinth of Life.* He had asked me to reserve a quiet place for our upcoming ten-day holiday, and I found just the thing: a self-contained cabin on his island of choice. The owner advertised his rental as having privacy, ocean views, and wonder of wonders, access to a small labyrinth he'd made, using rocks to outline the edges of the meandering spiral path.

This island had been on the top of Pierre's go-to list because he'd read in some book in his Mythical Creatures class at university about reported 1890 sightings of elusive flitterbits. He was keen to see if he could make contact and thought the Vancouver Aquarium might pay big bucks for one. "A flitterbit," he told me for the fifth time, as he packed his newly bought butterfly net with its extendable handle, "is a flying squirrel that moves through the air so fast it isn't visible to the human eye."

It sounded silly, but it was kind of sweet that he was so excited. I didn't want to put a damper on his enthusiasm. "Fascinating," I said, and went to look for my running shoes. I planned to do daily walking meditations in the labyrinth while I searched for the answer to that Oprah-style question: "What should I do with my life?" I confess my journal just wasn't cutting it these days. A recent "Ah ha!" moment involving a cup of coffee spilled on someone who considered themselves famous — another story for another time — had made me realize that I needed a change. The future loomed long in front of me, filled with more sameness.

The ferry ride over to the island helped me and my excited boyfriend say goodbye to the hustle and bustle of the city. Our cabin was everything I had hoped it would be, but Pierre wasn't pleased. My "It's so cozy!" became his "It's too small!" My appreciation of the quiet was met with a shocked, "What, no WiFi?" At least it was clean, with windows that looked out onto the ocean as promised, and it was very private, hidden by trees from the single dirt road that circled the island.

We opened the bottle of French wine I'd brought to drink with the delicious vegetarian dinner that the cabin's elderly owner set out on our porch overlooking the ocean. Randolph, or Randy to his friends, explained there were some oddities about the island, and that it was best if we didn't wander around outside at night. I pretended not to hear Pierre mutter, "Flitterbits! I knew it." Our dinner, the wine, and the sea air made the evening magical, even though my perkiness couldn't compete with Pierre's constant references to Dungeons &

Dragons and his wish for a Phantom Masher Mace to get rid of the mosquitoes. The bugs weren't bothering me, but I could see he was getting irritated. When I suggested we go for an evening walk to explore the forest path under the glowing full moon, he declined.

"This isn't all fun and games, you know," he told me as he started to line up his books according to their height. "This is a working holiday, and I need to be ready to start writing tomorrow morning. Besides, remember what Randy said. Maybe we can go flitterbit hunting in the afternoon."

Flitterbit hunting had not been what I had in mind. I sadly realized at that moment that a change in location didn't mean a change in nature. I sighed and set out on my own anyway. The air smelled of the tangy pine trees and the nearby salty sea and the full moon was like a flashlight illuminating the trail. The only sounds were the waves crashing against the rocky shoreline and the crunch of leaves and pine needles under my shoes. *I could live on this island forever*, I remember thinking. My breathing slowed, and my pace became a peaceful motion of one foot gliding beside the other.

As I walked down the shadow-filled forest path, I became aware of a faint buzzing and swatted the air with a flip of my hand. A flitterbit, that mystical flying squirrel, fell at my feet. The dazed creature shook itself and took flight again.

"Wait!" I called. *Surely this was a sign*, I thought, though I wasn't sure of what. To my pleased surprise, the creature stopped and settled on a nearby arbutus tree branch. I had my second surprise of the night when the flitterbit asked, well, more croaked — like someone who'd been a heavy smoker for fifty years — the question, "Who you?" We talked for a long time. Apparently, Pierre and I intrigued the flitterbit, whose name was Flo. It turned out that even though a flying life was fun, it could get lonely, and Flo craved community. I confessed that being able to fly was high on my bucket list, and that I wished I could launch myself and coast on the wind as easily as she did.

We were getting along superbly, and I had just worked up the nerve to ask her the big question, "Are there more of you?" when several things happened. Pierre, worried when I didn't return, had set out, braving the mosquitoes to search for me. The sound of his approaching footsteps startled Flo. She instinctively flew horizontally when she should have gone vertically and crashed into me again. I fell, but only hurt my butt and pride. Flo died on the spot. This was not an unusual consequence for her species when they slammed into objects or sentient beings at such high speeds.

When I sat up and looked at her tiny, lifeless body, I started crying. *Life can be so unfair at times.* That was when I heard a growl and realized a huge, wolf-like creature was watching me and making that deep-in-the-throat rumble noise I'd only heard in TV documentaries about wolf packs. When the creature went into a crouch, its tail twitching and its eyes gleaming a horrible yellow in the moonlight, I shut my eyes and cried even louder.

The seven-foot-tall loup-garou launched itself, tripped on a stone, and smashed into me. It instinctively bared its yellow fangs and bit me. Its tufted, pointy ears twitched. I only learned much later that twitching loup-garou ears are a sign of anxiety, not aggression. The creature was trying to figure out how to explain that its bite had serious consequences.

Pierre came around the path just in time to see the loup-garou grab the dead flitterbit and dash off into the forest. Then I started moaning and writhing on the ground as I began to transform into a hairy creature almost two feet taller than my now frightened boyfriend. Stunned, Pierre remembered the many loup-garou stories his French-Canadian grandmother had told him. He squatted beside me and explained in a breathless voice what lay ahead, while I, in my woozy state, tried to focus on what he was saying. "When a loup-garou bites you," he said, gently holding my increasingly hairy and clawed hand, "you are under a curse for 101 days. All you can do is let the curse run its course. As long as you don't eat human flesh — anything else goes, apparently — you return to your human form at the end of 2424 hours. If you succumb to your cannibalistic urges, you are doomed to stay a loup-garou, a member of the werewolf family, for life." I groaned in despair, but I guess it came out more like a growl because he quickly dropped my hand and stepped back. I was in too much pain to see him shudder as he looked down at me.

"Aren't there any other ways you can break or stop the spell?" I gasped.

"It's a curse, not a spell. Big difference!" He became aware of the moonlight shining down on us, filling the forest with shadows that could be hiding anyone or anything. He looked at me, growing hairier and bigger by the minute, and couldn't absorb what was happening.

I whimpered or maybe snarled, "I'm still your girlfriend," but he had already abandoned his role as my boyfriend and was running back to the cabin to pack his things.

Moments later, with a sad heart and suffering from a terrible migraine, I hid in the bushes and watched Pierre speed away to catch the last ferry of the day leaving the island. It was hard to be my regular perky self when I loped into our cabin. I'd just lost my boyfriend, probably my job, and I doubted my eyebrows would ever recover from this transformation. I scratched at a flea on my hindquarters and wondered what I should do next.

I read the note Pierre had left me, in which he explained again about the loup-garou curse, and that he'd arranged for the owner to deliver a daily meal — with meat thankfully, since I was starving — to our cabin. He'd asked Randy not to disturb me during what he'd described as my "101 days of silent retreat." My once-upon-a-time boyfriend had even paid the bill in advance, though using my credit card seemed a bit cheeky. His final scribbled words, "Hope it all works out," were underlined twice and barely legible.

I ate the note, licked my huge lips, and proceeded to spend night after night searching for the other loup-garou. I wondered if the creature was hiding from me. I wanted to meet it face to face and demand answers, but meanwhile got some comfort from knowing that the consequence of biting me meant it was stuck being a loup-garou forever. That would be satisfactory revenge.

I quickly discovered some positive aspects to this curse. Not only were the smells in the forest world tantalizing, but it also turned out howling was very cathartic, my night vision was fantastic, and the feel of the wind ruffling my back fur when I ran was surprisingly sensual.

Unfortunately, trotting was not as contemplative as I would have liked; it was hard to slowly walk when I was either plunking down on two huge feet or plodding along on four. I wandered the island at night, getting to know the animal paths, though all the other creatures fled when they saw or smelled me. My hope that I would meet another flitterbit or even the doubly cursed loup-garou never came to fruition. I walked the labyrinth many times each night, always waiting until I was sure there were no humans in the area. I began every meditative walk with the same question: "What should I do with my life?"

Answers came, but none of them felt right. When I was angry and wanted revenge, I considered going back to the city to bite Pierre and let him be the next loup-garou. When I felt sorry for myself, I stood in the centre circle of the labyrinth and howled under the stars.

I managed to control my powerful carnivorous urges every night and made it through three months without eating human flesh. Thankfully, most of the island tourists had left for the season, and the local population was so small I quickly realized if one of them disappeared, an island-wide search would not be good for me. Each dawn, after retreating to the cabin to hide and sleep during the day, I used one of my hooked claws to scratch a mark on the wall to keep track of the passing time. My hunting and the daily delivery of delicacies that appeared on my front porch — fried pork chops, barbecued hamburgers, roasted sweetbreads, raw kidneys, and stewed chicken gizzards — helped me resist attacking anyone, but by day ninety-four my body's fierce longing for a chomp on a gluteus maximus muscle was overwhelming.

With only seven days of the curse left, I admitted to myself I was as lonely — and hungry — as I had ever been in my life, so I did something I'd never done before. I snuck close to the front of the cabin where my landlord lived. *He's old. And he lives on his own. A little look wouldn't hurt, right?* I thought. When I squatted down to peek through Randy's large front window, I saw him reach out and pat the head of a monstrous dog sleeping at his feet. I stumbled back, knocking my head on a tree branch. (Being seven feet tall was a bit of a disadvantage when trying to be stealthy.) I took another, closer look. Yes, there they were, one asleep, the other reading. Could it be? No! The dog sensed me and, lifting its head, began to growl, leaving me no choice but to trot back to the safety of my little home.

As I put the latest scratch on the living room wall, I tried to understand what I had seen. There was no doubt about it. The "dog" was obviously the loup-garou who'd bitten me. Why wasn't the man afraid of the beast? A sudden, horrible thought came to me. *What if the creature had once been a member of Randy's family?* I was the one responsible for this irreversible consequence, but I quickly shook off any lingering sense of guilt. The loup-garou had bitten me, not the other way around.

I spent the last seven days doing what I had done for the previous ones, still no closer to finding an answer to "What should I do with my life?" I considered my options. No job, no boyfriend, and with the cost of the "meals with meat option," I was probably going home to a hefty credit-card bill.

Finally, it was day 101. I waited impatiently from dawn until dark, but nothing happened. As the moon rose above the sea, I returned to where I had been attacked, thinking there might be a loup-garou rule about returning there. I turned out to be right. At the exact moment my disaster had struck 101 days earlier, I began to transform back into a human. It happened surprisingly quickly, though it was as painful as the initial change. Once it was over, I shook myself, did a happy dance, and spread my arms wide, laughing in delight as I looked up at the stars.

When I returned to my cabin, I saw Randy sitting on my front porch, which meant I had to sneak around the back and climb through the bedroom window so I could put on some clothes. I discovered all those night-time runs had not only helped me lose some weight, but they'd also made my thigh muscles more pronounced than I would have liked. Even more bothersome, I discovered I had been right to worry about my eyebrows.

Randy was still waiting when I stepped through the front door and flicked on the porch light. We both flinched at the brightness, and I turned it off, wondering, *Maybe I'll get to keep my fantastic night vision*?

"Hope I didn't startle you," he said. "I did stay away at night, in case you weren't able to control your urges for human flesh." I was shocked, but he hadn't finished. "I didn't want to provide any temptation. Yes, I know about your ... condition" — he was a polite man and didn't say "curse" — "and hoped the food I provided helped satisfy your ... cravings."

He sort of sounded like he was saying he was sorry, but he still didn't look friendly. The reason for that came next. "When I saw what you had done to my son, Brad—" I sputtered, and he shrugged. "OK, what he had done to you, I was so angry. Brad is now lost to me forever, but he's helped me come to terms with things. He'd ... we'd like you to come for dinner."

It would have been rude to refuse. When we arrived at Randy's cabin, he flung open the door and called out, "She's here!" He introduced me to a shy Brad, who had to stoop because of the low cabin ceiling. Brad wouldn't make eye contact as he immediately began to apologize, his words tumbling out of his long mouth in a slurred way as he acknowledged his responsibility for my loup-garou experience. I thought of something Pierre's favourite movie star, martial artist Bruce Lee, once said: "Mistakes can be forgivable if one has the courage to admit them." I decided this apology would be the start of my forgiveness.

The three of us sat down to the most delicious and laughter-filled meal I'd ever had. Randy became friendlier when he saw how relaxed Brad was with me, and when I never mentioned — or blamed — his son for what I had just experienced, he thawed completely. At one point, Brad poked his father and nodded in my direction. Randy sighed. He told me they hadn't charged my credit card for any expenses. Patting Brad's paw gently, he continued, "It was Brad's fault you were in that state." Brad ducked his head, licked his lips, and twitched his ears. Any leftover anger I had slid away.

During a dessert of bacon-flavoured chocolates, Randy invited me to stay and work for them as a Jill-of-all-trades and a labyrinth workshop leader, since Brad could no longer help out like he used to. Brad's ears twitched again, but he didn't look away this time. I was welcome to continue living in the cabin and keeping Brad company if I wanted to carry on with my evening runs. I was still curious to know who'd bitten Brad in the first place and to find out if there were others. If not here on the island, then where? But I left my questions for another night. It didn't take me long to agree to stay. Journals, fickle boyfriends, and foreign-language films were things from my past — let them stay there.

These days we hold our labyrinth events in the summer, when the heat makes Brad the most lethargic, and leave the winters for our family time. I will never forget my essential loup-garou lesson, though. Brad may be my best friend, but he'll have to keep working at winning my trust, because "once bitten, twice shy."

Joy Thierry Llewellyn is a screenwriter, story editor, writing teacher, and creative non-fiction writer with a fondness for bohemians. She's explored the world as a journalist, filmmaker, biology technician, box stapler in Australia, angst-filled poet in the Northwest Territories, and a once-upon-a-time hippie in Mexico. Her interest in Intentional Communities has led to her living in Indian ashrams, a Tibetan Buddhist monastery in Nepal, an isolated co-op farm in the French Pyrenees, and sleeping in over 100 Camino hostels, but she has yet to spend time with a were-pack of loups-garous. You can find out more about Joy at **www.joythierryllewellyn.com**.

a time to reflect

by Colin Brezicki

It was February 29 again, and I was wondering which member of my family would try to kill me this time. I've been awake since midnight thinking about it. It's what I do once every four years — set my alarm for twelve and remain on red alert for twenty-four hours. I have to be ready for anything today.

It's also my birthday, so I only get a proper birthday every four years instead of every year like normal people.

Ingrid, my therapist, asks how old that makes me now.

Twelve, I tell her — forty-eight in real time.

In that case, she says, *you can die young and still live to a ripe old age.*

I look at her.

Sorry, she says. *You must get dumb remarks like that all the time.*

It's our inaugural session, and she's only trying to break the ice. As a clinical psychologist, I usually self-treat, but today I'm booked with Ingrid because I want a second opinion.

And my family can't get to me when I'm with her.

I already like Ingrid. She makes me think of the sister I never had. If I had a sister, I'm pretty sure she would never try to kill me, and neither would Ingrid, so I feel safe here. What I especially like about her is that once she breaks the ice, she doesn't beat about the bush.

Does your family try to kill you only on your birthday, or is this an ongoing thing? she asks.

Only on February 29, I tell her. Then they leave me alone for four years. In fact, I'd say we get on quite well, given that we're family. Odds are you'll be knocked off by someone you know rather than by a stranger, and who do we know better than family? I never know which one will try it on the day, so I have to watch out for them all.

How long has this been going on?

From the beginning.

The very beginning?

Absolutely. My mother told me she wished I'd been drowned at birth. Ingrid smiles, and I tell her I'm not joking.

Drowned at birth were her exact words, and the way she said it made me think she had actually tried to do it. She had postpartum, my father told me. That works, I thought. Probably why she never had another child after me, and so I never got the sister I wanted. My father must have intervened when my mother tried to drown me. He had my back then, not like on my second birthday when he tried to do it himself.

Seriously?

We were at Myrtle Beach. A late winter getaway I suppose. As I said, it was my second birthday, so I was eight in real time, and he decided I should learn to swim. He took me out in a boat and tossed me overboard. The hands-on method, he called it afterwards. He expected me to surface straightaway and start cutting through the waves like Mark Spitz.

What happened?

What do you think? I sank is what happened, right to the bottom, exactly as he intended. But someone on the shore must have seen what he did, and he figured that claiming to be my swimming coach wouldn't wash in a court of law — so he dove in and hauled me back up. I don't go anywhere near water now because of my hydrophobia.

What happened on your first birthday? When you turned four. Did anyone try to kill you then?

My brother Kenneth tried to electrocute me.

Go on.

I'm serious.

No, I mean carry on.

Sorry. I misunderstood. Anyway, my parents took us for a drive in the country. The weather must have been nice — an early spring, perhaps — because we took a picnic. I remember seeing cows in the fields and hearing birds sing, so maybe it was also my first time out of the city.

Anyway, after we had our picnic my brother wanted me to go for a walk with him. I wasn't sure. He was ten and not very nice. He was always doing things to make me cry, like giving me noogies, and locking me in the closet, and making me eat dirt. So I was suspicious when he asked me to walk with him, but my parents made me do it. I should have known then that something was up, but this was my first birthday and I was only four.

We walked down a lane and when we came to this field with cows in it, he dared me to climb the wire fence. He'd give me jellybeans, he said. The cows were at the far end of the field, so I didn't see a problem. I should have smelled a rat. I grabbed the fence with both hands and screamed. I got the worst shock you can imagine — it went right through me and knocked me to the ground. I started crying, got to my feet, and ran back to my parents. They looked a little disappointed when they saw me coming, I remember. They scolded my brother, but over time I had to ask myself, were they disappointed because he made me climb an electrified fence or because he had failed in his mission?

And he never gave me the jellybeans.

So you have a fear of fences now?

And cows.

What else?

You name it. After eleven birthdays I've got a long list of things that freak me out. Cars, for instance, after my mother backed hers out of the garage and almost ran over me in the driveway on birthday number three.

What else? Poultry. Fire. Bungee jumping. Confined spaces. Rottweilers. Cathedrals.

Why cathedrals?

You can thank my two children for that. Detlef and Dierdre — their mother named them — anyway, they're twins and they think exactly alike; that doubles the threat every birthday, now that I know they're in the game.

Anyway, we were in Paris, and they wanted me to take them to the top of Notre Dame, knowing full well I'm petrified of heights. Their mother had gone shopping, and I couldn't let them go up by themselves because they were only eight — same as me that day, you understand — so I had to climb the narrow winding staircase behind them. I was already close to panic because of my claustrophobia, and the climb was incredibly steep with only a vertical rope to hang on to. 387 steps, would you believe? I got to the top and nearly stepped right off the balcony, which was incredibly narrow and had only a small balustrade between me and the pavement two hundred metres down.

So, I'm already looking death in the face, and Detlef decides to straddle the balcony. He hoists himself up, planting one foot on the balustrade and the other on the roof. Then he starts goading me, and Dierdre's jumping up and down, shouting for me to copy her brother, "Do it, Daddy. Do it, Daddy."

I'm in a blind panic and I hit the deck because now I'm feeling the pull, like gravity's become this green fog slithering through the balustrade and coming to haul me over the edge. That's how it is with acrophobia. My legs turn to jelly and my stomach's a black hole. I'm sweating, even though it's February, and I'm shouting like a madman, down on my knees on a balcony packed with tourists. I try to crawl through all the legs to get to the stairs but no one's budging.

Eventually someone calls for emergency personnel. They clear the entire staircase so they can take me back down the 387 steps. The twins thought it was hilarious. I'm not sure exactly how they planned to have me end up dead that day — panic attack leading to cardiac arrest, a thirty-storey fall, or just embarrass myself to death — but it was depressing to discover my own children were now involved in the conspiracy.

So, yes, cathedrals.

What else?

Fire, as I said. It was the kids again, on my very next birthday — number nine — the day after their mother took them to a sci-fi movie that had flame-throwers in the combat scenes. I was painting window shutters in the garden shed when they burst through the door shouting, "Death to the alien," and pulled out these cans of hairspray and a lighter. I must have spilled some paint thinner on my clothes because I combusted pretty quickly, but I grabbed a fire extinguisher and put myself out. They ran off in hysterics.

Their mother told them she was very disappointed, though I wasn't exactly sure what it was that had disappointed her. You can see the burn scars on my neck.

What else? Parcels in the mail. My brother sent me one when he was away at law school, but I didn't open it because it arrived on the morning of my fifth birthday when I turned twenty. I took it to the bottom of the garden and buried it. He phoned later and asked how I liked my CDs. "CDs?" I said, "What CDs?" and then he claimed to have sent me a boxed set of Brahms' symphonies.

What could I say? "Wow. Thank you, Kenneth. Sorry, I was a little preoccupied just now, but I look forward to playing them." Maybe he didn't detect my sarcasm over the phone, but as far as I know the package is still in the ground, undetonated. Might have had a faulty timer, though you can never tell with mail bombs. Anyway, that was six birthdays ago and I still don't go near that part of the garden.

You live in the house you grew up in?

Yes. My parents agreed to give it to my wife and me if they could remain as tenants. The place is pretty crowded right now with the twins home for reading week, and I don't feel very safe at all.

Has your wife ever tried to kill you?

Just the once as far as I'm aware. The year we were married was a birthday year, and she roasted a chicken for my dinner (she's vegetarian, so she likely made some kind of salad for herself, but she knew I loved roast chicken). It was only the two of us because the twins weren't born yet. Anyway, the chicken smelled funny; when I checked inside, I found the plastic bag full of innards. I didn't accuse her of trying to poison me because she would just say she had forgotten to take out the plastic bag when she was preparing the chicken. She was very upset — disappointed, more like — when I insisted we go out for dinner. It's the same every birthday now. Just the two of us.

Did you go out tonight?

Yes. Before I came here.

How was it?

Awkward. I had to keep watching her so she couldn't slip anything into my bouillabaisse when I wasn't looking. The conversation was pretty strained.

How are things generally with her?

Not good. She finds reasons to go out when I'm home. Even with her social anxiety disorder and agoraphobia, she goes out a lot; I think she's avoiding me.

Anything else?

She doesn't ask about my day. I used to tell her about having as normal a day as possible with clients who are like mine. Maybe your clients aren't like mine, but mine sure are. "I know you like to be alone," she says to me now, like I'm reclusive or something. I see clients all day, I tell her, so who's alone? Maybe they don't have all their dogs on the same leash, but they're still people, right? All part of suffering humanity. Me? Reclusive? That's rich, I tell her. She's the one who needs help, but she won't get it. And that's normal with people who aren't, as you well know.

Does your wife have family living near?

Are you kidding? Her brother, Gunter, lives with her parents in the house next door. I discovered last birthday they were in on the plot to kill me when they invited me over for a drink and conveniently forgot to leash the Rottweilers in the backyard. They like you to come in the back way so you can leave your shoes in the mud room.

Gunter heard my screams but sure as hell took his time coming out the back door to call off his dogs. So I spent that birthday in Emergency getting a rabies shot and adding my in-laws to a growing list of family members to watch out for. I'm sure that planetary alignment has something to do with all this. Think about it. I've narrowly escaped being electrocuted, drowned, poisoned, immolated, run over, blown up, thrown from a great height, and savaged by killer dogs — all on the same day every four years. You think that's coincidence?

Happy birthday, by the way. I should have mentioned it earlier.

Thank you. I can't tell you how relieved I am to be here right now.

How has today gone so far, I mean apart from dinner with your wife? You've been up since midnight, and you say the whole family's with you this week?

Except for Kenneth, who lives in Oregon now. *And* he just sent me another parcel. My wife texted me this afternoon. I phoned her back right away and told her to take it to the bottom of the garden and call the police.

"But, Stephen, it's your birthday present from Kenneth," she says.

"Exactly," I say. "Call 911 and tell them to send the disposal unit right away."

"Don't be ridiculous," she says. "I'm going to open it right now and put an end to this nonsense once and for all."

Turns out this time he sent me a book. Albert Camus. *L'Étranger*. He knows I'm into the existentialists. Okay, a false alarm. I didn't tell her he'd tried it before. She'd only pretend not to believe me.

You were telling me about your day.

Sorry. Okay, from the get go. Midnight. I get up and go downstairs. I make coffee and take it back upstairs to my room. I lock the door again, then read my book until I hear the rest of the family moving around.

What book are you reading?

Kafka. *The Metamorphosis*. It's amazing. Gregor, the protagonist, wakes up one morning and discovers he's turned into a cockroach. He's afraid his family will find out, so he locks himself inside his room. Eventually his sister finds out and brings him food and cleans his room, which is filthy because he's a cockroach. See? That's a sister for you. Not a lot of laughs in the book so far, but I'm enjoying it. I've got several reclusive patients who'd benefit from reading it.

Later, when I hear movement, I make breakfast for everyone, because that way I can keep an eye on the food while I'm preparing it:

waffles, maple syrup, peameal bacon. I pour tea and coffee for everyone, and they're all eating by the time I sit down, so I know it's safe to eat the food. After breakfast I open their cards and presents.

Did you get some nice presents? Besides the Camus?

I thought I did, but all day I've been rethinking them and I believe now I've cottoned on to something. Take my wife — please! Sorry, old joke — anyway, she knitted me a scarf. It's a beautiful scarf, alpaca, and it's very long. I mean like *really* long, even for a scarf. It would take a whole alpaca to produce the wool for that scarf. So, think about that for a moment.

You mean, it was generous of her to knit you such a beautiful scarf?

No, no. *Long.* Such a *long* scarf. I could wrap it around my neck three times and the ends would still come down to my knees. Think about *that* is what I mean.

You mean you could hang yourself with it?

From the balcony. The catalpa tree in the backyard. Anywhere.

A change of strategy, then?

Exactly. Instead of killing me, they supply me with the means to do it myself.

Do they think you might be suicidal?

They suspect I'm not happy and they're nudging me in that direction, my wife by knitting me one inordinately long scarf.

Isn't that stretching things just a little?

Ha! Good one. No, not at all. My son gives me a deluxe Swiss Army knife — a dozen ways to end your life right there, wouldn't you say? — and my daughter some expensive cologne to which, by the way, I've become very allergic. My father buys me a bottle of single malt — a large bottle, so what's he thinking about there? I get a shirt from my mother, which is safe enough you say, though what they can do with fabrics now is scary. You can see why I wish I had a sister. Did I tell you that you make me think of her?

In what way?

I can't put my finger on it, but when I look at you I think of my sister. At least, I think of the sister I would have if I had one. It's kind of like transference, maybe, do you think?

It's hard to say because this is only our first session. But tell me, did your brother-in-law and his parents come for breakfast, or give you a present?

Gunter goes to work very early, and his parents never leave the house. I can't remember when I last saw them. Maybe when they set their Rottweilers on me? Gunter's one weird guy, I can tell you. This evening before my wife and I went out for dinner, I watched him put his car in the garage.

Why?

It's hilarious. Parking his car is like the moon landing for this guy. You have no idea how complicated it gets. Whenever I hear his garage door open, I go straight over to my window. This one was a doozy, I can tell you.

So tell me.

Okay, he's already opened the garage door with his remote, but he doesn't just drive in. Oh no. Not Gunter. He stops, gets out of the car, and walks into the garage to see how much space he'll have on either side of the car. Right away I'm thinking two things. *One*, why have an automatic door when you don't drive straight in? And *B*, if you want to check the space on each side, you stand *behind* the car and look *into* the garage — you don't stand *inside* the garage looking *out*. Right?

I guess.

Then he climbs back into the car and inches it forward. And I'm thinking, Gunter, you could *push* the car faster than this. After stopping inside the garage, he gets out again and walks to the front of the car out of my view. I figure he's checking that he hasn't driven it into his lawn mower or workbench or maybe his parents because living with them must drive him mad.

Now he comes around to the back of the car to see if the rear wheels have overshot the paint stripe. He painted this white stripe across the floor so he'd know when the car's in far enough and the automatic door won't chop off its ass-end. Anyway, he's not in far enough yet because even *I* can't see the paint stripe, so he climbs back in and moves the car forward a few more inches. He gets out again to check the stripe, and now I can see it, so he's okay — in a manner of speaking.

Then he moves from one side of the car to the other to check that it's evenly spaced. This time he's got it right, but some days he backs the car out again because it's not evenly spaced and so he has to do the whole thing all over, including the lawnmower-workbench-parents-thing in front and the paint stripe behind. Four times he did it the other day. In and out, in and out, check the front, check the back, check the sides, in and out. Four times. I figured a couple more and it would be tomorrow morning, so he could just back out of the garage again and go to work without having to worry about the paint stripe or being evenly spaced. It's better than Formula One, I'm telling you.

Then he waves his remote and watches the door come down. He waits for the door to close completely before he goes into the house. Like if he doesn't stand there and watch the door come all the way down, it'll stop halfway and go back up again, just to be awkward, as garage doors can be. Same with elevators that go up to the fortieth floor even though you pressed for the lobby when you got in on the sixth. Garage doors and elevators have minds of their own.

Anyway, I stay at the window because I know we're not finished. Sure enough, out he comes. He opens the garage door and does the left-right-even-space-check all over again. Does he think the car might have shifted in those two minutes just to annoy him? Then he closes the door and walks into the house looking disconsolate, like he's upset with himself for getting his car evenly spaced the first time so now he has to find something else to occupy his evening. His head's not evenly spaced, I can tell you. And his elevator doesn't go anywhere *near* the fortieth floor. Anyway, I'm happy he got it the first time because my wife was shouting up the stairs for me so we could go for dinner.

Did Gunter see you?

No. I look out through my Venetian blinds. I angle them just so. I've made some notes on the guy over the years, and by now I know his pathology. I used to think he was thirty percent obsessive-compulsive and the rest paranoid. But today I nailed it. *Atelophobia,* in a nutshell. Fear of imperfection. He lives with his parents, right? There is no Frau Gunter. When you live with parents, even if they drive you crazy, you can get away, not like when you live with your wife and you can never get away. Living with parents means you can spend half your day perfectly parking your car and giving your atelophobia a free rein. I should send him the invoice for my analysis.

Are you sure his parents are still living with him? I mean, you say you haven't seen them for four years.

You mean he might have murdered them? No, I don't think so. My wife would have said something. They're her parents too.

Actually, I was thinking maybe they'd moved to a retirement home or something, though I guess your wife would have mentioned that too. Anyway, tell me how the week's going with your son and daughter?

I'm worried. They haven't done anything obvious since they set me on fire, but the steak knives and cologne tell me they're up to something. Sure, they're writing essays and preparing for midterms this week, and, being millennials, they're preoccupied with themselves and their devices. But I think it's all a ruse. Technology — there's a whole new ball game.

What do you mean?

Seriously, there are apps now that can hack into a car's computer and basically take it over. An app can drive your car, even park it for you — I should tell Gunter — set off your air bags, accelerate at will, override your braking system — everything. Millennials know all about apps. Anyway, here's the thing.

Tell me.

My phone went missing last weekend after they came home. Stupidly, I left it on the hall table — I absolutely know that's where I left it — and it disappeared. I couldn't find it for a whole day. Then that same evening I found it in the pocket of my coat hanging in the hall closet. No question but they used it to hack into my car's computer before they returned it. Sneaky, eh? So, today, being the twenty-ninth, I took a taxi to work and then another one home.

I thought you were afraid of cars.

Other people's cars. And only of being outside them. I'm okay inside a car because I'm — well — inside. And driving my own car is fine because I control what it's doing. At least I did until my phone went missing for a day and my kids hacked the whole system. No way I was driving anywhere today. Tomorrow I'll be fine because it's March 1, and four years from now I'll have a different car.

Did you come here by taxi?

No, I walked. It's not that far.

It concerns me that you're unhappy on your birthday.

It could be worse. So far, so good, and it's what, nearly nine o'clock. Only three hours to go. *Ha.* You know I mean it literally when I tell you I'm just getting through the day.

It's got a whole new slant, for sure.

As for not being happy, who is anymore? I swear if I didn't run every day I'd go mad.

You still run every day?

Treadmill now. In my clinic, when I'm between patients.

Why the change?

I don't get stressed on a treadmill. When you run on the street you have to deal with other people running, or walking to work or maybe from work, shopping, trying to control their kids and not doing a good job of it, or just standing on the sidewalk talking to each other about running, working, shopping, and trying to control their kids.

What else?

Cars, obviously. Fumes. Noise, generally. Scary buses. A treadmill's safer, and calmer too, with my earbuds. You can't wear buds running outside because a cement truck could run up on the sidewalk and take you right out, or someone could drive by and shoot you, and you wouldn't know. Not until after you were flattened or shot, and then it would be too late. But I can wear my buds on the treadmill. Is there someone outside your door?

I don't hear anything. What music do you listen to when you're exercising?

I thought I heard someone. Anyway, Mozart, now. I could run all day listening to Mozart.

Most people listen to rock or hip-hop when they run. Why Mozart?

The way I see it, you spend most of your day doing stuff you don't like — standing in line for your double espresso, riding the elevator, being put on hold — and you have to listen to crap music. When I run, I listen to real music. I run *from* crap music and I run *to* Mozart. Am I going too fast for you?

No. I'm right with you. When you're running to Mozart, are you running from anything else besides crap music?

Life. Most people think they're running from death. I'm the opposite.

How does that work? You say you're running to death?

Think about it. Most people diet, quit smoking and drinking, and take pills so they can live longer, but they hate their lives. You tell me how *that* works. They pay an outrageous fee to sit in my office for an hour and tell me how much they hate their lives. And when they think that running will lengthen their lives, they're wrong. It won't.

Why not?

Simple. The heart is programmed to beat only so many times in anyone's lifetime. Running makes it beat faster, right? So you use up those heartbeats in a shorter time. In other words, they're shortening their lives when all the time they think they're prolonging them.

I, on the other hand, don't delude myself. I run to live better, not longer. One day when I'm pushing myself way more than I should because Mozart makes me think I can do the higher, faster, farther thing, my heartbeat allocation will expire and so will I. Right in the middle of, say, the Jupiter Symphony, with the notes tumbling over each other, soaring into the ether and taking me with them, I'll flatline just like that and never know what hit me. What a way to go.

An apotheosis of sorts, wouldn't you say?

I hadn't thought about it like that. Interesting. But how do you think your family would feel about your apotheosis?

If it happened today — on February 29 — they'd be ecstatic, obviously. On any other day? I don't know. You'd have to ask them.

Right. If you could do whatever you wanted right now, what would it be?

Just walk away. They call it *Sannyasa* in Hindi. I've researched it. The old man wraps up some basics in a cloth and walks away. He carries an empty bowl in his hand and his worldly possessions on a stick. He's preparing for eternity, you see. People toss coins into his bowl while he goes from village to village preparing for death and the life beyond. Makes sense to me. I'm not old, but I think I'm ready for it — okay, now I'm hearing someone at the door. There's someone out there.

I still don't hear anything.

It's my wife. She eavesdrops all the time. Whenever I'm talking to myself, for instance, I know she's at the door. So I say stuff loud enough for her to hear and then she thinks I'm crazy. It's a game, you see.

You talk to yourself?

Who doesn't? It used to bother me because I thought maybe I *was* losing my mind. But everyone talks to themselves. You stub your toe or bang your head or pee blood — what do you do? You say something to yourself. *God damn,* or something. It's natural. It's called thinking out loud, and it's normal. How do I know what I think until I hear what I've said? Like right now. Am I talking to you or to myself, and how do we tell the difference? Are we preaching to the choir or playing to the gallery? It's all to do with *perceptual* versus *conceptual.* Is the car backing out of the garage or is the garage moving away from the car? Wouldn't it look the same either way? I should run that one by Gunter while he's parking his car. It would freak him out.

It would give him something to think about.

I'm the same when I listen to people. I let them ramble on while I make mental notes, like you are right now, because we both know the therapy is in letting the person talk. Is he talking to me or to himself?

And how would it look any different?

It's okay to think that.

So, yes, that was my wife outside the door. She probably wants to use the bathroom. We have four in the house and she can use any of them, but she's stubborn. I use this bathroom because I like the mirror. It's a *Who's the fairest of us all* kind of mirror. The queen spoke to the mirror and it spoke back. This is my mirror. And *you're* okay with it, right?

Right.

So I don't see why she can't use another bathroom with just any old mirror. But now she's out there and she thinks we're talking about her. Well, we are *now*, because I've just realized she's out there, but she would think we were talking about her even if we *weren't* talking about her. What we're really talking about here is paranoia, straight up. There's a lot that's wrong with my wife — enough for a whole symposium. So, I'm going to cut this short and do the whole floss and gargle thing before bed or she'll think I'm letting myself go again. I've got a couple of hours until midnight, and tomorrow's a whole new day. All I have to do is make it to my bedroom and lock the door behind me. Do you think I can do it?

I think you can do it.

Will I see you next time?

February 29, right?

I should be fine until then. Thank you, Ingrid.

After teaching in England and Canada for thirty-seven years, Colin Brezicki returned to writing to try and make sense of the world — still a work in progress. *A Case for Dr. Palindrome* (2017) and *All That Remains* (2018) were published by Michael Terence (UK). His short fiction has won awards in Canada and the U.S., while some whimsical articles have appeared in *The Globe and Mail* and *Voice of Pelham*. He enjoyed writing "A Time to Reflect" and is grateful to have it included in the anthology. He never knows where a story will end up until it gets there. **colinbrezicki.com**

blood is thicker than scotland (until we leap)

by Jess Skoog

It was February 29 again, and I was wondering which member of my family would try to kill me this time. I imagine most of you are completely certain I'm, at the very least, exaggerating my predicament. More than likely, you think I've recently escaped from some institution. I'm not sure that such institutions even exist anymore, not in these days of cutbacks and political correctness. Now the challenged are housed in jails. Oh my, how easily I run off topic.

But thinking of jails brings me to a topic that arises whenever I feel the need to tell my story. If my family tries once every four years to kill me, why have I not pursued their incarceration? And how is it that I can sit here and record my story so calmly, considering today is February 29, 2016?

Surely you're sitting in your most comfortable chair while playing this recording of my story. If not, please get comfortable, because my predicament is unlike any you've ever heard before. It not only deals with my family dynamics, but also the balance of power worldwide.

The first thing all my listeners must accept is that my family is not at all like your family. At least, I have never been made aware of any other family that shares the circumstances that my brothers and I do. If another family was blessed with our destiny, surely someone would already have sold the movie rights. Perhaps a visual would help, my fine listener. Picture me as an even fitter Harrison Ford. Allow me this leeway. I have my charm, but maybe not quite his strong manly gaze.

It makes sense to start at my birth. I was born on the evening of February 29, 1928, in the magnificent city of Dunfermline, Scotland. Maybe you've heard of it? To completely understand, it's important to know Dunfermline was once the capital of Scotland and therefore possessed magical powers bestowed upon it by fairies. Fairies have always roamed the city, protecting and blessing the city and its dwellers. Dunfermline, however, is often left out of listings of previous capitals of Scotland, due to the need for some to bury history and escape superstition.

Dunfermline ceased to be the capital with the death of James I in 1437. James I was a man far ahead of his time. A real Renaissance man, if you'll excuse the pun, since the Renaissance did not occur in the British Isles for another few decades. But I digress.

James I, despite being a king, was a "prince" of a man. A well-loved poet, master debater, avid sportsman, and talented musician. All of his talents were surely due to the city's fairies. There were few such charismatic men around at that time, which helped him to emerge as a fine leader for Scotland. At the time, a strong sense of entitlement was common among the well-to-do. But James I had revolutionary thoughts; he believed that no one, no matter their title, should hold themselves above the law, which endeared him to the masses. Oh, the powerhouse Scotland could have been, had he lived! Unfortunately for my homeland, he was murdered.

What does this sad tale of a life cut short have to do with my family trying to kill me every four years? Well, as time passes, things often change. Frankly, no one is around to dispute facts that have been buried or rewritten. Think of the 1400s as an ever-changing Wiki page that's constantly being modified by know-it-alls. However, I remain here to document the truth as I — and all of my kin — know it. Since their role in the story sets their destiny as murderers, you can easily see why I'm sitting here recording the facts.

Our honourable James I was not in fact killed on February 21, 1437, as the history books tell you. Rather, the magic he brought to Scotland was extinguished on February 29, 1436. Surely you see the significance of the change, as 1436 was a leap year, allowing for the date — my date, February 29 — to occur. The instigators, hoping to diminish the Scots' glorious future — which was most assuredly to come under James I —

picked the worst day to murder him. As a result, the murderers felt the wrath of the fairies, which imposed the unluckiest of spells on the men who did the deed.

Without any obvious solution to rid themselves of the fairy magic, they simply pretended the murder hadn't happened that day. The powers that be simply moved the year of James' death to 1437 and for good measure subtracted a week. Think of it: millions of tests have been written by British schoolchildren with the wrong correct answer of when James I died. The fairies allowed this change, but everyone in Dunfermline knows the true date of his death. By design, I believe they did not want to draw any attention to the leap-year date of February 29, as it has been the foundation of their plans for Scotland's future.

Fairies are regularly portrayed as lovely, light-filled creatures, but believe me, they have their dark side. They've always intended for Scotland to rise and become a powerful nation, not only in Europe but in the world. You will be astonished to learn that they've always been working behind the scenes politically. Please listen intently, as the secret I am about to divulge will shock everyone.

Fairies are the masterminds behind the Scottish vote in the upcoming Brexit referendum four months from now. The fairies will engineer it so the vast majority of Scotland votes to remain in the European Union. Their ultimate objective: Scotland as the leading nation of the Union.

I know what you're thinking: why in the world would the fairies want Scotland to remain in the EU if their goal is for Scotland to become a powerhouse? Economically, they are small potatoes when compared to other nations housed under the Union. Well, those fairies are always thinking outside the box. Without getting too political, there is logic to their plan. The wheels have been in motion since the European Union was formed: Scotland will first be the most powerful nation in the Union and then the world.

And that is where I come in. My humble yet blessed birth in

Dunfermline — on February 29, 1928 — was a notable day. It is special to have a leap-year birthday, as only around a quarter of one percent of the world's population is born on February 29. That's not many when you look at the big picture of the world's population. But it is more remarkable that, ever since the demise of James I, only one baby has been born in Dunfermline on February 29. That miracle is me. And now dear listener, this is how my fate was first revealed to me.

One fateful evening, my friend John took ale from his uncle and we set off to the woods to enjoy it. We came across a fairy, the most beautiful thing I had ever seen. I was a mere three leap years — or a little over thirteen years — old at the time. Apparently, the fairies' plan for setting Scotland back on its proper path was set to begin. This beautiful, beguiling woman sowed the seeds for my family taking turns trying to kill me each and every February 29.

These are the words she spoke:

Our king was taken one timely leap day.
He was not only of royal blood, but one we chose.
The man one saw was inspired by the gifts we gave.

So when the time arrives, Scotland just may
rise above, and the world all will bestow.
Destiny was always ours, as we are the brave.

But evil took our king, much to our dismay.
All will right, with the death of the leap child, so it goes,
by a family hand. Mighty Scots will uphold a new wave.

The woman's words struck fear in me. Her words reached deep down to my soul, as there was no doubt she believed Scotland would rise only if a member of my family killed me, the only child of Dunfermline born in a leap year. While I'll admit that I had always felt special because of my birthday, and I was confident that my destiny was more extraordinary than that of my brothers or my friends, I did not want to be Scotland's saviour. I envied my brothers and their ordinary births. I imagine anyone in my shoes would feel the same.

My brothers grew tired of hearing of my fateful birth. Most people viewed the day as unlucky, due to the acts of those murdering bastards, but my parents thought differently. After all, my connection to the date was my birth, so what could possibly be unlucky about that? Plus, it was a necessary balancing day for the calendar. My mother always assured me that it was a blessing to have been born on such an important date. She was a convincing woman, and the community generally ran with the notion that I was a lucky lad. And so it always seemed. Until that meeting with the fairy, I was always grateful when opportunities fell into my lap.

WWII had brought lean times and hardship to us all, but at least I was too young to serve. Many lads enlisted by lying about their age, but I was too well-known to get away with any such deception. But no one could say that I didn't love my country or was not brave enough to fight. I held a job in a factory that supplied shirts for our men at war.

I worked diligently, always being careful not to let any substandard stitching slip through. Before the term even existed, I was a quality-control manager. I wanted desperately to do my part by serving my country the only way possible. The work was satisfying, and I felt very good about myself — until my mother received a dreaded envelope with the black border. Back then it was the universal marking notifying the family a loved one had died.

My older brother Lloyd had died heroically in battle. We heard first from one of his platoon members, and later it was confirmed by two soldiers whose sole job was to inform families of their loss. Things were much different back then. It was that fateful sadness that drove my family to a festival. We were dragged there by my mother's closest friend, who had also received an envelope. A strange time it was, mourning our Lloyd and going to a festival full of music and drink. My two remaining brothers, one a year older and one a year younger than me, attended with my mother and me. By that time my father had passed, blessed be his soul.

Late that night, we were approached by a slight woman who turned out to be a fairy. She gathered my family in a circle while she spoke her truth. Her eyes glistened as she spoke, mesmerizing each of us. As they listened intently to the fairy's words, my family was very quiet. My mother dismissed her as a drunk. My brothers remained conspicuously silent. I only started paying attention when she said the fairies were watching me as I grew.

I do remember my head hurting beyond belief, and feeling numb, Memories of Lloyd kept flashing through my mind. The fairy talk was simply something to keep myself distracted from thoughts of my dead brother, but her words remained with all of us. I have never admitted it before today, but she spoke the same words the fairy had spoken that fateful night with John. On the way home, we did not speak of this encounter; it was far easier to pretend our ears had never heard her words.

The war wore on, and I felt a distance grow between my brothers and me. How I longed for Lloyd, who was far more fun than Peter and Malcolm. When I was sixteen, my dear brothers came to me with a piece of paper in their hands. It was a copy of the very words I read to you earlier, recited by the beautiful fairy woman and then repeated at the festival. They wanted me to have a copy. At first, I thought it was strange; in fact, I had forgotten about the oddness of that evening. The words, while not quite a song, are now indelibly etched in my mind. I preserved the actual copy by having it laminated. You will undoubtedly have found it as you began listening to these tapes.

Malcolm spoke first. "Brother, will you do the honourable thing for Scotland?"

I remember being confused, as my mother and brothers were all loyal Scots, proud of our country and our clan. Knowing their tempers,

I allowed them to explain, but inside I grew angry at the preposterous idea that I was not loyal to my country.

"Read the words again," he said.

I knew exactly what he was getting at, and the indelible words of the fairy played over and over in my head.

But evil took our king, much to our dismay.
All will right, with the death of the leap child, so it goes,
by a family hand. Mighty Scots will uphold a new wave.

My pride at being a leap child was now nothing to be proud of. Instead, it posed a big problem.

My brothers tried to reason with me. They wished I would make it easier for them to take my life for the sake of Scotland. Perhaps if you have not had exposure to fairies or any magic in general, you would find this story a bit farfetched. But long before this quandary of the verse landed on my lap, I had experienced the magic performed by the fairies.

Often at the factory, I'd felt I was a chosen one and that the fairies were helping me. They provided me with sunny days when I needed to do intricate drafting work; on days when we were all desperately hungry, chickens appeared in the open yard of the factory, and I easily rounded them up and prepared them for cooking. Our factory was deemed one of the most productive. What more can I say about this tangible evidence? When the workers were hungry, food appeared. I chalked it up to my blessed birthday. I can imagine what you're thinking: I'm a braggart. Perhaps in this day and age, finding stray chickens does sound trite, but during the war, these blessings were counted and given thanks for.

As my brothers continued to try to convince me to make it easier on them, I always had the same answer. I wanted to live. "Life is a blessing," I would almost chant at them. They would leave, heads hanging, and give no response to my reasoning. Perhaps they were feeling pressure from the fairies. By my twentieth year, even my mother, while she would still speak to me, avoided eye contact, making life quite uncomfortable. One day Peter finally blurted out, "Why do you think your life is more important than seeing Scotland rise?"

I had prepared for this situation to come to a head, and I simply stated that it was not unreasonable for me to expect to live out my years naturally. Yes, my birth occurred on the most unusual of days, but perhaps I was meant to serve Scotland with my talents. I pointed out the contributions I had made at the factory, and the lives I had saved by noticing the errors in one shipment of poorly stitched seams. They would have burst open with the slightest movement. My brothers thanked me for my service. But they reiterated that the fairy felt strongly that my death could do even more for my country than my keen eye at the factory.

I knew my life would never be the same, so the only logical thing to do was to move out of the family home. The fairies, of course, knew where I was; I could still feel their presence and their blessings helping me, but the fairy's prophecy remained indelible in my mind. All I could conclude was that the fairies desired me to live well until one of my family members would kill me one February 29.

I made my way to Cornwall, England. I found a thatched cottage by the ocean and took up farming with my wife. We never had any children, for whatever reason, but we were happy. I am forever grateful that she passed away before this momentous day. We had a content existence, and I felt a large degree of protection.

It did not take long for my brothers to find me. My wife greeted my brothers with open arms when they showed up at our door. She had already prepared a delicious stew and invited them to stay and tell their side of the story. I knew from the sadness enveloping her face that she truly believed me. She chased Peter and Malcolm out of our home with a broom and insisted they never return. But return they did. At first, all their attempts on my life were easy to thwart. In all honesty, they could have tried harder, put a bit more effort into it. But all I can attribute my survival to is my cottage. It had been built by quite the superstitious bunch.

The previous owners had etched the beams with spirals and other protective figures, which are referred to as apotropaic markings. Scots have their fairies for protection; the English, their markings. Oddly, I did not dismiss the marks, as I had dismissed the similar spirals I'd drawn at my factory drafting table years earlier. Make of that what you may; both foreshadowing and destiny suit in my mind. Mark me a man who has always believed fairies and etchings have the power to keep evil at bay.

But here I sit. Today I am eighty-eight years old, and I am preparing this recording. Is it treasonous for me to leave these facts to be found? After much thought, my answer is no, I think not. History, where I am concerned, did change with the recording of James I's death. But if need be, my tape here will prove as evidence of my story, of the goals of fairies and the perseverance of my brothers to follow through on what is required of them.

I am not entirely sure which one of them will show up here today, but I am certain one of them will, as it is February 29, 2016. I will inform them of this tape. While I haven't been unreasonable to want to successfully thwart each of their attempts, it is now reasonable for me not to deny that the time of my death is near.

The framework has been laid, the foundation poured by the fairies. They will have their desires granted, and Scotland will vote to remain in the European Union. The fairies have their plan, and they have moved forward without my cooperation … until today.

Today, I, James Wilson, am twenty-two leap years old and I freely give my life to be taken on this day. Twenty-two is the atomic number for titanium, a metal synonymous with strength, and it is perhaps not coincidentally found here in my home of Cornwall. I cannot deny my destiny any longer. Like my mother had insisted, February 29 was created for balance. It is now time to fulfill my role in balancing what was always meant to be. Large dreams rest on my demise, and today, my death will bring strength to Scotland.

There's a knock at the door. Did you hear it? I've been sitting for far too long; these old bones don't want to help me up. Ah, there I am, I'm up.

I will keep the tape running.

"Peter, so glad to see you. Do come in."

"No elusive disappearance or such this year, dear brother?"

"Aye, no, not this year. In fact, there's some tea in the kitchen. Now it's time for you to prepare it for me and only me."

"Truly? James, are you sure?"

"The future is clear, and the time is now. The fairies can rejoice. Long live Scotland."

[Tape one ends.]

Jess Skoog lives in Waterloo Region with her husband and daughter. Her love of writing stems from her parents exposing her to a wide variety of authors. Top influencers throughout the years ranged from Carolyn Keene to Camus. She is a firm believer that as the sun rises, solid, thoughtful words abound. As a result, she is a regular member of the #5amwritersclub. You can find Jess on Twitter at @jessskoog.

the race

by Judith Pettersen

It was February 29 again, and I was wondering which member of my family would try to kill me this time. I glanced over my shoulder to see Megan closing in on me, her arms pumping, eyes searching the crowd of runners. Our schoolmate, Jacob, was ten paces back and catching up fast. Scores of people were on the trail ahead, but Megan and I were still within the top third of participants. She caught up to me, her stride matching mine, her gaze fixed on the racing path winding through the trees in the distance. The temperature was just above freezing, and clouds of moisture circled our heads as we breathed.

"Have you seen him?"

"Shhh," I said. "Don't waste your energy." Wisely, she didn't reply, just gave me a measured glance. We ran side by side, our breath rising and falling in unison. We didn't need to win. We just couldn't be last. It's been four years since we first stumbled across the leap year finish line, completely wet, shaking with cold and fatigue, barely making it in time. We're much better prepared this year. Megan and I were just twelve-year-old girls then. That might have been the older side of childhood, but we were still at a disadvantage. Yet there's no point in complaining. The event is mandatory for townsfolk aged twelve to forty.

Our final practice took place two days ago. I'd barely finished tightening the laces on my racing boots when Megan rocketed past, her heels kicking snow into my face. I yanked on the laces one last time and took off after her. "No fair," I hollered. "We run together, remember?" In spite of the distance between us, I could hear her giggling.

"Who said anything about fair?" she cried, putting on more speed in an effort to stay out front. "You think your cousin Roman will be fair? Or Rudy?"

"They're family," I said, catching up to run alongside her, our breath billowing around our heads.

"Yeah?" she asked, starting to pant. I've always said we need to run without talking, but she never listens. In preparation for this year's race, we'd trained relentlessly after school and on weekends, both in the creek and on the track my dad made that weaves through the woods around our farm. We never know what kind of route the race committee will choose. Running through snow is hardest. We took yesterday off, but the day before that we ran for hours to work on our stamina.

Four years ago, my parents saved me when I fell during the race. They'd never gotten over the death of my brother, Ben, and it had made them extra vigilant. Ben was a really fast runner and thought he'd win for sure — boys can be overconfident like that. But he fell in his very first race, four years before mine, and my parents never knew until it was all over. He'd run off with his best friend, Jon, and he'd gotten lost in the crowd. And then Jon showed up alone. After everyone else was counted, the community searched for hours before finding his body hidden beneath a snow-covered patch of ice, snagged by a tree root after he'd drifted with the current. The general consensus was that Ben had tripped and hit his head. Because it happened during the race, the officials counted it as a righteous death. I can still see the poorly concealed relief on the face of the woman who'd finished last. Her life was saved, and her family rejoiced. Only mine was left to grieve.

In my first race, I tripped because of my cousin, Roman. He raced past, his shoulder hitting mine, and turned his head to make a rude face. I was so startled that I forgot to watch my feet. When I tripped over a boulder in the creek, a cold rush of water soaked through the sleeves of my racing jacket right up to my shoulders. Pebbles scraped my palms, and a sharp rock ripped my pants at the knee. I never told my parents why I fell. My father would never have forgiven the betrayal. But I've come to believe that Roman wanted it to happen. Luckily, my parents were close enough to snatch me up and half carry me until I got my breath back. I can't help thinking it might happen again. Roman's brothers are just as cunning, but he's the one to watch.

Megan has been my best friend since grade school. That's why we're sticking together during the race. My parents are over forty, so they don't have to run anymore. Megan's are too. For the rest of our lives, they're safe. It comforts me. Knowing Megan and I are watching out for each other reassures our families.

My Uncle Ronnie is just like his sons. He's never lost an immediate family member and he's arrogant about it, as if his own superiority protects the people he loves. When Ben died, Uncle Ronnie patted my father's back while gesturing toward Rudy, his eldest son, as if saying, how can anyone compete with this guy? I bet when he and my father ran, Ronnie did everything he could to throw his brother in harm's way. He's like that. Roman is the same. But my father and mother both survived. It's possible that I understand my dad's relatives better than Ben did. We'll see.

My mother's sister, Elizabeth, was here yesterday along with her two children, Nate and Alice, who are eight and ten. Elizabeth turned forty last year. She's alone except for the kids because her husband, Ed, died during the race four years ago. He was at the head of the pack when he stumbled over a slimy rock on his way out of the creek and died of a broken neck. My parents were too busy saving me from the same fate, and my uncle and aunt had gotten separated. The race is naturally crowded, and if you spend too much time looking around, you lose. I hope we don't have to run through the creek this year, but it seems to happen more often than not.

Aunt Elizabeth talks about Ed in a cheerful voice, as if saying his name over and over again will bring him back. I wish it could. He was so kind. So funny. While they worked in the kitchen, my mother put her arm around my aunt's shoulders, letting her babble on about how she and Ed had met and then married on the sly. We all know the story, but it makes her feel better to tell it again.

My parents and I had set up trestle tables in our large farmhouse kitchen. Dad and Ronnie inherited the place from their parents. After Dad paid his brother for his share, it was all ours. The stone barn across from the house is over 200 years old, the house a century younger. We've had to do quite a bit of repair work over the years. My grandparents replaced the old stone fireplace with a brick one, and we try to paint the white clapboard siding every ten years or so. The roof is steep, so in the winter the snow slides right off. Two dormer windows peek out from the roof on each side of the house. My bedroom faces the barn. Ben's did too, but now it's my mother's sewing room.

In the clearing out front, the branches of the beech trees meet overhead like they're holding hands. I love the sound of the leaves rustling on a summer night, as if they've been waiting all day for us to go to bed so they can whisper their secrets. I used to stay awake and try to figure out what they were saying. In February, the branches are frozen and bare, and anyway, with all the training I've been doing, I'm barely undressed and under the covers before falling asleep.

Everyone brought food to yesterday's family gathering, even my Uncle Dan. He gave my mom and Aunt Elizabeth a big hug, first thing. They were always close. That's one of the reasons they won the race when they were my age, my mom said. They helped each other through it. Uncle Dan never married. His sweetheart, a fine girl named Rosemary, died after the race twelve years ago. He never got over her. Maybe that's why Uncle Ronnie ignores us all. He doesn't want to feel the pain of our loss. That part I understand.

I was only eight when Ben died. All I have left of him is the memory of a messy, brown-haired whirlwind tearing through the house. Perhaps my poor recall is for the best. I can't imagine the agony of losing a child or a sweetheart. I broke a rib once when I fell off my horse, and I bet it's just like that. Sudden and sharp, and you hope the pain will go away, but it stays for a long time and makes breathing hard and sleeping even worse. For my parents' sake, I'm going to live. So is Megan.

After dinner, when everyone had toasted this year's racers, Roman brushed past me to have a word with my father. He's never spoken to me, not even when we were little, but for some reason he really likes my dad. I don't blame him. Who would want to be stuck with Uncle Ronnie for a father? Mine treats everyone with kindness and respect. I watched my dad speak with his brother just before everyone left. His face seemed to sink and I could tell that my uncle was crowing about something. I wanted to go up to Uncle Ronnie and shove him hard. "Stop talking," I'd have said. "Just stop it." The man has no conception of anyone else's feelings.

Ronnie's wife, my aunt Melinda, is kind to me. Perhaps she would have liked to have a daughter. We don't talk for long because what is there to say? But she smiles at me and seems to prefer my company to my mother's. Aunt Melinda has never lost a child. Her relief may be tainted by guilt. Some people lose every single member of their family. Every four years another person dies — a child, a teenager, or someone's parent. A friend of my mother's, Grace, lost her husband and both daughters over the last twenty years. She died a couple of months ago, and I can't help thinking she wanted it to happen. Who wants to live without family? Not me. But at least my parents are safe.

My three cousins, Roman, seventeen, Rudy, nineteen, and young Ronald, just thirteen, carried the hot dishes from the stove to the tables. I set out the plates and cutlery as the brothers marched back and forth, filled with their own sense of importance. I must have made a face because my father's twinkling eyes met mine. I grinned back and he winked. In spite of the difficulties with his brother, these meals are important to him. The gathering of our clan, small as it is, is a family tradition dating back to my great-great-great-grandfather, who built the original farmhouse after clearing the land with only a few horses and his wife and five sons. We have a daguerreotype of them on our dining-room wall. Everyone's face is very stern, which surprises me. They didn't have to race back then. What was there to frown about?

The food was excellent because my mother is a wonderful cook. The large roast pork sat on my grandmother's oval platter like an island in a sea of roasted potatoes and carrots. A huge salad of fresh greens from our nursery took centre stage, along with freshly baked bread from Aunt Elizabeth, large crusty loaves sliced and calling out for butter. Sometimes my hunger takes me by surprise. It seems like I'll never fill up, no matter how much I eat. I'm a little on the skinny side, so maybe that's it. Megan is a curvy girl who looks well-fed even though she just picks at her food. All the boys like her a lot. I don't have anyone like that. Maybe I'm too preoccupied with the race.

The clock ticked over the mantel until, with a heavy sigh, my father said it was time to go. My parents and I were sitting in the living room drinking green tea. I'd eaten hours before to avoid cramps during the race. Nervously I pulled on waterproof pants and grabbed my racing boots. Ankle-high and lightweight, they're guaranteed to stay dry. My mother was trying to be cheerful so I avoided eye contact. I couldn't let her fear get into my head. It would only ignite the worries I've been trying to subdue.

I zipped my jacket against the cold wind as we headed out the door. The temperature was warmer than usual, but the sunshine was not a good thing. My father rushed back into the house to bring me a peaked cap to shield my eyes. There are no rules about head gear, and snow blindness is a concern. It was almost four o'clock but the sun was still high.

We drove to the main street of our town where everyone congregates before the race. A huge red ribbon for the mayor to cut blocked the way — the race doesn't start without him. The youngest runners were placed at the very front and behind them teenagers under eighteen. The oldest racers came next. I looked up and saw Megan pushing her way through the crowd. She took her place next to me and we exchanged looks but didn't speak. Nervous giggles broke out from some of the younger kids, but most participants were quiet. I didn't bother looking for my parents, just breathed slowly, calming myself and picturing my final dash through the finish line well ahead of everyone else. The mayor raised his starting pistol.

Over 500 of us filled the street like silent protestors, some folks jumping up and down to build up energy, others bending in a low crouch, one foot behind the other. Megan reached over and squeezed my hand just before the gun went off. A surge of movement came from the first line of runners. A space before me opened and I took the opportunity to cut in. Megan was right behind me as I barrelled through the opening, slipping between two runners before increasing my speed. My breathing was slow and even. The race was only five kilometres, and I was determined to save most of my energy for the last two. We passed one of my dad's friends, Burt, just a few years younger than him. He glanced sideways at me as he ran, a resigned look on his face. It made me angry.

"For your family!" I shouted as I shot past him. Megan caught up, and we found the space to run side by side, falling into a good rhythm, breathing almost in unison. There were a number of people ahead of us, but far more lagged behind. We had to follow the trail guides because the course changed every four years. They didn't want people practising on the official trail before February 29. Up ahead, I saw Jacobson's Hill in the distance. I prayed for that to be the route. A struggle, that's for certain. But worth it.

We weren't that lucky. At the last minute, the trail veered to the left and we pounded our way through snow just beginning to melt. We headed for the creek, and it looked as if a good portion of our run would take place there. I heard Megan mutter something but didn't catch the words. I wanted to tell her to hush, that we needed all our energy for running. Legs pumped up and down, arms moved in sync as we increased our stride. We needed to make up time before moving into the creek.

Megan stopped for a second when we reached the creek and I leapt first, landing with a splash in the creek bed. The trick was to step between the rocks. It slowed a runner down but was better than falling. *For you, Ben*, I thought, as I picked my way down the course. *For you, Mom and Dad.* I practically flew from one spot to the next, finding my footing with uncanny ease. Then I heard Megan cry out. She'd stumbled and her foot became wedged between a boulder and a smaller rock almost the same colour as the creek bed. Worse, my cousin Roman came up behind her and propelled himself forward by pushing down on her back. She fell into the water. I reached for her hand just as Jacob, the boy from our class, grabbed the other and yanked her upward. Foot freed, she didn't hesitate but dashed ahead, the best thanks she could give us. Jacob didn't reply, just kept running through the creek toward the finish line.

It seemed to be taking forever to reach the end of the creek. I was feeling less sure of myself after Megan's fall. But she'd regained her confidence. As I was carefully skirting a large boulder, she even slapped me on the butt. "For Ben," she cried. My heart surged and I moved faster. Up ahead we could see Roman behind his brothers. Even thirteen-year-old Ronnie was ahead of us. We passed the spot where my brother's body was found, but I didn't look. I kept my gaze focused on Roman's back, as if I had the power to trip him with my thoughts.

And then it happened. He hit something with his boot and went crashing down about ten metres ahead of us. Before he had a chance to recover, Megan had stepped onto his back and sprung off, landing evenly on both feet. Jacob surged ahead of me to do the same. I wanted to but didn't. Instead, I tried to avoid him but accidentally stepped on his leg, stumbling as a result. Megan reached back and took my hand. More people had raced past us, mostly teenagers. I longed to look back and watch Roman's recovery, but it was too risky. *Focus,* I told myself. *Keep your head.* At last we reached the point where the race exited the creek. I was too worked up to feel the cold, and fortunately, my boots kept my feet dry.

Far in the distance, the crowd was waiting for us, the red finish-line ribbon stretching across the road. We weren't too far from our farm. I couldn't help noticing that the old beech trees, like the ones around our house, met overhead as if they were clapping and cheering us on. Jacob was keeping pace, the three of us running full out.

We moved closer and closer to the race's end until finally I saw my parents jumping up and down in excitement. Megan's parents were there, too, and the look on their faces was all we needed for the last sprint. The ribbon across the road had been taken down by the first runner, so I headed straight for my mother's arms. She hugged me hard, and then my father picked me up and swung me around. "You did it!" He said it over and over. "I told you," I said. I wasn't feeling smug. I knew that Megan and I had been lucky. Though I'd promised my parents to put myself first, there's no way I could have left her. Jacob looked over at me, his face creasing in a wide grin.

It startled me. I looked around for Megan and saw her hugging her little brother, Eric. I waited for Jacob to walk over to her, but he stayed nearby, glancing at me every now and again. It made me feel self-conscious but warm, too. Like he'd given me a blanket.

Uncle Ronnie and Aunt Melinda stood off to the side, anxious looks darkening their faces. Young Ronnie was jumping up and down. He had done very well for his first race, and his brother Rudy proudly clapped him on the back. "Roman isn't here," my dad muttered. "We saw him fall," I said, glancing over at Jacob, who closed one eye in a subtle wink. My dad nodded soberly.

Roman was a big, strong boy. He'd be fine. It was another twenty minutes before all the racers came through. When my dad's friend, Burt, crossed the finish line, he headed over and hugged me before embracing his wife. I don't think they have any children. So many young couples were picking that option that there's talk about the race being cancelled every second leap year. Otherwise, we might run out of people.

We waited an extra ten minutes, but Roman didn't show up. The officials gathered in a huddle. When they were done, they made an announcement to those left waiting. "We're going to look for the boy," they said. "Either way, he's last." Aunt Melinda started to sob, and Uncle Ronnie ran his hands through his hair like he wanted to pull it out. "Not possible," he stuttered, over and over again. I couldn't help my words from spilling out. "He fell in the creek," I said. "Perhaps he'll end up in the same spot as Ben." My uncle's face whitened at the cruelty of my words and, for a moment, I was shocked at myself. Then Jacob returned. "My parents are hosting a post-race party," he said. "Would you like to come?" I must have looked undecided because he added that Megan was invited, too. I nodded and told my parents.

Before we left, I headed over to where my aunt and uncle stood waiting for more news. They weren't allowed to look for their son. Uncle Ronnie turned and his eyes met mine. I saw the pain there, the same look I'd seen on my own face after a night of bad dreams. One I saw every leap year on my parents' faces. I put a hand on his arm and he burst into tears. "I know," I said. I started to walk away — Jacob was waiting for me — then turned back. "You've still got Ronnie and Rudy," I said. "And us." As we headed for Jacob's house, I said aloud what I knew to be true. "Family is important, no matter what."

Judith Pettersen is a writer from Flin Flon, Manitoba. On her blog, "This Northern Life," on her website at **judithpettersen.com**, she writes philosophically about her husband's wardrobe, speaks her truth about hipster beards, and lectures on how to go to the bathroom on the side of the road when it's thirty below. Judith is currently querying her young adult novel, *Ellinor*, a contemporary fairy tale about a girl, a boy, a wicked stepbrother, and a 1964 Volkswagen.

costumes and wild mushrooms

by Heather Bonin MacIntosh

"It was February 29 again, and I was wondering which member of my family would try to kill me this time."

I rolled my eyes; I couldn't help it. Could my sister be any more dramatic? Of course she brought up the date — her birthday. I waited for the television interviewer to fall into Belinda's sugar-coated trap.

"I'm a leap-year baby, only seven years old!"

A groan seeped from my throat and the cat looked up.

"So what happened on February 29?" The interviewer reached for the baited morsel.

"My sister tried to poison me at my own birthday celebration. Wild mushrooms."

The mushrooms were a poor choice, I'll admit. Yet I do love the names of the most sinister fungi: Death Cap (*Amanita phalloides* ... a phallic symbol?!), Autumn Skull Cap (*Galerina marginata*), and Destroying Angel (*Amanita species*). My favourite is Deadly Dapperling (*Lepiota brunneoincarnata*) because it's toxic to the liver. Did I mention my sister is a recovering alcoholic? The complementarity is delicious.

"It was ghastly!" Belinda said.

Who says *ghastly*? I'm surprised she didn't feign a British accent. Although, she did a stellar Irish lilt in the film *Island Fairy*. The cinematography was magnificent — desolate stones covered in mist and moss, as emerald as a travel writer's promise.

The interview continued. Next project, most difficult co-star, exciting new Canadian talent ... blah, blah, blah. I pulled out my cellphone and began a game of Candy Smash. You're probably wondering why I didn't turn off the television. What can I say? Sibling rivalry is compelling, even when it's my own. Mid-multitask, I heard my name and my attention veered back to the monitor.

"Bianca? No, I don't believe my sister and I will work together anytime soon."

I pitched the phone at her.

I used to like her. When we were little, Belinda and I put on plays in our basement and enacted stories of sister princesses, sister explorers, sister animals.

"I want to be the black horse this time," I said.

"I always get the dark mane," she replied. It was true.

"Not fair!"

"You can choose the best costume."

I had a weakness for sequins. I raced for a bin bursting with old clothes. The tulle skirt swished as I flung it to the side. A Red Riding Hood cape in satin skimmed across my fingers. Shiny beads peeked up at me and I tugged at them. A gold, sequined dress too large for either of our small frames hid underneath a wizard's hat. I pulled the sparkling frock over my clothing and tied a long sash around my waist. A tail.

"You look beautiful, horsey," Belinda said. Her approval enveloped me. "Now put on the wig."

A tangle of long, blonde hair sat limp in a corner. It was more unruly than my own dark curls.

"Are you sure I can't be Black Beauty?"

"The other horsey has golden hair to match the dress, Bianca," Belinda said, as though her chief concern were a well-matched ensemble.

The wig refused to stretch over my skull, but I twisted the fibres into submission and clipped the hairpiece in place with a barrette.

Belinda yanked a netted skirt over her pants and pulled on a peasant-style top covered in embroidered roses.

"My horsey likes flowers," she said.

Belinda braided her straight, dark hair down the back of her skull and wrapped an elastic band at the nape of the neck, leaving a pony tail. As always, her hair-mane shimmered.

I neighed and pranced with my older sibling until our mother called us for lunch.

"Belinda, your hair is lovely," our mother said. "Are you Black Beauty?"

My sister galloped around the kitchen and thrust her nose in the air.

I spun in a circle so my sequins would catch the light. I tossed my golden mane and whinnied.

"Don't wear that dreadful wig at the table, Bianca." Mom wagged a finger at me. "You'll drag hair through your soup."

Belinda and I used to work together, mostly in the early years.

On her second major film, I was a costume designer at NBN Pictures, a production house in Los Angeles. As a Canadian in the industry, I was surprised — and delighted — to receive an offer to lead a department south of the border. The fact that Belinda Cross was my sister may have helped.

Corridors at NBN Pictures showcased movie posters from their award winners and blockbusters, and breathtaking costumes sparkled in display cases. I was drawn to clothing worn by women who had suffered tragic deaths.

Belinda negotiated a three-film contract for NBN Pictures. Her first role was Felicity, a mother who finds her son and the neighbour's daughter in bed in the bonus room above the garage. She calls the girl's father, who storms in and kills Felicity's progeny in a parental rage. The film was sensational and tragic. I dressed Belinda in wide-legged jeans and a modest pastel blouse. She changed into tight-fit denim and unbuttoned the blouse a bit more than I'd planned. I tried to re-button her on set.

"Bianca, what the hell are you doing?"

"Fixing your costume."

"Making me into some dowdy housewife."

"Your character is conservative."

"How dare you tell me what my character is like!" Belinda's voice echoed through the cavernous studio.

"The costume fits the role." I refrained from mentioning the pants.

"I know what Felicity would wear or not wear!"

"Felicity would be in wide-legged jeans!" Restraint disappeared.

"You bitch!" My sister whirled to face the director. "I want her off the set!"

He nodded and an attendant walked toward me. I reached out my hand to slap Belinda across the cheek. Instead, I turned my palm up and moved to the sideline.

The next day Belinda filmed a segment where she fingers a necklace and pendant her dead son gave her, quite a touching moment in the story. The spectacular jewellery I chose stole the scene. Belinda developed a terrible rash around her neck and they had to stop filming. Her skin burned and itched for days. The director reordered the sequencing and shot other scenes without Belinda until her swelling subsided and red skin could be concealed by makeup. The burning did help her acting, though — her grimace and death grip on the pendant added emotional realism.

A couple of years later, NBN Pictures brought us together once more. Shooting began a few months after Belinda's stint in *Island Fairy*, a heartwarming movie. My sister, the crew, and the local actors visited the pub daily after work. I didn't realize how heavily she'd been drinking until production started.

I was leery of working with her.

"Don't worry, she'll never blow up at you again in front of everyone," my assistant, Floyd, said. "She looked like a spoiled brat."

"Not sure that'll stop her. I'll hide among the feather boas and stay out of her way."

"You can't avoid each other. Find a way to interact civilly," Floyd said. "At least when everyone else is around."

"She partied a lot in Ireland." I hadn't intended to confide in him. "Dad wants me to keep an eye on her."

"Sounds risky."

"Floyd, she's my sister. I might not like her much, but I still love her."

In the new film, Belinda portrayed a gambling addict who ran a tanning salon in Las Vegas. The plot was kind of ridiculous: who needs an artificial tan in the middle of the desert? I felt a little sorry for her.

I decided to stop by my sister's trailer on the way to work in order to see her at her best: she was a morning person. To Belinda, sunrise was a watercolour of light splashed across the sky for her alone.

When I knocked, she opened the door in her bathrobe.

"Sorry, did I catch you too early?"

"Come in. You can share a mimosa with me," Belinda said.

"How was your run?"

"I'm not running these days."

I stared. Belinda had been a runner for a decade.

"What happened? Did you fall?"

"Oh, don't be an idiot. I decided I like the extra sleep." She shrugged. "Late nights."

We shared a drink. She told me about the pubs in Ireland and an affair with a key grip named Marty.

For the rest of the week I stopped by her temporary home each morning. She poured a mimosa every time.

"Can I have a coffee?" I asked.

She eyed me, slack-jawed, eyebrows raised, head tilted left. I took the mimosa.

On another day, I pointed to a box on the floor. "A case of champagne?"

"Screw you." She held the door open for me to leave.

I avoided Belinda for a week. Rumours flew around the studio: she'd come drunk to rehearsal on Tuesday; she threw a shoe at the props manager; the director ordered her back to bed and cancelled the film shoot.

Dad called me at home one evening.

"Your mother and I are worried about Belinda. Can you check on her again?"

"She tossed me out of her trailer because I asked why she had a case of booze in the kitchen. I'm not up for the abuse, Dad. Liquid breakfast is a helluva way to start the day." Maybe I exaggerated a little; I wanted Dad's sympathy.

"Bianca, your sister is in trouble and she needs you. Call me and tell me how it goes." He hung up.

I frequented Belinda's trailer again. I insisted she give me a spare key so I could let myself in. I made coffee for us both each day and we swirled possibilities around in matching mugs. Twice I found her passed out in her clothes atop the bed. The reek of stale alcohol suffused the claustrophobic space. I urged her to bathe and bought her jasmine-scented body wash. Weeks passed and hangovers endured. I called Belinda's agent to commiserate. That was a mistake.

"You called my agent? You bitch!"

"Belinda, you're not okay. You need help."

"You've gone too far, Bianca. You're interfering with my career!"

"I'm trying to save your career. I'm saving you."

"It's what you always wanted, isn't it? To be the darling of the family, for Mom and Dad to say, 'Isn't Bianca wonderful, intervening with her out-of-control sister?' Always jealous, clinging to me like lint. You hate to stand in my shadow."

I stormed out. It was true, what she said.

Three days afterward, the director came to the costume department.

"Can I talk to you?" he asked.

I nodded. Floyd rounded up the staff, hustled them out of the room, and edged the door closed.

The director was a hefty man who moved like a bird. He alighted on a stool and pushed a bolt of cloth out of the way.

"It's Belinda. She's been sloshed on set a few times. Hungover most days."

"She doesn't want my help."

"Doesn't want mine either, but this can't go on. Crew says you were making her coffee. Go back, try again."

I mulled over his request. A part of me enjoyed this sabbatical from my overbearing, overwrought sibling. I wondered how long it might last.

"We're three-quarters through the movie," he said. "You appreciate what going over budget will do to NBN. This is already costing too much with the delays. I want to finish."

The trailer door squawked open and jasmine drifted through the air. *At least she bathed*, I thought. I stepped inside and saw the bathroom door ajar. In the shower, Belinda mumbled and swayed and gripped the taps holding her upright. A young man thrust his pelvis behind her. I think he was on the painting unit.

"Get off her! She's drunk." My stomach contracted.

The young man's face paled and he stepped back, shrivelling before my eyes. He opened the glass shower door, snatched a towel, and dashed into the tiny bedroom, drawing the curtain behind him.

"Oh, Belinda." I started to cry.

"Bianca, I hate you. You ruined a fun shower."

I concentrated and sifted through her soft syllables and blurred phrases.

"You're the worst thing that's ever happened to me, and I'm going to make sure you're fired," she said.

She was angry. She didn't comprehend what she was saying. Once she sobered up, she would be back on set again, regain the esteem of the Director, and thank me for all I had done.

"Get out!"

Sympathy ebbed away. *Let the painter dry her off and wrestle her into her clothes*, I thought.

The next day, the director peeked around my door again. Floyd offered to buy everyone a latte at the coffee shop.

"I need to take you off the film. She's refusing to work with you here."

"What? You're letting me go?"

"Leave of absence. Think of it as a break. And she wants your name off the credits," he said.

"But those are my designs!" I dropped my scissors to the floor. "NBN Pictures agreed with her demand?" I gripped the cutting table with both hands.

"You know movie stars." He tilted his head and shrugged.

"I know my sister." Black Beauty: glorious, superior, untouchable.

I hid out for a week, organizing, sorting, labelling. The tasks gave me a sense of order and control. I didn't dare cut any patterns or stitch any fine details; my accuracy was awful when I was upset.

I ran into Belinda in a seldom-used corridor. Her face was pale and her eyes bloodshot.

"Are you okay?" I asked.

"Leave me alone." She stumbled into the washroom.

I followed. Retching echoed off the metal partitions.

"Belinda, I can call someone for you. Mom? Rehab?"

She emerged from the stall and her sour breath assaulted my face. I wanted to retch too.

"If you say anything to anybody, you'll never work here again!" Belinda's threat reverberated along the stalls and reflected from the washroom mirrors.

Dad telephoned the same evening.

Not long after, the head of the studio called.

"We're going to need you out of the building," she told me.

"But why? I haven't even seen her!" She didn't ask to whom I referred.

"We're putting you on leave. Sixty percent pay, Bianca. Sorry. Miniscule budget. Or you can use up your holiday time. Up to you. I think this will be temporary."

I hung up the telephone and leaned against a sewing machine. The room swayed. Belinda's smock for the water-fight scene in the tanning salon taunted me from a wall hook. I touched the fabric, checked the pockets, fingered the seams. I imagined slicing through the smock with a knife.

An antique wooden pharmacy cabinet across the room held our supplies. I searched through small drawers until I found the bottle I wanted, an acid-wash chemical that reacted with water. I took the vial over to the smock.

Then I packed things from my desk. A picture of me holding a gleaming Oscar positioned in a gold-leaf frame, helmet sketches for a television series located on the international space station, and a calendar of adorable puppies and kittens: treasures and trash.

It took weeks for Belinda's burns to heal after the water-fight scene. A formal letter from NBN Pictures arrived in the mail, firing me permanently. Belinda's lawyer advised of a lawsuit against me. Mom and Dad left voicemails; I never responded.

I miss NBN Pictures. I miss the team and Floyd and the movie posters, even the bad coffee. I miss the strange odours emanating from the construction zone — the cleanness of plaster, the burnt smell of hot tar.

A few years earlier, I won an Oscar for costume design for a modern film, which was impressive if I do say so myself, as the Academy adores period pieces. Our film, *Urban Jungle*, had an edgy vibe, a fresh take on Gothic style. I paired traditional black and studded pieces in leather with unexpected rainforest references like feathers and florals in bold, vibrant shades. A bird of paradise plant inspired me. NBN Pictures supported my vision.

My costume design team attended the ceremony together. A simple yet elegant black dress caressed my hips and a ruched centre panel hid my stomach curves. A floral scarf draped across my shoulders — upscale *Urban Jungle* couture.

Belinda came with us. She sparkled in a butter-coloured gown by a new Canadian design house. Her dark hair cascaded toward the nadir of the low-cut back. She was not in the movie, but she added celebrity excitement to our entourage. My sister breezed onto the red carpet. Her signature scent, a dense floral, wafted ahead and heralded her arrival.

"Belinda, give us a pose!"

She smiled, thrust out a hip, and lightly balanced a hand on it, very practised.

"Who are you wearing?"

"Christian and Moletti," she said.

"Show us the back!" the photographers called.

Stance reversed, she peered over her shoulder at them, the seductress. Hair swished across her olive skin then settled into place; perfect, like when we were horses.

"Your sister is up for an Oscar," one said.

"Yes, Bianca, come," she beckoned.

I took my sister's outstretched hand and her warmth tingled my fingers. We posed for a photograph. She slung a slender, bare arm across my more substantial back. I shrank. My black gown seemed too dark, my shawl too bright, my neatly pinned hair somehow unkempt.

"Another shot!" the photographers called.

She let go of my hand and I was eclipsed.

Inside, we found the seats relegated to costume, lighting, and cinematography. Belinda was an anomaly, the only recognizable actor in our area. Her peers waved as we walked by en route to the theatrical equivalent of the nosebleed section at a sports stadium. She blew air kisses at them and winked. That wink bothered me, a sort of "look at me slumming with the staff."

I'll never forget when they called my name.

"And the winner for best costume design in a motion picture is ... Bianca Cross!"

I put my hands to my mouth. We cheered and threw arms into the air as one. Belinda embraced me. Flashes burst across my eyelids.

I signalled to my colleagues, and they rose to walk with me to the stage. The music circled back on itself, a trumpet caught up in a whirlwind of strings and woodwinds, until finally we reached the stairs. As we climbed, a scene from *Urban Jungle* welcomed us. There stood my main character clad in a biker-style hat with a scarf not unlike my own wrapped tightly around her neck.

"I'd like to thank the Academy, my phenomenal creative team at NBN Pictures, and my family," I said into the microphone.

"Belinda!" A shout from the floor sped round the venue.

My sister's face dominated the towering screen behind me. Gone was my stunning design. My mouth went dry. I moved away to let others take a turn.

Weeks later, Belinda framed a photograph of the two of us on the red carpet at the Academy Awards ceremony. She penned "All our love, Belinda and Bianca," and couriered it to our parents. The autographed image sits on their mantel; I see it whenever I go home.

My mother likes to tell people her daughters were at the Oscars together.

"You know my daughter, Belinda Cross, the actor," she says to new friends and strangers alike.

Six months after I was fired from NBN Pictures, I found work again in Montreal; French-immersion school and its endless verb conjugations served me well after all. The French-Canadian film and television industry was much more forgiving of past sins and far less actor-oriented than Hollywood. I thrived. An avant-garde weekly series required a new approach to accoutrements, which fed my creative beast, and I loved the collaboration of the production group. My remuneration was a pittance compared to my previous salary, but I managed to cover my bills. I explored the old city on my free time and became friends with local artists. Together we hung paintings for temporary exhibits and roamed galleries, scouting new opportunities and assessing emerging talent.

I didn't speak to my sister for nine months. She curbed her drinking and her star skyrocketed. Her agent underscored Belinda's struggle with the bottle and resiliency in overcoming addiction. Belinda appeared on the cover of magazines, and received offers of strong female characters. In interviews, she mentioned her portrayal of a gambling addict in Las Vegas, so inevitably the story of her violent sister and the acid-burn incident was rehashed.

Dad called.

"What're you up to for the February long weekend? Mom and I are heading to the Muskokas. Join us. It'd be great."

"Will Belinda be there?"

"No, sweetie, your sister can't make it."

"Isn't it her birthday?" I had my suspicions.

"You know her work schedule. It's such a challenge."

I agreed to meet them at our family cabin on Thursday. I gave my keys to a friend who offered to check on my cat. Snow skiffed the road, wispy and insubstantial. I selected a jazz compilation on the car stereo and buzzed along the highway to saxophone riffs.

Memory assailed me when I pulled up to the familiar cottage. A juniper bush brushed a hello across my shin. Creaks on the front steps welcomed me in. The door latch stuck a little, perpetually in need of oil. Inside, a fire spit and sputtered, held back by a mesh screen. Smoke and citrus mingled in the entry.

"Hi Mom, Dad!"

"Just me," Dad called back from the interior. "Your mother is out for a walk. Let me pour you a mulled wine."

I doffed my coat, boots, toque, and mitts and sorted the outerwear into designated cubbyholes. When I found my sister's jacket wasn't in the closet, my posture mellowed and I took a deep breath.

We perched on stools at the kitchen island. Dad told me about their curling league and I updated him on friends' gallery successes and failures. We avoided show-business topics. During a lull, he gulped his mulled wine and said, "Belinda is here."

I plopped down my mug.

"You need to make up with your sister. Leave the past behind."

"Dad, she got me fired."

"Bianca, you put acid on her apron."

If Dad were taking Belinda's side, I could imagine what my biased mother might say.

"I can find a nearby bed and breakfast." I stood. "Nice seeing you, Dad."

The door opened and in bounded the dog, followed by my mother and sister. Their laughter tinkled through the opening.

"So I said, 'You're too adorable, Brad' and he flashed me that gorgeous grin!" It was Belinda's voice.

Mom giggled. "I'm so excited for you, darling." She saw me. "Bianca! Come say hello to your sister."

Junior high again.

"I'm just leaving."

I yanked my coat from its hanger. No one spoke.

"All the rental places are full," Dad said.

I glanced at my watch: 4:30 in the afternoon, a little late for the drive to Montreal but reasonable to reach a neighbouring town.

"I'll find something."

"Can't you at least stay for Belinda's birthday dinner?" my mother said. "Don't be so selfish."

"It's been a long time, Bianca," Belinda said. "Stay for supper. It'll mean so much to Mom and Dad. I won't be putting on an apron to do the cooking, though." Her voice was sharp; I tasted its bitterness in my mouth.

I pivoted to my father. His face was all creases and lines.

"The least you can do is help cook," my mother said. "After all you've done."

Belinda flaunted a satisfied smile that did nothing for her features.

I ground my teeth to keep from exploding with anger. I stood there for a long time, looking at the three of them.

"How about if I sauté some of last year's wild mushrooms for supper?" I said. *Champignons sauvages* waited in the cold room. I'd picked them myself, had studied each bulbous head and slender stem, had separated the toxic from the intoxicating.

I turned to my father. "Sorry, Dad, I know you don't care for them. I'll make something else for you."

"That's okay, honey. I'll have salad. Your sister likes wild mushrooms," he said.

I hoped he'd say that.

I'm not longing for NBN Pictures anymore. Montreal fits me like a comfortable pair of moccasins. I love my apartment, my cat, and my remarkable man, an artist named Serge. He works in mixed media. Sometimes we shop for fabrics. We're talking about moving in together.

Belinda is back in Toronto. She started a television series based in the Thousand Islands of the St. Lawrence Seaway. Dad updated me, but I can't quite recall the details: something about a friend of a wealthy heiress. She repeated her story of the poisonous fungi in another interview. I don't pay attention anymore; she's being offered smaller roles and the scandal keeps her in the entertainment news, so who can blame her?

Mom and Dad are divorcing. Dad is taking the cottage in the Muskokas and will try to work remotely. They've sold the house and Mom lives in a condominium downtown, near the theatre district. I think it suits her.

I talked to Dad last night. I told him I'll come and pick wild mushrooms again this year. He didn't laugh.

Heather Bonin MacIntosh is a Calgary-based aspiring writer passionate about family, travel, and living well together, locally and globally. Her article, "All the Wrong Moves," outlines her creative journey and was published in the Writer's Guild of Alberta newsletter in summer 2017. This is her first published short story. She tweets at @greenheadmac.

the metamorphosis of nova

by J. F. Garrard

It was February 29 again, and I was wondering which member of my family would try to kill me this time.

Last weekend, we ate at our usual Cantonese restaurant. We ordered pots of black bo lei tea and ordered a range of dim sum, from soy sauce covered beef rice rolls to the more delicate ginger milk custards. Instead of gossip about friends and the latest shopping deals, an unusual silence hung over the table. The six children accompanying us giggled enthusiastically while playing with their toys or tablets, and we adults would occasionally smile in their direction, but most of the time we studied each other with awkward smiles, knowing that the day was coming.

There were three of us: me — Nova — and my two sisters, Rose and Jade. There was no doubt we were related, as we resembled one another, with our silky manes of black hair and porcelain faces highlighted by red painted lips.

Rose was a delicate-looking woman, the most feminine of the three of us, in a flowing yellow chiffon dress. She broke the silence, casually dropping a bombshell as she poured me some tea. "Do you have your affairs in place?"

"What do you mean?" I scoffed and crossed my arms, covering the large cartoon cat on my sweatshirt. "You guys cannot be serious. Mom and Dad have been gone for a while. Their estate is settled. I gave you my share already. Isn't that good enough?"

"No, it isn't," Jade, the youngest sister, said bluntly. Although she was dressed in a warm teal dress decorated with embroidered flowers, she was hard as the stone that was her namesake and did not mince words. "Look, Rose and I have three kids each. Do you know how much university costs? We'll never be able to retire at this rate."

"Last time you guys tried to kill me, it took me weeks to learn how to properly walk again. Mom told you February 29, but you tried on February 28. What kind of selfish creatures are you?" I scowled at them. I used my chopsticks to pick up a siu mai from a bamboo basket and set it on a plate. I cut it into little pieces so I could feed Rose's young child Jackie, who was sitting next to me busily playing with trains.

"Wow, you sound like you can actually feel pain." Rose raised an eyebrow.

"I can, thank you very much. My nervous system may not be the same as yours, but it does work, and I can feel pain!"

Rose scowled. "Come on! Our family created you, took care of you, and gave you everything you ever wanted! Before Dad died, he even made you a free person! You should be grateful and willing to give us what we want!"

I wiped up the siu mai bits Jackie spat out and sighed. Father had been a marvellous scientist, engineer, and adventurer. He had made me, a half-organic and half-metal AI person, from a custom order bot kit in his basement before my sisters were born. An otaku obsessed with the film *Tetsuo, the Iron Man*, Father considered me his life's greatest achievement. On more than one occasion, he credited my uniqueness to the fact that I had an organic heart, compared to other robots made of pure metal, believing it made me feel empathy and provided me the courage to save him from death more than once on our dangerous treasure-hunting adventures. Father was obsessed with the twenty-first century, the period before AI breakthroughs changed the world. He confided many secrets to me, and we were the closest of friends, drawing ire from my mother and sisters. When my sisters became teenagers, he resculpted my face so I would resemble his flesh and blood daughters more. The majority of AI robots were still considered property, but if the owner wished, they could apply for "free person" status for their robots, granting them the equivalent of human rights.

My patience grew thin. "Professor Maureen and Mother were just toying with you two. It's not logical to think that opening me up on a certain date would bring Father back so he can tell you where the lost chest of gold is. They didn't even mention in their wills where the diary with details about this silly treasure can be found. Isn't that suspicious?"

"Mother would not have lied to us. She told us just before she died that Father hid a message inside you. We just have to find it." Jade glared at me.

Lately Jade had been obsessed with buying Korean facial injections to reduce the lines between her brows. She wanted to look younger in order to attract a new mate. She also started dressing in more fashionable clothing and spent the days exercising to make herself thinner instead of working. Although I was the oldest, I looked the youngest, given my skin was constantly being rejuvenated. Father had made a fortune by selling hopes of immortality to women with a cream made from a substance generated by my skin cells, and my stake in the company — which I relinquished — was worth quite a bit. However, the more the sisters had, the more they spent.

"Last year, you guys ripped me apart and found nothing. My computer chips were damaged from your hacking, and it took so long to reprogram new chips. I have no special message or contraption inside me that would spring out Father's ghost to tell you where the stupid gold is. He would have left the information in his will or programmed me with a map if it were true." A dim sum android rolled by with another cart of rice noodles, and I hailed them down to get the ones stuffed with fried fish and shrimp for the children.

"Well, we found nothing because we did it on the wrong date. Why would we need to attack her on February 29 on the Western calendar? That matches an odd day on the Chinese lunar calendar. Why would this matter?" Rose mused out loud.

"Exactly," I said sarcastically. "Committing murder on any day of the year should be acceptable. This is a totally illogical situation and a pointless exercise!"

"There is probably some formula based on certain times Father can come out through a spacetime dimensional rift ... or something like that. There must be a reason behind all this we don't understand." Jade began stuffing her face with the rice noodles before her kids could get to them.

Frowning, I snatched the dish back from Jade and divided them among her children, who were all dressed in clothing either too large or too small for their developing bodies. I am a free person and could have left after Father died, but I chose to live in a large house with both of my sisters' families to take care of everyone. Their husbands had been sent off to space when the war started against a potentially invasive alien species. They left three years ago and never came home, nor sent paychecks. Sometimes I think a combination of loneliness and tragedy in my sisters' lives made them act rashly, without thought. Such as now, in this conversation about tearing me apart again.

"I've been on all of Father's excursions to find treasure. The most valuable things he found were those two antique porcelain cups, which I gave to you."

Jackie, the child next to me, rolled a train toward me on the table and I rolled it back. Lisa, Jade's firstborn, was immersed in a book about robotics. Out of all the children, she was the most mature, and my favourite, as her intelligent nature always ensured we had interesting conversations on topics ranging from what the first landed aliens look like to why sugar tasted so good to humans. The other children all sat with their headphones on, watching the latest music videos, and another child played tea with a small doll made in my likeness. All the kids had one, a plastic rendition of my body, with long black hair, light peach skin, in an adventurer outfit. It had been a gift from their grandfather. He'd been hopeful it would encourage them to form a strong bond with me.

"It wasn't worth that much," Jade rubbed her eyes. "But it was enough to pay for this year's tuition for my little monsters. That's about it."

"You sold it! How could you?!" Rose's cheeks flushed red, and her eyes were ablaze.

"Don't judge me!" Jade raised her voice. "Your husband left you with a lot more than mine did. I can't let my kids starve while I hold on to a stupid cup. The kids were going to break it anyway."

Rose turned to me. "We're both running out of money and supplies. My hours at the factory have been reduced. Are you sure Father didn't leave you any clues about the gold?"

"Stop talking to her! We'll find out on February 29." Jade poured herself some tea.

I shook my head slowly. "You know that Mother always hated me because I got along with Father so well. You're both my sisters; can't you see this was a ploy to tear us apart even when she isn't here?"

The two women grew silent, and I spent the rest of the meal tending to the children. Strangers would not have been able to tell that I was not completely human. Father had made me out of his flesh and blood and had set reminders in my daily programming that my loyalty will always lie with family. Somehow, I don't think the same message made it into my sisters' consciousness.

Professor Maureen was my mother's closest friend and a mentor to my two sisters. An anti-AI advocate, she loathed my presence and constantly berated me for serving her the wrong tea, even though I brought her what she asked for. Both she and mother had developed Alzheimer's, and over time their minds and personalities faded. However, their dislike of me remained, giving some comfort to other family members at my expense.

Today was Sunday, February 29. The children were all in different extracurricular classes, ranging from toddler swimming classes to robotics for the teenagers. I set the lock on my door and refused to come out regardless of the pleading from both the mothers and children.

My heart was aching again. The disadvantage of organic material was limited longevity. Father said that having a real heart made me human and that I had to be careful not to become too cynical or else my metallic compounds would take over the heart cells. This was a ludicrous theory, likely his ploy to help me keep a steady head in an emotional household.

For most of the day, I set myself on sleep mode so I could ignore the pain that shot from the centre of my chest and ran down the middle of my limbs. Owners had the choice to give their AIs a central nervous system with pain conduits and to include any organic material they wished. For many owners, choosing organic skin for their bots was important, to cover metallic skeletons and make their help appear more human. I am not sure why that is important. Father always told me that pain, as annoying as it was, was an important feedback mechanism pointing to change in the body.

After donning my favourite baggy sweater and jeans, I sat comfortably in a large lounge chair while multiple clear plastic tubes with different coloured liquids ran into my veins from buckets on the floor filled with synthetic polymers, metals, and cellular material. The movement of material was not visible to the human eye, but if I focused my micro lens I could see little nanobots scurrying about, repairing and replacing parts. My body would be rejuvenated once the process was complete, and I would be good for another few months, unless damage were to occur.

Toward the afternoon I made the decision not to run. To exist within a family meant sacrifice, and the bonds that held me to my sisters were too strong. It pained me that my role in the family was reduced to being a pile of scrap metal and that my wellbeing meant nothing to them. This emotional pain was worse than any physical pain I have ever endured. I wish Father could have incorporated a switch to turn off my emotional intelligence, though I understand that not giving me one ensures that I won't hurt the family. Regardless of how I suffer, I always know that in the big picture, what matters is that the children have the best future possible. I ran algorithms in my head while filling in forms on a tablet.

The sun was low in the sky, and the beautiful shades of purple and pink made me forget for a moment about my throbbing heart and impending death. I knew all the kids had been fed and sent to bed when my sisters knocked on my door.

"Open the door, Nova! You weren't around to help us all day! Lisa needed help in her robotics class, and the kids laughed at her when her robot blew up. This wouldn't have happened if you were there!" Jade's angry tone made me roll my eyes.

"Oh crap!" I could hear Rose fumbling with something, which dropped to the floor with a clang. No doubt they were holding all sorts of metal tools to rip me apart.

I remember asking Father once if I could die. He'd answered in an amused tone, "Of course. Everything that lives must die. Just make the best choices possible and enjoy life while you can." The thought of his calm face made me sad now. I knew he would be very disappointed that the cause of my death would be my two sisters.

I walked to the door and entered my code. It opened to reveal the two women gathering objects that had fallen out of a large tool box. I picked up a wrench, hammer, and screwdriver from the floor to hand to Rose. The sight of a chainsaw on the floor behind Jade made me wince as I thought about the last time they attacked me, metal teeth sinking into my body. Both were dressed in jeans and T-shirts and wore clear garbage bags over their clothing, their hair tied up in ponytails under shower caps.

A sharp piercing spasm ripped through my chest, making me stumble backward slightly.

"Are you OK?" Rose held my arm and walked me back to my chair. "You were repairing yourself today. Are things OK?" Her voice wavered slightly.

"This stuff will probably give us a month's worth of food when we sell it," Jade said, peering at all the equipment in my room. "You shouldn't have used any today," she scolded me. "Now we'll have less to sell!"

"Before we start, can we go over again why we are doing this?" I clutched my chest as I sank deeper into the chair.

"Mom and Professor Maureen told us before they died that you had a message from Dad about a chest of gold inside you," Jade scowled. "We've been over this a million times. Look, we're running out of money, and we have many mouths to feed. Think of this as helping the children."

"You do realize that you are listening to messages from people who had dementia," I pointed out. "Their memories are unreliable!"

"Mom did get pretty confused. She couldn't even remember her own name toward the end," Rose said. She crossed her arms, her brows furrowing. "Maybe Nova's right, we could be killing her for nothing. Besides she is a free person, we could be arrested."

"I've thought this through!" Jade said triumphantly, holding a small box up in the air. "If Nova does die in the process, I bought a new microprocessor brain to put in her body. Technically she can't die, so it'll be OK."

"Where did you get that?" I groaned. "The parts inside me are specific to my operations. Any disruption would mean my body won't be able to function properly."

"Look, this is the best I could do on the black market. If things don't work out, then we'll bury you next to Dad," Jade shrugged.

"Right, give me a minute to send in this form to the government to wrap up my affairs. I still have that trust account that has to be dealt with." I gestured to a tablet sitting on my desk, and Rose brought it over to me. Up until this moment I had held off on submitting my documents, but after this conversation, all my doubts were erased. I hit *Send*.

Jade left my room and came back with a tarp, which she put on the floor. "This might be messy," she explained. "Last time it took a long time to clean the blood, or whatever is inside you, off the floor."

"Before you start, I wanted to let you know that the household budget spreadsheets are saved in this folder." I took my time showing

Rose the different files on the tablet. "I've also created schedules for the children's meals and activities for the week. Recipes for their favourite meals are saved here."

"I don't know if I can do this…" Rose put her hands to her face and sobbed, tears dripping onto the floor. "We need all the help we can get with the children. They're energy leeches!"

"Stop crying! Nova isn't a person. She's a robot Dad made to take care of the family. Once we get that gold, we can pay someone to fix her, and she can be a proper nanny bot that doesn't talk back." Jade turned the chainsaw she held in her arm several times, studying it closely.

"Instead of a one-time influx of gold, you could also get a job," I pointed out to Jade. "The whole reason for me staying after Mom and Dad died was so I could take care of the children while you two worked. You know what? Never mind. If something goes wrong after you tear me apart, you will have to take care of the kids full-time. You won't have time to work."

Jade wrinkled her nose at these words. "Nothing's going to happen. Just lie down and let us see if we can find the message about where to find the gold. We'll be fine." Her voice sounded monotone and hollow.

I shrugged and lay down on the floor. To be honest, I was tired of pleading for my life. Over the last fifty years, since I came to be, I was charged with all things domestic, from making all the meals to cleaning to maintaining the lawn. Here with my sisters, work was given to me 24/7, and I only got one day off every quarter for maintenance. When Father was alive, at least I could go on excursions with him, but since his death, I had not taken any vacations.

The minutes on the large digital clock above my bedroom door went by very slowly as my sisters chattered about how to conduct their business. There was a loud noise when Jade finally figured out how to rev up the chainsaw. Sighing, I took off my sweater to reveal pale flesh with notable scars on my chest from Rose clumsily stitching my skin together and bumpy ridges from metal plates damaged by the chainsaw last year. Although at this moment I felt tears would have been appropriate to show my extreme disappointment and devastation at the demise of our sisterhood, nothing erupted from my eyes. Crying was a feature omitted from my design to prevent potential water damage. Made in the image of humans, but not human. Perhaps rejection of me was inevitable from the beginning.

"Are you sure you want to do this? I'm your sister and I've known you all your life." I tried one last time to reason with them. Surely our relationship of over forty years must count for something.

"Yes … I … are you stalling?" Jade squinted as she considered where to cut.

"Would you stall if I had a chainsaw aimed at your stomach?"

"Mom, what are you doing?" Lisa, Jade's eldest, appeared in the doorway in fuzzy blue pyjamas, carrying a small robot with wires dangling out of it. It had been charred black by a blowout of some sort.

"We're doing an experiment," Jade said sheepishly, turning off and putting down the chainsaw. "Get back to bed!"

"But I need Nova's help. My robot blew up in class today!" Instead of leaving, Lisa brazenly walked into the room and knelt down next to me. "Oh my gosh, why do you have all these scars?"

"They were from the last time your mom stabbed me," I sighed.

"What?" Jade looked so incredulous that I didn't have the decency to lie.

"There was a ticking noise, and your mom was trying to fix me with a knife," I offered weakly.

"Mom, Nova is very complicated inside. You can't just use knives or chainsaws to hack at her! And you need to put her to sleep mode too so she doesn't feel pain!" The child glared at her mother.

"Oh no! What is happening?" Jackie, one of Rose's girls, shouted from the door before running into the room. She wore a thin pink nightgown and held her doll replica of me. "Why are you hurting Nova?" She let out a loud wail and burst into tears.

"Shit," Jade muttered, "We should have shut the door…"

Rose walked over to her daughter and hugged her. "We aren't hurting Nova. We're opening her up to look for a secret message from your grandpa."

"Oh," Jackie wiped her eyes. "You mean like the message we all have from Grandpa?"

"What?" Rose looked stunned.

"Let me show you, Mommy." Jackie held up her doll and pressed on it several times but nothing happened.

Lisa put down her burnt robot and gestured for Jackie to give her the doll. The older girl took off the small fabric jacket, turned the doll over, and pressed a button protruding on the doll's back. There was a tiny popping noise when a square-shaped flap in the chest of the doll opened. A tiny scroll was hidden inside.

"This is Grandpa's message in all the dolls," Lisa offered, handing the miniature beige coloured scroll to Jade.

"This message is from your grandpa, Eric Chan," Jade said, gingerly unravelling the scroll and squinting at the tiny handwriting. "Your auntie Nova is worth more than a chest of gold. Love her, treat her well, and her heart will thrive. Otherwise, her heart will harden to metal, and the family bonds will be broken. Celebrate every February 29 on the odd lunar calendar date, for her birthday fell on such an exquisite day."

"I showed this to Grandma and asked her what it meant, but she didn't know," Jackie said, taking back the scroll and putting it back into the doll.

Jade looked devastated. "This can't be it. We really need more money … there has to be gold…" She started up the chainsaw again causing the two girls to scream.

"Stop it!" Rose tried to approach her sister, but jumped to the side when Jade swung about manically with the large tool.

The children put their bodies on top of me and yelled at Jade to stop what she was doing. Eventually, she shut the chainsaw off, slowly put it down, and collapsed to the ground, sobbing.

A loud announcement filled the house. "Incoming! Incoming!

Military craft landing on roof. Military craft landing on roof."

I pushed the children off my chest gently and stood up. I grabbed my sweater off the floor and put it back on. Ignoring the gaping open mouths of my sisters, I took a small canvas bag, packed up a few essentials, and quickly walked out into the hallway elevator. On the rooftop, I was met by two military droids who asked to confirm my identity by scanning my retina and the computer chip embedded in the back of my neck.

"What are you doing?" Rose grabbed my arm when she caught up with me. The children and Jade trailed behind her.

"Jade is right. The family is running out of resources. Out of the three of us, I would earn the most taking part in the war. You both have access to my account; take as much as you need for the children." I made my voice cold and logical.

"I'm so sorry. You don't have to go, really…" Rose tightened her hand on my arm but I shrugged her off.

I walked over to Jackie and Lisa and hugged and kissed them.

"Will you come back to visit us?" Lisa asked.

"Maybe. You can always video call me when you need help with homework." I ruffled Lisa's hair, making her squirm.

Jade opened her mouth to say something to me, but I turned my back and walked away. I gritted my teeth as another sharp pain seared my heart, but it was brief, and then I felt nothing. The nanobots running through my system issued a message informing me that the replacement of the organic heart was complete and from now on, extra metal will be required during every maintenance cycle.

As the military craft rose in the air, the children and Rose waved goodbye to me. I waved back.

"Your family?" A man sitting inside the craft spoke to me as I took a seat on the bench opposite of him.

"We share blood," I offered. A quick scan told me that he was of similar build to me, a hybrid of metal and flesh.

"Might as well be water," he scoffed.

His face and hands were full of scars, but I was too tired to ask him about his story and closed my eyes instead. An image of my father speaking his last words on his deathbed came to me: "Take care of them at all costs." To the others, he had spoken of love and life.

Even if my heart had hardened, my memories and promises lingered. Father knew me well. For a moment I feared that I had made the wrong choice. I had never ventured out into the world without a family member before. Then the taste of freedom overwhelmed my senses as I realized how narrowly I had avoided death. Another day, another adventure. I smiled at this thought and went into sleep mode.

J. F. Garrard is the founder of Dark Helix Press, marketing strategist for *Ricepaper Magazine*, and an assistant editor for *Amazing Stories Magazine*. She is an editor and writer of speculative fiction (*Trump: Utopia or Dystopia* and *The Undead Sorceress*) and non-fiction (*The Literary Elephant*). Her contributions to business, diversity, and health subjects have been published in *Entrepreneur*, Huffington Post, Moneyish, Monster.com, *Women's Health* and *Cosmopolitan*, and elsewhere. Her background is in Nuclear Medicine and she has a MBA in Marketing and Strategy. Currently she is pursuing a Creative Writing certificate from Ryerson University. **www.jfgarrard.com**

rotting away

by Karen Ralph

It was February 29 again, and I was wondering which member of my family would try to kill me this time. Well, it was almost February 29. I watched the seconds on the clock tick closer and closer. Five. Four. Three. Two. One.

I rose to my feet, crossing the small, one-room cabin in four strides, and peeked out the curtain. A shadow moved beyond the gated graveyard.

I snagged a dark hoodie, even though the cold hadn't affected me in a long time, and stepped out into the night; sheets of snow fell from the sky slowly and silently with no wind to hurry them along. I unzipped my hoodie, grimacing as I tried to pull it on. My arm hadn't been right for months and my left eye was getting blurrier by the day, but it was the smell that was always the most bothersome. The ripe, rotting smell clung to me, and strips of my skin were beginning to tear like tissue paper, dangling until I got some bandages on them.

Someone had been buried today, and I needed to eat soon. I grabbed the shovel leaning against the cabin and set out. I rotated my bad arm slowly, the appendage grinding in its socket as I trudged to the cemetery. The forest surrounding me was completely silent. With the village miles away, though, it was always quiet, even when it wasn't night.

As caretaker of the graveyard, I had easy access. Pulling the keys from my dark jeans, I selected the largest one, inserting it into the lock on the fancy, sweeping gates, which opened with a rusted groan. I followed the indentations in the snow, the path the funeral procession had carved, almost buried again, to the mound of fresh dirt peeking out from the blanket of white. Kneeling, I brushed the loose flakes off, revealing the rich overturned earth beneath. I bent my head, burying my fingers in the soil.

"May your soul be as light as the snow and as free as the birds." I repeated the prayer I'd invented years ago, although the words were now just habit. "May you rest well and receive my thanks for the gift you may offer me, even in your passing. Blessed be this hallowed grave, dug for death and disturbed for life."

I stood and pushed the shovel through the first layer of dirt. Placing the first shovelful to one side, I then took another, the motion even and well-practised. About halfway down, I felt something pop in my bad arm. I switched the shovel to my other hand and continued digging, my right arm now dangling uselessly.

On the next dig down, I hit something. I brushed the dirt away to reveal a polished, wooden coffin. Digging my fingers into the top left corner, I pried open the lid with my good hand. The wood groaned as the nails gave way and the wood along the edges splintered. The man in the casket looked like he was sleeping. He wasn't. Embalming fluid, wax, and makeup hid the fact that he was decomposing. But I knew where it was best to eat.

I hopped out of the hole a few minutes later. Slamming the lid shut, I rolled my arm back into its socket until it felt normal, my hand running along the raised skin of the scar there, twin circles stacked on top of each other and run through with three wavy lines. My vision cleared and my complexion, I knew from experience, shifted from "corpse" to "very fair skinned."

I glanced to the east and saw the shadow from before. "I know you're there."

"You're looking worse than ever." A man stepped closer, his skin as pale and smooth as my own had once been. His eyes so blue they almost glowed in the night. His ears, buried behind a slick of thick, chestnut hair, I knew would be a little pointed, just like my own. *Derek.* "Hello, Nyssa." He stepped closer.

I turned away from him, digging my shovel into the mound of earth and placing it back in the hole. Then the next shovelful. Then the next.

I was careful to pack the layers down every few times so the earth wouldn't protrude.

"I come all this way to see you and not even a 'hello'?" Derek leaned against the tombstone beside me, casually crossing his legs.

"Hello." Shovel. Shovel. Shovel.

He chuckled. "And I thought you were quiet before."

I packed down the next layer before continuing.

"I hate when you ignore me. I'm not the bad guy. I'm just trying to help you," he said.

Shovel. Shovel. Shovel. Pack.

Derek tossed his head back. "Look, I know you know how this normally goes. One of us tries to kill you, you're somehow unaffected, you wander off, and then we go back and explain it to everyone and wait until the *next* leap year to try again. I'm starting to feel like Wile E. Coyote at the Olympics or something. But I'm not here for that now." He glanced around before turning back. "*She's* coming this year. I don't know why, but..."

I paused mid shovel.

Derek scratched his neck. "Yeah, I was surprised too."

She. Our leader, the most beautiful, powerful, and successful of us all. The only one of us who was a quarter fae and grew up learning about our culture and had inherited the knowledge of her forbearers. The one who taught us who we were and the ritualistic power we could harness for luck and good fortune. *Islanda*.

"Look, she's been losing it for years now," Derek continued. "She's been trying to keep us from seeing it, but the cracks are getting worse. Last month at the ritual, her makeup was so thick you could count the layers, like one of those rock formations down at the gorge. And she looked haggard. *Islanda*. I mean, I've seen her stay up for days at a time, and she never had a hair out of place. I was convinced she had mastered the art of sleeping while awake. She keeps saying you upset the balance.

"And all of us have been feeling it more and more. Bad luck, bad coincidences. Jerrand found a grey hair last year and he's only thirty-two. That's early for a *normal* human. Suzanna lost half her fortune in a bad investment. With the flooding down south, it's been a bad year for corn. Do you know the last time it was a bad year for corn? The dark ages. It's corn. And there was a fuel leakage at my main plant; half our transport trucks and the entire western shipment for the year went up in flames. I literally stood there and watched it all burn. We don't *do* bad luck, Nyssa.

"She's coming today. I just thought I would give you the heads up. It's maybe a good time to make peace with…" he gestured at me vaguely, "and let us restore the balance. We can help you be free, or whatever you want to call it. It has to be better than *this*."

"I don't need help." I kept shovelling, layering the last bit of dirt on.

Derek kicked the snow at his feet. "I know you hate us. But none of us really know what's happening half the time. Most of us didn't even really believe all of this before." He gestured to his ears.

I began to pull the snow back onto the grave.

"We thought all the *rituals* and *initiations* were just secret-society stuff," he continued. "We found a place to belong and a cool backstory: we're special and gifted and beautiful because we're descendants of fairies and we have a magical connection to chance and fortune. I think most of us just got sucked into the story. Then we're told you got in over your head, one of the rituals 'went wrong,' and you're like a zombie, and all of a sudden everything's dangerous and real and we're all ready to bolt, but Islanda says you messed with magic, like *real* magic, that could affect all of us through the bond we formed from some stupid blood oath we took back when it was all just pretend. And now it's started affecting our lives, and we're just trying to put everything right again. So just let her make things right, Nyssa. Please."

I kicked the last bit of snow back. "Good night, Derek."

I returned to my cabin and perched in my chair in front of the window. The shadow that was Derek disappeared into the snow shortly after, but I watched as the night stretched then dwindled, and light began to stretch across the sky.

It was well into the afternoon before anyone else would be seen.

As the dark clouds lightened to a deep grey, a figure made its way around the graveyard.

She meandered closer as I sat, watching.

Islanda was now close enough that I could see her face. New, fine creases lined her eyes and mouth. Eyes, once purple like twin amethysts, as she often liked to remind the men ogling her, were now like sugary-sweet grape juice. The type with artificial flavour that only young children seemed to enjoy. I met her at the door as she took the last few steps to stand at my stoop.

Neither of us spoke, both openly taking in each other's appearance. Her slightly pointed ears protruded from her long, fair hair, her skin pale and flawless. She had always had a high-maintenance kind of beauty, but now up close I could see the layers of hasty makeup.

I used to adore her, just like everyone else in the cluster. The fae blood often skipped a few generations, so it was common for one to be born completely alone in a family. We had all felt different and outcast growing up, enduring the mocking of others at our slightly tipped ears or vibrant eyes, casting us out for being too effortlessly successful at so many things. Islanda had given us a home and a heritage. Then she'd abandoned me.

Islanda spoke first, as she always did. "Nyssa, I thought I had the wrong house when you first answered the door."

"No, you have the right house."

Islanda's face remained a mask of indifference, but her nostrils flared a fraction. "Well, I'm glad to see you again. It's been too long. You look … it's so nice to see you again."

"Is it?" I cocked my head.

"I would have preferred it to be under better circumstances." She reached out, squeezing my hands, her face crumpling. "I'm sorry,

Nyssa. You must think I've abandoned you all these years. Written you off."

I stepped back, tugging my hands free. "That's a safe assumption, considering you've been sending Derek and the others to try and kill me. Goodbye." I began to close the door.

Her hand snaked through the crack, impeding the door's movement. "Yes, well, some of us are cursed to bear the immense burdens that others thrust unfairly upon us." Islanda pushed the door open further, pushing past me and striding in, pulling my only chair from in front of the window to the kitchen table and flopping down. "Sorry. I don't mean to be snappy." She kneaded the bridge of her nose. "There's just been a lot going on lately. We've all been facing a lot of … backlash, so to speak."

"I can't imagine how awful that must be for all of you. The stress of everyday, *normal* life." I turned to the cupboard above my sink, pulling out a cup.

"Yes, it's been taking a toll on all of us. More and more, Nyssa."

I filled the cup with water and placed it in front of Islanda. She pushed the cup away with a small shake of her head.

"That's why I'm hoping to resolve it *this* year." Islanda tried to catch my gaze, but I picked up her cup, turning back to the sink to empty it. "I don't know if any of us," she grabbed my arm, "and I mean *any* of us, can last another four years."

"I've lasted the past twelve just fine." I pulled away, dumping the water out. It was none of her business that the rotting had been getting worse lately.

"Nyssa, we're all connected. If we're seeing worse conditions, then I know you must be as well. Blood kin, right?" She held up her hand, palm out, displaying a thin, light scar that ran from her fingers to her wrist. I had one on my palm. From the bonding ceremony we'd all gone through when we were initiated into the cluster.

"It took me years to understand." I stared at her hand.

"Understand what, dear one?"

"Why you only send our family on leap year day. Your little loophole is only good for one day every four years."

"I'm not sure what—"

"The loyalty oath we all took, bound in blood, your careful wording. *We shall never harm one another on this year or any other like it until the day we leave for our final sleep.* None of us were initiated in a leap year, so you'd have a loophole. That's why Marissa had to wait to be inducted, not to cleanse her aura as you had claimed, but because the year you found her was a leap year. Now you can have me killed today without breaking the oath."

Islanda grinned, shaking her head. "You're the only one to spot that, you know. I think you're the only one who really believed in all of this fae and ritual stuff before all of this happened. I didn't want to mislead them, but I've learned it's usually for the best if you give people a reason to need their leader. It keeps dissent from the ranks, so to speak."

"You lied to us all."

"To protect you all. It is sometimes the burden of a leader to do what's best for the group, even if it doesn't always seem right. The others are running scared and confused. The last thing we need is for them to turn on each other. But while we have a moment to ourselves, there is one thing I would like to go over. Walk me through it." Islanda's eyes bore into mine. "Everything you remember leading up to…" she gestured to me. "I never did get your account of that night."

My hands clenched into fists. "Twelve years, Islanda. Twelve years ago, I tried to talk to you and you wouldn't listen. You tried to kill me. All these leap years you sent Derek and the others, never any interest in anything other than seeing me dead, and *now* you decide you want to listen to me? Why are you even here?"

Islanda rose to her feet. She was actually a little shorter than me, but she had a way of looking down at you that made her seem like a giant. She crowded my space, but I was leaning against the counter and had nowhere to go, even if I planned to back down. I raised an eyebrow at her, and she narrowed her eyes into twin slits. It felt like all the air had been sucked out of the room, but luckily for me I didn't need to breathe.

A grin split Islanda's face.

"You've always been different, haven't you, Nyssa? Even among us oddballs. The 'blaze my own trail' type, not from any real defiance, not usually, but just by wandering off and getting lost. How I've missed you." She patted my cheek then turned back to the chair. "I know you think I abandoned you, but I have my reasons for sending the others in my place. But you deserve closure. Coming today was a risk worth taking to get this resolved for *all* of us."

There was a tap at the door.

"You didn't come alone." I wasn't surprised in the slightest.

"No. I've heard their reports. Stabbing. Poison. Suffocation. None of it has been effective. I'm afraid we may need more drastic measures. Enter!" Islanda called out.

The door swung open, revealing a hulking figure with slicked-back, dark hair framing his pointed ears and tired, indigo eyes. Charles. Right behind him was the same electric-eyed figure from the graveyard, Derek.

The two men shuffled in, and suddenly my cozy one-room house felt like a coffin. Then Charles stepped a little closer and I saw the axe, sharpened to a glint, clenched in his shaking hands. "Sorry, Nyssa. But it's for your own good. I've been practising. It'll be quick." He wouldn't look at me.

A strange tickle started in my throat at the mere thought of that axe near my neck. I straightened, wanting to back away further, but I had nowhere left to go. I turned to Islanda. "You wanted to talk before. About that night. Let's talk."

Charles paused, shooting Islanda a pleading glance. "We do have all day, Islanda."

She shot him an icy glare and he shrunk back. I blinked. Charles had always been the closest thing Islanda had to a favourite in our cluster; she'd always at least considered his opinion. And Charles had always been blindingly loyal to her in return. Smitten, almost.

"No more stalling. I already know enough of what happened that night. Just get this done." She beckoned Derek forward. "Hold her steady. Neck extended."

Derek swallowed, going very pale. He took a hesitant half-step forward.

"Derek, don't do this," I begged. He tried to look away, but I could see his resolve, as tenuous as it had been, slipping. I felt almost cold as I tried to back up, but there was simply nowhere else to go. "I thought we were friends."

"Islanda, are you sure we need to resort to *beheading?* I just … trying to poison her was one thing, but all the blood? And the screaming? I just … I can't. I can't." Derek shook his head violently, turning on his heel and fleeing from the house, leaving the door wide open as the sounds of retching drifted into the house.

"Islanda…?" Charles watched me, obviously waiting for orders, his hands shaking harder, but I knew if she gave the word, Charles wouldn't falter. Not at Islanda's prompting.

"Go check on him." She waved Charles off, but it sounded more like a dismissal than mercy.

Charles dropped the axe with a resounding clang, barrelling out the door right behind Derek. I didn't miss the look of venom Islanda shot at his fleeing back.

Islanda pinched the bridge of her nose, sighing as she flopped back onto the chair. "Apparently we have a few minutes to talk after all."

I glanced at the axe on the ground, but it was quite evident that Islanda had no intention of trying anything herself. I eyed the door, wondering if everyone would be just busy enough I could make a run for it.

"Stay." The one word was sighed, but it was a very dangerous syllable and I found myself leaning back against the counter without even processing what I had done. "Maybe some details could be useful. Start talking."

The words slipped out like she'd taken a pair of pliers to my tongue. "I've replayed that night every day in my mind, but I still can't figure it out. We met for the ceremony. We had to unexpectedly meet up a few days sooner than planned because Suzanna had that conference to fly to. I got there late, but I was still the first one there. I came in and you told me to help you set up the ritual — the candles, the book, the chalk, everything in its place. I'd never done any of that before, but you seemed to be in a hurry, so I wanted to help. Then everything kind of goes blurry and distorted." I paused, only hesitating a fraction of a second, wondering if I should tell her about waking up with the odd scar on my shoulder. It obviously meant something, but I didn't exactly want to help her when she had a man standing outside of my own house to decapitate me. "I woke up to you trying to stab me. Charles, just standing by the door, pale and—"

Islanda was shaking her head. "You were there hours early, not late. That's why no one else was there, and *you* insisted on helping me set up. You said you wanted to learn more about the ritual. Asking a million questions, such a sudden interest in what I do."

The memories in between arriving and waking up with a knife aimed at me were fuzzy, but none of that sounded right. I had never had any particular interest in how the ritual was set up.

"I went out of the room to get the door when Charles came," Islanda continued, "and we came back to you convulsing with the book in hand. The page was open to some spell even I had never learned. You must have tried something you couldn't handle. How can you be so stupid, Nyssa? Your magic might seem slight, but it's not something to mess with. Those spells are for fuller bloods such as myself, not for the rest of you with barely a drop of fair folk blood between you. When I walked in, your eyes were already getting cloudy and there was a knife in your back. You had fallen back onto the table. What were you even trying to do?"

I shook my head. "No, no. I was there late. I remember having to leave without eating that night."

"I don't know, Nyssa. Maybe you got the times mixed up—"

"Eight o'clock. It was already after seven when you called, but you insisted we be there for eight o'clock sharp."

"We never meet that early. It's always after eleven."

"I remember you said eight because Suzanna had to go to the airport that night."

"She left in the morning. What kind of flight would leave that late?"

The whole night had been a little hazy, but I did remember a few things, and eight o'clock was one of the clearest.

"I talked to my family, Nyssa." Islanda waved me off. "I showed them that spell you messed with, and none of them had ever tried it either. It's dark magic, a perversion of everything we stand for, the type that can leave festering lashes on the magic of the entire cluster for a lifetime. If the book weren't a family heirloom, we would have torn that page out and burnt it a long time ago. There are a few like that in there; that's why I'm the one who sets up and I'm the one who reads. That kind of magic can have a pull on people. You probably started reading it without even realizing what you were doing. You would have been stressed and tired from rushing over, and it wouldn't take much to draw someone like that in." She paused, choosing her next words carefully. "I'm sorry that it can't be fixed in you; it's taken root, so to speak. But we can still help the others out. Remove the blight. The reason I've been avoiding you, dear one, is that I'm the core of our cluster. If you infect my magic directly, it will only spread faster and more fully to the others. It's why I was in such a hurry today. I was trying to mitigate the damage by staying back and having others correct what I couldn't myself. Blood is a powerful thing. I'm afraid if yours touches my skin even for a second, the blight could transfer to me directly and even your passing couldn't correct that. But it almost killed me, knowing you were scared and suffering on your own because of my mistake. I shouldn't have ever left you alone with that book. I'm so sorry, Nyssa. If I could fix it, pull the rot out of you, I would do it in a heartbeat. But you died that night on the table, and death is something even we can't fix. This is just a final mercy." She stood, walking to standing in front of me, running her hand tenderly down my cheek like she were wiping tears away. It was sort of nice, like I could almost pretend I could still cry.

And it was like everything had been pulled out of me, like I was being hollowed out. Years of hating her, years of feeling like she betrayed me, like she did something to me, that everything was somehow her fault, and in the end, it was all on me? Because I stupidly touched a book I didn't understand? I bowed my head, resting it on her shoulder. Suddenly I felt very tired. "I'm sorry."

"No, *I'm* sorry, Nyssa. I failed to protect you. That is a burden I will bear until the day I die. Please, just let me make it right." She gently grasped my chin and tilted my head up to meet her gaze. I felt my heart swell but this time not in a panic. "You've always had the most beautiful eyes." She rubbed under my eyelid. "Like twin galaxies. I've heard so many in the cluster say that. *The heavens are trapped in her gaze* and that's coming from a species known for their unique and stunning eyes. How could amethysts ever compare to the stars?" She laughed softly. "I always heard things like that. *Nyssa is so beautiful, Nyssa is so smart, Nyssa is so kind.* In a cluster of doctors and lawyers and politicians and CEOs, they still came to you for advice, didn't they? The librarian who never held the same ambition as the others. Different even among a group of outcasts, and you only shined brighter for it. Humble and unassuming and so kind in a family of self-centred egotists and champions. I will miss your calming presence." Islanda kissed my forehead.

"There must be some other way, Islanda. I don't want to d-die." My lip trembled, and my eyes pricked, but they remained as dry as my tongue as it tripped on that last word.

"None of us do. But we must accept when it is our time and go out with dignity and grace. Come with me. I'll be with you until the end." She held her hand out to me.

I hesitated.

"Let me be your strength today, my dear one." She reached for my arm, shouldering the axe on her other side, and pulled me out into the snow.

I stumbled out, Derek and Charles turning to face us. She tossed Charles the axe, stepping away. Charles turned to face me, still pale and shaking. I tried to steady myself with a huge, shuddering breath. I didn't know if decapitation would kill me or if I could recover from it like I had with my arm earlier that night. But it would be slow and messy, maybe even excruciatingly painful. As Charles approached, the wicked-sharp metal gleamed even in the low light as he raised the weapon over his head, his other arm reaching for my neck. This could be it. I could really die here, tonight. Then what? Would I just disappear? Had my soul been corrupted by the magic too? Would I be trapped somewhere, suffering agonizing pain alone for eternity? Decapitation could be the easy part. I was running before I even realized I had moved.

Now it was late afternoon, and little could be seen through the blanket of white flakes gusting in the wind. I raced to the gates, unlocking them with practised ease, and slipped inside, slamming them shut as the others reached them. Charles, always bigger and stronger than me, strained to pull the gates open, but I held them shut one-handed, using the other to lock them with little trouble. My current state had at least one advantage: the increased strength.

I took off for the heart of the cemetery, leaving a damning trail of footsteps a blind man could follow, but I had no time to be subtle. In my peripheral vision, I saw Charles and Derek along the outside of the graveyard each take one side of the fence. I moved deeper into the cemetery, huddling against a tree almost dead centre. I waited, pulling my knees to my face, watching as the two distant figures made their way. They seemed to be heading for the other end. Seeing my opportunity, I slipped back the way I came, heading for the same gates I had entered. I knew the area, so if I could get out without them seeing me, I could lose them in the forest. There were old forgotten church ruins tucked up in a clearing that would be sheltered from the elements. If I could get there, I could wait out the rest of the day.

I moved quickly but carefully, knowing holes and tombstones can get buried very quickly in this weather.

I might have to move house this time. Islanda seemed so desperate this time, she might not even wait for the next leap year. I didn't know if she would risk the blood oath, or what the consequences would be if she did.

I stepped carefully around a small tombstone. I knew I should just stop running. Islanda was right, I was getting worse too, and it wasn't fair the rest of the cluster had to suffer for what had apparently been my mistake. But I couldn't just stand there and let them hack off my head, especially with this corrupt magic still rotting inside me. I glanced around before stepping out into the open, back onto the main pathway. If all of this was caused by a spell, there must be a way to undo it. Islanda was only a quarter fae. There must be someone out there more powerful, maybe even a pure-blooded fae. I *wasn't* dead, my pulse was still there, albeit a bit slower. I was still alive, so there must be a cure somewhere.

I reached the gate. Checking over my shoulders, I didn't see either man along the sides, so I opened the gate and slipped out, locking it behind me. Hopefully they'd be here a while trying to spot me before they realized I was gone. I turned back to the pathway, sliding the keys into my pocket, when something wrapped around my throat, lifting me clear off my feet. Islanda stood in front of me, angrier than I had ever seen her. "Never send morons to do an important job," she hissed.

My throat felt tight and my pulse hammered, but my body just didn't need air like it used to. It didn't feel any more serious than someone squeezing my shoulder, even with my mind screaming to break loose on pure ingrained instinct. "W-wait, I have an…" I tried to speak as her grip tightened.

Footsteps approached from behind me. Islanda looked over my shoulder, a sneer on her face letting me know that in seconds we would no longer be alone, and moving on autopilot, I wrenched her hand off my neck, falling back onto my feet. I looked up, prepared to defend myself again, but all thought of fighting died as quick as it rose.

Islanda's hand was frozen midair in front of her, not just broken but mangled, two of her fingers dangling by tendons. Apparently, I had forgotten my own strength.

A gasp came from my other side. Charles had a look of horror on his face. Islanda yanked her hand to her chest, but no flash of pain crossed her face, no scream of agony escaped her lips, and no drops of blood fell. Just like when my arm had been falling off the previous night.

"What is…" Charles pointed vaguely at Islanda.

She buried her hand in her shirt, hiding the mangled but bloodless limb. The collar of her shirt dipped down ever so slightly and a familiar sight greeted me. What looked like the top of a circle with several squiggly lines running through it.

And in that moment, I knew. The missing, hazy pieces of that night twelve years ago finally made sense. "It was *you*." I couldn't look away. "*You* were the one reading from the book that night. You did tell me to come for eight, knowing we'd be alone until eleven."

Derek skidded up beside Islanda, resting his hands on his knees to catch his breath.

"We cornered her, Derek. Give Nyssa her peace now." Islanda drew a dagger from the folds of her coat, the wicked blade curved like a lazy river, and gave it to Derek. I knew that blade. It was the one that had been sticking out of my back the night it all started.

"A few quick saws and we can put this behind us." Islanda shoved Derek closer.

"Show us your hand." Charles looked ashen, swallowing more than necessary, but his eyes were hard and steady. "The one Nyssa damaged. Show us."

Derek turned back to their leader with a look of complete confusion.

"She broke my hand, Derek. She mangled it." Islanda held her hand tightly to her chest, keeping her sleeve firmly over it. "She's losing herself more and more. We need to end this before it gets any worse."

"Maybe we should get you to a hospital." Derek eyed her hand warily. "Figure this all out later."

"Show us your hand." Charles stepped closer to Islanda. Islanda wobbled back a pace.

"You're telling me what to do now?" Islanda hissed, sending Charles a look of pure venom.

Charles' face fell ever so slightly. He never could go against Islanda.

"You *did* tell me eight that night," I continued. "That is the one thing I remember clearly. I was late, but no one was there because you'd only invited me. I was never the first one to our meetings, even when I did get there early … Charles was always there first." I turned on Charles. He had been there that night when I woke up. Was he in on it too? Had they been planning something together? But he didn't even acknowledge me, all his attention riveted on our leader, his face a storm of indecision, a hint of … hurt, maybe, lurking in his eyes.

"Charles, I told her eleven. She's confused," Islanda repeated firmly, staring deeply into his eyes.

"You're always so careful not to blink when you're lying, Islanda." Charles' face turned stony. "I followed you everywhere, I did whatever you asked of me. But you've barely even looked at me since Nyssa left. You don't touch me anymore. I thought you blamed me for coming over unexpectedly that night. That it was because of me you left her alone with that book, and you felt it was my fault for arriving unannounced. Do you know how awful I felt? I lost a sister and a lov— you that night because I didn't call ahead when I skipped my stupid meeting at work to come see you before the ritual. I thought it was my fault we fell apart, and Nyssa's condition…" he gestured vaguely in my direction, "but it was something else, wasn't it? Guilt? Are you even capable of feeling guilt? Or were you just afraid I might notice your body rotting away?"

"You want to know the truth?" Islanda snapped. "Yes, I have been rotting away, because I have been the one siphoning the sickness out of our bond. I have sacrificed myself all of these years to keep you *all* safe." She wrenched her mangled hand out of her sleeve, waving the flopping appendage around. "I stayed away to protect you. If anyone got too close it would start really spreading." Islanda spoke directly to Charles as if Derek and I weren't even there.

Derek went very pale, his gaze morbidly fixated on the dangling flesh of her waving hand. "Spreading...?" He scuttled away from Islanda, joining Charles on his other side.

Charles' anger wavered, his eyes flicking to her hand, his shoulders starting to slump. Then the skin on her hand began to wrinkle and became grey and withered, her one pinky that was still intact curling over like it was plagued with arthritis.

"I-I've never had that before." I stepped back, like it was contagious. Maybe it was.

"It's getting worse because you're too close to me," Islanda hissed, snatching her hand back.

Charles' eyes narrowed as he stalked closer to Islanda. "You're still lying. You know what's funny?" Charles stepped into Islanda's space. "This morning, I would have believed every word you said. I would have killed Nyssa, even though it would have destroyed me, and I would have never resented you for any of it. But now, I think things are becoming clearer. Nyssa's not the problem; you are. I had an extra key that night. I was getting it out when you didn't answer right away. You didn't need to leave her with the book. But you did have to leave her if you didn't want me walking in with you standing over her body. Those symbols you painted, which are now scarred on your shoulder, you said they were the usual ones for the ritual, but you just hadn't finished them. But they were different, weren't they? I think you were going to sacrifice Nyssa for some dark spell and I interrupted you. But why? What could you possibly want that badly? What couldn't I — we give you?"

"That's why I can't die. " I breathed. "I'm tied to you somehow, aren't I? I finally pulled my shirt down a bit, revealing the odd marks on my own shoulder. "And you're at the root of all of this, so you must be rotting even faster than me."

Islanda chuckled. Her head shot up and she lunged for me, wrapping her good hand around my neck again, and dragged me to the ground. "I don't even need an axe, I can just tear your head off myself and complete the ritual. Set everything right again."

I rolled out from under her. "You did this to me!" I yelled, diving back for her. "All those years, leaving me alone and scared and it was all your fault! It wasn't even an accident; you did this to me on purpose!" I grabbed her around the middle, dragging her to the ground. She thrashed, squirming loose, but Derek was there. She lunged for him and he stumbled back, hands raised. She turned back to me.

"Don't be so dramatic, child." She rolled her eyes. "I needed a life force to sustain me and yours was the most annoying. You've always been a disgrace to the fae; unambitious, uncompetitive, you just meandered through life and they all adored you. Even Charles. Don't think I didn't see it." She turned on Charles with a snarl. "A shy librarian who always wore her hair in that messy ponytail, nose buried in a book, a walking cliché if there ever was one. Everything our kind is not, and all of *my* cluster adored you. *I* found them, *I* recruited them, *I* gave them a home. *I* advised them and led them with my 400 years of experience and more fae blood than all of you combined and doubled and they seek out the child."

"Four hundred?" Charles face was awash with pure disbelief.

"Yes, and a *half* blood, not some quarter blood. My mother was a pure-blooded fair folk, and she taught me everything I know."

"Except how to properly run a ritual apparently," Derek said, shifting back on his heels.

"Well, I'll rectify that soon enough. I've found, in my experience, that very few creatures can live without a heart and a head. I suspect that will be the case for you as well." Islanda turned to me.

"You're outnumbered." Charles stepped up beside me.

Derek backed away. "I am *not* fighting a 400-year-old half blood." He shook his head vigorously. "If any of you have any smarts left, you'll follow my lead." He turned and fled into the storm.

Charles shook his head. "It doesn't matter. You're still outnumbered."

Islanda lunged for his shoulder, bringing her dagger down, but he darted away at the last second. She moved faster than we'd ever seen her move before, a whirling dervish of knife and snarl. Straightening up, Islanda faced us once more. She held the knife in front of her face like a villain on a horror-movie poster.

"There may be two of you, but I'm the one with the knife. One slice and your flesh will begin to rot whether you're living or dead. After all, it's the one I used on you the first time, Nyssa." Then she dove at me.

I braced myself, meeting her attack and holding her back. Charles chopped at her wrist and with a sickening crack, the knife fell to the snow. Growling, she lunged sideways, going for Charles. I rummaged in the snow until my hands closed on the handle. I held it in my palm. This is what had caused all of this. The scar of our cluster bond stretched across my palm. *The bond.* That's what the scar on my shoulder must be too.

Taking a deep breath to steady myself, I pulled the neck of my shirt down again, revealing the mark, no, the *bond,* just below my collarbone. She had bonded us then started to kill me but hadn't finished the job. She had been feeding on my life force for years, draining me, and trapping me somewhere between life and death. We had been keeping each other alive.

I moved to drag the knife along the bond when something collided with me. I was suddenly on my back, buried in the snow, Islanda's snarling, almost inhuman, face glaring down at me. I brought my feet up, resting them on her stomach, and heaved with all my might. She sailed through the air, almost twenty feet above. The wind howled as she fell back down, impaling herself on a spike of the cemetery fence.

The black spike had come through her chest. She thrashed, trying to get loose. I snatched up the curved knife again, slicing along the mark on my chest. The twin circles began to grey and fade from my skin. I rose to go toward Islanda but Charles intervened.

"Give me the knife." He held his hand out, not looking away from her prone form.

I hesitated then placed the blade gently in his hand. "Aim for her mark."

Charles stalked forward, coming to a stop at her head. Islanda's eyes flashed with recognition.

"Charles. Save me." She reached a hand out. He ignored her feebly waving hand.

"I know you think love is weak because in its purest form it's selfless by nature. But I think I loved you."

Islanda stilled. "I think love suited you."

Islanda sighed as Charles plunged the knife through her scar, the bond mark fading with the storm around them. She smiled, stroking his cheek as blood cascaded down the spikes.

Islanda did not move anymore.

I began to cough as my throat felt on fire, tearing itself up as my bruised throat finally made itself known. A wave of nausea rolled through me and I heaved up things I didn't care to look at, my system slowly beginning to purge itself. After I took a few minutes to catch my breath, I looked up at Charles, sprawled in the snow, watching the sky above as the clouds began to clear. I staggered over, flopping down beside him, relishing feeling my body wracked with shivers because I felt *cold*. We sat there long after it got dark and the stars appeared. And without either of us realizing it, February 29 died, making way for a new day.

Karen Ralph is a graduate of the Creative Writing Certificate programs at both the University of Guelph and Conestoga College. She placed in the top percent of the 2015 international NYC Midnight Challenge flash fiction competition, and she was a writer for the University of Guelph's online newspaper *The Cannon*. Karen is living in her hometown of Guelph, while working on her debut novel, *Dragon Kin*. She has always loved fantasy stories with a bit of a dark twist. You can find out more about Karen at **kaelra.wordpress.com**.

CPSIA information can be obtained
at www.ICGtesting.com
Printed in the USA
LVHW04s0823300518
578919LV00002B/3/P

9 781771 802680